Sam met her eyes. "I
anyone here before."

Dana reached for his hand. "I'm honored."

He held her gaze for a long moment before he stepped closer and slowly lowered his head. Her lips parted in a tiny gasp just before he pressed his mouth against hers. She closed her eyes and let her entire focus shift to the sensation of their lips meeting. His hands settled on her waist; her arms reached up around his neck. She pushed her fingers into his thick hair and pulled him closer. He responded, tilting his head and deepening the kiss.

He didn't rush, simply kissed her as though it was the one and only purpose of his life. Dana had dated a few other men, and yet somehow she'd never truly been kissed.

Not like this.

Dear Reader,

Welcome to Anchorage. I'm thrilled to be able to share my hometown with you in my very first Harlequin, *The Alaskan Catch*. It's the first story in my Northern Lights series, all about life and love in Alaska.

Anchorage is the kind of city where you can dine on grilled king salmon with béarnaise sauce prepared by a master chef or catch your own salmon in one of the creeks that run through the city—maybe on the same day. This mix of wild and refined is one of the reasons people fall in love with the place. A story I've heard over and over is "I came to Alaska for a summer and I never left." They found home.

I wanted to capture that feeling in this story. Dana, the heroine, has been the glue holding her family together, especially since her brother's unexplained departure nineteen years ago. After her father's death, she heads to Alaska to find her brother and get some answers.

But pinning her brother down is more complicated than she anticipated. While she's waiting, his roommate, Sam, shows up and takes charge. When Sam shares his favorite wild Alaskan places with her, Dana discovers an adventurous streak she never knew she had. And with Sam, she feels confident enough to let it out, knowing she'll treasure these memories once she returns home. Only her heart isn't sure where home is anymore.

If you enjoy *The Alaskan Catch*, keep an eye out for the next Northern Lights novel, coming this Christmas.

Happy reading!

Beth Carpenter

HEARTWARMING

The Alaskan Catch

———

Beth Carpenter

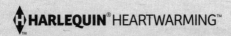

Recycling programs
for this product may
not exist in your area.

ISBN-13: 978-0-373-36849-5

The Alaskan Catch

Copyright © 2017 by Lisa Deckert

Printed in U.S.A.

Beth Carpenter is thankful for good books, a good dog, a good man and a dream job creating happily-ever-afters. She and her husband now split their time between Alaska and Arizona, where she occasionally encounters a moose in the yard or a scorpion in the basement. She prefers the moose.

To my mother. For all those Scholastic books you let me order, all the trips to the library, all the years of unwavering support and so much more...thank you.

CHAPTER ONE

NOT AN IGLOO in sight. Dana wasn't sure whether to be relieved or disappointed. Somehow she'd expected…maybe not an igloo, but something more exotic than the sage-green split-level at the end of a cul-de-sac. Only the dense spruce forest behind the house and towering mountains in the background hinted she wasn't in Kansas anymore. That and the salmon-shaped mailbox across the street.

The house number matched the address the private investigator employed by the estate had given her. This was it. She paid the taxi driver, collected her suitcase, climbed the three steps to the porch and stood there, staring at the doorbell. Nineteen years. Fifty-four percent of her life. A lot could change in nineteen years, although apparently not her brother's taste in vehicles. The battered blue pickup in the driveway wasn't too different from the one he'd been in the last time she saw him, through the crack in her bedroom curtains. She could still picture Dad scowling in the driveway, his arms folded across his chest, while Chris burned rubber and burned bridges, roaring out of their lives.

How would Chris react after all this time? Clearly, he had no overwhelming desire to see her. He could have gotten in touch with her anytime, right where he left her all those years ago. She wasn't the one who ran away to Alaska, who changed her name. Who obviously didn't want to be found.

But, after a long and expensive search, she had found him. Letters from the lawyer had garnered no response, so she came in person. Would she even know him after all this time? What if he slammed the door in her face? But she hadn't flown thirty-six hundred miles to chicken out now. Maybe he still felt something for the home where they'd been raised. After all, it was only forty-seven percent of Chris's life since he left. Less than half.

As always, the mental calculation calmed her. She set down her suitcase and reached for the bell, but before she could push the button, the door flew open and a big brown dog rushed out. Dana stepped back and might have fallen down the steps if the man hadn't grabbed her arm.

"Hey, careful there." The bean pole she remembered had filled out, with a wide chest and shoulders that looked as though he could carry a moose. In spite of the two inches she'd grown after he left, Chris was still a foot taller than her, his rust-colored hair wild and curly with a beard to match. His blue eyes held an expression of puzzlement as he looked at her.

She studied his face, waiting for a spark of recognition. "Hello, Chris."

After a moment, a grin spread across his face and laugh lines formed around his eyes. "Dana!" He dropped the duffel bag he was carrying and crushed her into a bear hug, lifting her from the ground, just as he always had when he came home from college and she would run to greet him. The years melted away as she hugged her big brother.

Finally, he set her back on her feet. His eyes skimmed over her. "You grew up."

"That happens."

"I guess so." He shook his head in wonder. "I can't believe it's you. How did you get here?"

"The usual. Airplane. Taxi." She glanced at the duffel at his feet. "I see you were on your way out."

"Yeah, actually." His face grew more pensive. "But I have a few minutes. Come in. Do you want something to drink? Coffee, maybe?"

"Okay. Thanks."

He picked up her suitcase and led her up the short flight of stairs. A brown leather couch and two recliners faced a giant television. Snowshoes decorated the wall above a rough stone fireplace in the corner. Behind them, a butcher-block island with four barstools divided the living room from the kitchen. "Have a seat. Is instant okay?"

"That's fine." She perched on the edge of the couch. The dog picked a rubber bone from the floor and dropped it into her lap, then sat and tilted his head, looking up at her.

"That's Kimmik."

"Hi, Kimmik." Dana stroked the dog's head, and his tail thumped against the floor. Yellow eyes met hers. "What kind of dog is he?"

"A chocolate-brown Lab. At least that's the general consensus. He was a stray." Chris poured boiling water into two mugs, stirred and set them on the slate coffee table. "I hope black is okay. I don't have any milk."

"Black is fine." She really didn't want coffee, but since he offered, she didn't want to refuse.

He sat down on the chair next to her. "So—" his mouth quirked "—did you ever get your driver's license?"

She laughed. Thanks to his inexpert coaching on driving a stick, she'd failed the driving test the first time. "I did, finally. What have you been up to all this time?" She looked around the room but saw no signs of a feminine influence. "Married? Kids?"

"Nope. Near miss once. How about you?"

She shook her head. "Not even close. I went to college and then went to work for Dad." She'd planned to teach math, but Dad insisted he wanted her there, in the business. Sometimes she wondered why.

Chris raised his eyebrows. "The old man know you're here?"

She pulled a piece of paper from her pocket. "Actually, that's what I came to tell you." She licked her lips. "He died about three months ago." She handed Chris the obituary.

He didn't take it. Instead, his face went blank, his eyes staring into the distance. She set the clipping on the coffee table. After a moment, he blinked and turned to look at her. "Three months, huh?" He picked up the scrap of paper and read it over, his face impassive, but his jaw grew tighter as he read. Dana had helped write the article, all about her father's success in tool rentals, his contributions to the community and his surviving wife and two children. It, of course, didn't mention Chris's absence from the family. When Chris was done, he let the paper flutter to the table, saying nothing.

After a moment, Dana spoke. "The lawyers tried to contact you, but you didn't answer their letters."

He frowned. "I remember some sort of letters with a return address for a law office, but I assumed they were some sort of scam and threw them away. What did they want with me?"

"You're his son."

"I'm not." He shook his head firmly. "We dissolved that relationship a long time ago."

"Is that something you can dissolve?"

He shrugged. "He did."

Dana leaned forward. Maybe she was finally going to get some answers. "What was that all about, anyway? The big fight."

Chris looked away. "He didn't want me to come to Alaska."

"That's it?"

"In a nutshell. He said if I stepped foot in Alaska, I was no longer his son. I came, anyway."

There had to be more to it than that. Yeah, Dad could be a little dictatorial, but he'd overlooked much more blatant disobedience from Chris than an unauthorized destination. Like when he was thirteen and drove Mom's car three towns over to visit a girl he'd met at a basketball game. Or the secret party he'd thrown at the warehouse his senior year of high school that turned out not to be so secret. She was tempted to point that out, but confronting Chris directly had never been the way to get him to talk. She tried another tack. "You're in his will."

His eyebrows rose. "What did he leave me, a cyanide pill?"

"Same as he left me—fifty thousand dollars."

He stared at her. "No way."

"I have the papers you need to sign. They say the estate—"

"What about Mom?"

"She got the house, the business and all the investments. In trust."

He sat very still, as though he was taking it all in. Kimmik whined and laid his head in

Chris's lap. He rubbed the dog's ears. Dana picked up the mug and took a sip of coffee. After a moment, Chris turned to her. "It was good of you to go to all this trouble to find me, but I don't want anything from him."

"But—"

"No. Thanks for the offer, but I'm doing fine on my own."

This wasn't how it was supposed to go. This inheritance was supposed to bring them together, to reunite the family. To show Chris his father cared enough to leave him money. At least that's the picture Dana had imagined when she had decided to make the trip.

"Come on, Chris. He wanted you to have it."

Chris stared into the empty fireplace, working his jaw. Dana sat very still and watched him. Her hand trembled, threatening to spill the coffee. She set the mug on the table.

Chris turned toward her. "When did he make this will?"

Dana couldn't meet his eyes. "The year I was born." She looked up. "But that doesn't mean he didn't want you to have the money. He had plenty of time to change it if he'd wanted to."

"What happens if I decline my share?"

Dana shrugged. "It goes to me. But I don't want that. He's your father as much as he is mine."

He tilted his head. "You came all the way up to Alaska to convince me to take the money, when it's in your best interest if I don't?"

"I came to find you." And to find out what happened between him and Dad nineteen years ago, but she wouldn't push. Yet. "Also, I wanted to look into some letters the lawyers found in Dad's safe."

Chris tightened his hand into a ball. "What kind of letters?"

"From some woman named Ruth. No last name. She claimed Dad owed money. The lawyers aren't worried. They posted a notice, and if no one has filed a claim within four months, it's too late. But there was something—I don't know—desperate in that letter. It sounded sincere to me. Anyway, I thought I'd look into it. I just have to find the son of someone called Roy Petrov."

He jerked his head toward her. "Who?"

"Roy Petrov. From Fairbanks. Why? Do you recognize the name?"

Chris rose abruptly, pushing the dog away,

and walked into the kitchen to set his mug on the counter. "Sorry, but I'm not going to be able to help you. I don't want anything to do with that money."

She stood and followed him. "Think it over before you decide."

"I'm not changing my mind, and I have to go." He slung his duffel over his shoulder. "Look, Dana, thanks, but no thanks. I appreciate that you came all the way here, and I wish I could spend some time with you, but you should have called first or something. I have people waiting for me. I'm sorry you wasted a trip."

He started for the door, but after two steps he turned back and looked at her, indecision written on his face. "Where are you staying?"

She shrugged. "I don't know yet."

"No reservations? You won't find anything last minute at a reasonable price this time of year." He sighed and pulled out a key ring from the kitchen drawer. "I'll tell you what. You came all the way to Alaska—you might as well have a little vacation." He tossed her the keys. "You can stay here and use my car until you're ready to go home. It's in the garage. Take the first bedroom on the left down that hallway. You'll find clean sheets in the hall closet." He whistled. The dog jumped up and followed him out the door.

What just happened? Dana ran to the porch and watched Kimmik jump into the truck. Chris climbed in after. She'd found her brother after nineteen years and he was walking out on her? "Where are you going?"

He leaned out the open window as he backed out of the driveway. "Fishing."

She stood on the porch until his truck turned the corner and disappeared, all her hopes disappearing along with him. Fishing? Really? She thought she'd prepared for all possible outcomes, but this wasn't one of them. Not for Chris to ignore her like this.

They'd been close once. Chris was the golden boy, honor student, gifted athlete. Their father didn't spend a lot of time with them, but she used to hear him brag to their neighbors and friends about Chris's accomplishments. The fact that her GPA was actually higher than Chris's didn't seem to register on Dad's radar. But Chris noticed. He encouraged her to take honors classes, to compete in Math Olympics, to enter the science fair.

She was sixteen when it all fell apart, the summer between Chris's junior and senior years of college. On Saturday, Chris was his usual cheerful self, putting some things in the attic at Mom's request. Dana went to a movie with friends that night. On Sunday morning, after some muffled yelling behind the closed doors of Dad's study, Chris left without saying goodbye. From that day forward, her dad refused to talk about him. It was as though she'd never had a brother.

She wandered into the house and collapsed onto the sofa. What now? Tuck her tail between her legs and go home? She probably should be there, making sure her mother wasn't in negotiations for the Taj Mahal, but she'd come all the way to Alaska for answers, and she wasn't going to leave without them.

She would just have to wait for Chris to come back from his fishing trip and try again. Surely, once they sat down and really talked, Chris would understand why she needed to know what happened. He could accept the inheritance, and they could make up and be a family once again.

Her cell phone vibrated in her pocket. She checked the screen and braced herself. "Hi, Mom."

"I got a bill for that new étagère I'm having made. Should I send a check?"

Of course she'd be worried about something she was buying. "If the amount looks right, just put it in the basket for Ginny to handle next week."

"But what if someone else's check arrives first and I lose my place in line? This is a handcrafted artisanal piece. He only makes so many."

Considering there was hardly room to walk in her mother's bedroom now, Dana didn't see the urgency to acquire another piece of furniture. But if she said so, Mom would explain why this piece was a bargain or one of a kind or some other reason she had to have it. By the time the piece was delivered, she would have forgotten all about it and moved on to her next acquisition.

Her mother had never even learned to write a check until Dad died. Dana taught her how so she would be able to pay the bills, but she was beginning to think that had been a mistake. Mom seemed to delight in it, like a kid with a new toy. However, she wasn't so eager for a lesson on balancing a checkbook. There was a good reason Dad had doled out Mom's weekly spending allowance in cash; cash couldn't be overdrawn.

That's why Dana hired someone to handle

her mother's bills and checkbook while she was out of town. She would only be gone a week or two, most likely. How much trouble could Mom get into in that amount of time? "If you think it's important, go ahead. Just make a note for Ginny with the check number and amount."

"I'll do that." Mom's voice relaxed. "What is it you're doing again?"

Dana repressed a sigh. "I told you, I was going on a trip to look for Chris."

"Oh, yes. Did you find him?" Honestly. She asked about the son she hadn't seen in almost two decades with the same level of interest as asking about a misplaced sock. Dana would suspect senility except Mom wasn't that old, and Dana could never remember her being any other way. Only things mattered to her, never people.

"I did find him. In Anchorage."

"Anchorage, Alaska?" This time, some emotion sounded in her voice. It almost sounded like fear. "What are you doing in Alaska?"

"I told you. Chris is here." Dana stood and paced across the living room.

"Did you talk to him?"

"Briefly. He was on his way out."

"So he hasn't agreed to accept the bequest?"

"Not yet. I'll talk to him again later."

"I don't know why you had to go all that way. Isn't that what we pay the lawyers for?"

"I volunteered. Since I'm not working—"

"Why did you quit, anyway? Doesn't the business your father built mean anything to you?"

It used to. Dana had worked her tail off in her father's business, Reliable Equipment and Tool Rental, and due in no small part to her efforts, it thrived. She kept waiting for Dad to notice. But then he got sick and appointed his golf buddy as manager. Dana had tried to tell Dad she could handle it, but he said he didn't want her to put in the extra hours in the office when he needed her at home taking care of him. And somehow, he'd never gotten around to updating the will. "I just couldn't work under Jerry."

"You worked under him for two years after Wayne had his first heart attack."

"Yes, but that was when I thought— Never mind. It shouldn't take too long to finish up my business here. I'll be home before you know it. In the meantime, Ginny can take care of everything. You'll be okay, won't you?"

"I suppose so." Her mother hesitated. "Just be careful. Don't they have wild animals or something up there?"

Dana glanced out the window at the suburban neighborhood. A pair of birds soared in front of the green mountains rising behind it. She'd never seen a more peaceful vista in her life. Still, Mom had shown a smidge of concern for someone besides herself. That was progress. Dana smiled. "I'll be careful. Bye, Mom."

Dana set her phone on the table. Some things never changed. Shopping was her mother's overriding passion. Almost every day brought another shopping bag of stuff into the house. Once Dana was old enough, her after-school job was to find the items that still carried price tags and return them to the store so Mom would have enough cash to buy groceries and household supplies. Fortunately, Mom's favorite department store was still downtown then, within walking distance of their house.

Dana hated the walk of shame to the customer service window every other day, but the employees were understanding, all except one. When Mrs. Valens, the owner's wife, happened to be working returns, she always threw out a catty comment guaranteed to turn Dana's face crimson.

But in spite of Dana's efforts, the house overflowed with furniture, clothes, knick-knacks and decorations. That was one of the reasons Dana loved her own little cottage, with a minimum amount of clutter despite all the gifts Mom tried to foist onto her. She'd lined up her favorite books in neat rows on the bookshelves, sorted kitchen utensils into bins in the drawers and corralled pens and pencils into pretty mugs. It was comfortable, and she could use some of that comfort right now.

But what Dana needed was a plan of action. She wasn't going home until she'd come to some sort of understanding with Chris. With her father gone, she was determined to bring Chris back into the family. He said she could stay in his house and use his car, so he must have a soft spot for her somewhere. She could just wait here until he came back. How long did fishing trips usually last, anyway? A day or two?

In the meantime, she might as well settle in. She carried the cold mug of coffee to the kitchen, poured it down the sink and opened the refrigerator door. Mustard, ketchup and three bottles of beer. Definitely a bachelor's place.

She found a pad in a drawer and started a list. Milk, bread, eggs and a few more staples. And she'd get ingredients for chocolate chip cookies, Chris's favorite. Homemade food always softened him up. After washing the mugs, she grabbed her purse and Chris's key ring and stepped through the kitchen door into the garage.

A gleaming red convertible greeted her, parked in the shadow of a pickup with a camper shell. Wow. Maybe Chris's taste in cars had evolved. But how could he afford a house and three cars on a job that allowed him to start a fishing trip on a Tuesday afternoon? A few unwelcome possibilities flitted through her mind. Was "fishing" a euphemism for something else?

Chris wouldn't do anything…illegal. Would he? Not the Chris she knew. But then, she didn't know him anymore. Still, if he were some sort of criminal, he would have jumped at the offer of ready cash. Right?

She slid onto the soft leather seats of the car. A big step-up from her six-year-old compact. She rested her hand on the stick shift and smiled, remembering Chris's patient, if ineffective, tutoring. With the press of a button, the garage door opened. After a little fumbling, trying to decipher the key system, she located a start button and the engine roared to life, then settled into a smooth purr. Cool.

The car prowled up the street. Dana slowed to a crawl and inched over an unusually large speed bump. She didn't want to take a chance on messing up Chris's gorgeous car. She almost felt guilty for using it to run errands. It was designed for something much less mundane, like swooping around the curves of a scenic highway in a dramatic chase scene for a movie.

She'd passed a grocery store in the taxi on the way, so she headed in that direction and found what she needed.

After arriving home and putting away the groceries, Dana nibbled on a salad from the store deli. In spite of the daylight still gleaming through the windows, the clock on the microwave read nine thirty, which would make it well after midnight in Kansas, where she'd started the day. She yawned and found the sheets Chris had mentioned and then carried them into a spare bedroom. A large desk dominated one side of the room, with a single bed beside the thick curtain covering the window on the other side. She made the bed, changed into pajamas and opened the closet door to set her suitcase inside.

A blue canvas bag took up the floor space. She tried to push it with her foot but found it surprisingly heavy. Curious, she unzipped the top. It seemed to be filled with heavy ropes mostly, but also two helmets. She lifted one of the helmets and drew back. A red pistol sat atop the ropes. Dropping the helmet back inside, she zipped the bag closed. Her suitcase would be fine under the bed.

She slipped between the sheets and closed her eyes. Maybe Chris would be back tomorrow. Maybe he would have changed his mind. Maybe everything would be okay. Maybe.

SAM YAWNED AS he dug American bills from the back of his wallet to pay for the taxi. The aggravations of travel on top of twenty-eight straight days of twelve-hour shifts always left him feeling like a bowl of mashed potatoes. He usually spent his first two days at home catching up on sleep.

He hefted the huge duffel over his shoulder

and climbed the steps to the front door. Even at three in the morning, enough predawn light leaked over the mountains to allow him to fit his key into the keyhole.

He flicked on the lights, dumped his bag and wandered up to the kitchen. Might as well wind down with a beer before bed. He had to rearrange milk and eggs to reach the bottle. Odd. Chris's truck was missing, so he'd assumed Chris would have cleaned out the fridge before going. He scavenged through a drawer, searching for the bottle opener.

"Hold it right there."

Sam blinked. He knew he was tired, but was he hallucinating? A woman wearing flowery shorts and a pink tank top stood in his living room, near the hallway. She couldn't have been more than five-two or -three, but the red gun in her hands more than made up for her petite size. Especially since the hands seemed to be shaking.

He set the beer bottle on the counter. "Easy, there."

"Put your hands up."

He raised his hands, slowly. "Who are you?"

"Never mind who I am. Who are you and what are you doing here?"

"I'm Sam MacKettrick. This is my house."

"This is Chris's house."

Sam nodded. "Yes, Chris lives here, too. You know Chris?" He spoke slowly and gently, as he would to a timid child.

"Chris is my brother. He said I could stay here."

Sam raised his eyebrows. "I didn't know Chris had a sister."

The gun wobbled. "Maybe you don't know Chris at all. Maybe you're making it all up. Maybe you're here to rob the place."

"Calm down. That's not a real gun, you know. It's a flare gun." Not that he found that reassuring. Flare guns weren't particularly accurate, but if she managed to hit him with a flare, it wouldn't be pretty. Even if she missed, she might burn the house down.

Her gaze wavered, but then she raised her chin. "I suspect it could still do a lot of damage."

"No doubt, if you actually loaded a flare inside." He guessed by the flicker in her eyes she hadn't, but he wasn't about to bet his life on it. After a quick scan of the room, he located the pile of envelopes in the corner of the island. "If you check the mail, I'm sure you'll find some bills in my name at this address."

She glanced uneasily at the letters, then at him. "You back away and I'll check."

"All right. I'm just going to get my wallet from my pocket so you can see my driver's license, okay?"

"Slowly."

Sam set the open wallet on the counter beside the mail and eased toward the front door to give himself a chance to escape, in case she wasn't convinced. She crept to the island and looked over everything while keeping the pistol trained on him. Finally, her shoulders relaxed a fraction, and she set the gun on the island, her hand trembling. "Sorry. Chris didn't tell me about you."

"So I gathered." She didn't look nearly as tough without the gun. In fact, she was kind of cute, with glossy brown hair, big dark eyes and a little pink mouth. "Now it's my turn. Chris never mentioned a sister. How do I know you are who you say you are? For that matter, who are you?"

"Dana." She hesitated and then stepped forward to offer her hand as if they were in a business meeting. Her small hand was soft inside his.

"Hello, Dana. So, prove to me you're Chris's sister. When is his birthday?"

"February 15."

He cast around in his mind for another test. "First pet?"

She frowned. "We never had any pets. Well, except Chris used to have a betta in a bowl in his room. He always wanted a dog, but Dad wouldn't let him get one."

That checked out. Weird that Chris would mention his fish, but not his sister. But Sam was too tired to worry about that right now, and he had trouble seeing the girl in pink pajamas as much of a threat now that she was disarmed. He picked up the pistol to take with him, just in case. "Well, Dana, I've been traveling for three days and I'm wiped out. Make yourself at home. I'm going to bed."

CHAPTER TWO

THE SMELL OF bacon lured Sam into consciousness and started his mouth watering. He yawned and checked the clock. Almost noon. He considered turning over and going back to sleep, but his hunger overruled his exhaustion.

The red flare gun rested on his nightstand, reminding him not to go stumbling into the kitchen in his boxer shorts. A houseguest. Just what he needed after a particularly exhausting hitch. The least Chris could have done was text him a warning that there would be a strange woman in his house. Or maybe he had. Did Sam remember to turn his phone on after the flight?

Sure enough, a message waited when he powered up the phone.

Gone fishing. Girl staying at the house a few days. Should be gone before you're home.

Apparently, Chris had lost track of Sam's work rotation schedule, which wasn't unusual. Chris had enough trouble keeping track of his own.

If it were anyone but his sister, Sam might suspect Chris was setting him up. He'd been needling Sam lately about the scarcity of women in his life. But what was the point of dating when Sam spent half his life out of the country? And assuming everything fell the way he wanted, he would eventually get promoted to a full-time posting overseas, in Dubai or Norway or the UK. A girlfriend would only get in the way of his career. Chris knew that as well as he did.

In the meantime, Sam was a supervising drilling engineer on the Siberian project, with a big fat budget and big fat expectations. Not bad for the kid who used to wear thrift-store clothes and eat on the free lunch program.

Early on, Sam had learned not to ask for things he saw in the store, for new snow boots or a football, because whenever he did, his mom would get angry and mutter under her breath about Raynott. For a long time, Sam thought Raynott was a curse word, but it turned out to be a name.

He'd only seen it written once, one day

when he got off the school bus and picked up the mail on the way to the apartment. The landlord was there at the mailboxes, growling something about reminding his mom the rent was late, again. Like she didn't know that. They were always late. Chances were they'd be moving on soon, the way they always did when landlords started getting persistent.

The envelope on top had the name Raynott in the corner with a return address from some other state. When his mom opened it, Sam got a glimpse of a check, and for a moment, he believed in miracles. But Mom swore and tore the check into confetti, yelling something about blood money. He knew better than to ask questions when she was in a mood, so he kept silent.

But that was a long time ago and he'd come a long way. He'd burned the mortgage on this house last year and had substantial equity in a property on the Kenai Peninsula. His job paid well, and according to his boss, Ethan, the company had big plans for him. And it was summer in Alaska, with four weeks off to play. Of course, thanks to Chris, he had a houseguest to consider. He caught another whiff of something cooking and his stomach growled, convincing him it was time to face his unexpected visitor. But first, he needed a shower.

Fifteen minutes later, his hair still damp, Sam stepped into the living room. Chris's sister stood behind the island, stirring a pot. Apparently, she'd taken him at his word to make herself at home. What was her name again? Dana, that was it. Today, she'd pulled her hair back into a ponytail, making her brown eyes appear huge. She favored him with a sheepish smile. "Good morning."

"Morning."

"About last night—"

"Don't worry about it."

"I'm so embarrassed. I don't know why Chris didn't tell me you'd be coming home."

"My travel schedule isn't always reliable. Chris doesn't keep track of exactly when I'm due in."

"Well, anyway, I'm sorry. Believe me when I say I don't usually go around waving guns. I found a great fish shop this morning, and I'm making seafood chowder and smoked salmon BLTs for lunch. Are you hungry?"

"Starving. But you didn't have to cook for me."

"I like cooking. Coffee's made if you want some."

Sure enough, fresh brew dripped into the pot of the coffee maker. Sam filled a mug and took his first sip. She must have picked up a quality blend somewhere. Much better than that instant powder Chris used, and a whole different animal than the vile stuff that passed for coffee at the rig. Dana popped some bread into the toaster. Today she wore a denim skirt and pink T-shirt. Pink seemed to be a theme with her. He went to perch on a barstool on the far side of the island and watched Dana assemble sandwiches.

She worked with an economy of motion, slicing tomatoes, zesting a lemon, patting lettuce leaves dry. Within a few minutes, she had two professional-looking sandwiches arranged on plates, each with a bowl of creamy chowder. She set one in front of him and handed him a spoon. "Enjoy."

Sam bit into the sandwich. It had never occurred to him to pair salmon and bacon, but the result was amazing. The lemon mayo was the perfect counterpoint to the smoky flavors. He nodded as he chewed. "This is good." He took another enthusiastic bite.

"Thanks." She set her plate in front of another barstool, but instead of coming around, she stopped to watch him, a little smirk on her face. "You really were starved, weren't you? Would you like another sandwich?"

Sam set what was left of his sandwich on his plate and grabbed a napkin to wipe his mouth. You'd think after all these years he would have learned not to gobble. He no longer had to worry that he wouldn't get enough food, that the other kids at the shelter would take his if he didn't eat fast. Ursula's efforts to civilize him had been met with mixed results.

He tried for a carefree smile. "One is plenty." He tasted the chowder and laid down his spoon. "This is excellent. You're a good cook."

"Thanks." She smiled back and came to sit beside him. "So, you said you'd been traveling. Did you have a nice vacation?"

He shook his head. "It wasn't vacation. I'm working a twenty-eight-day rotation in Siberia."

"Siberia?" She stared at him as if he'd said Mars.

"Yeah. We're doing some infill drilling."

"What does a rotation mean?"

"I work for four weeks straight, and then my alternate takes over and I have the next four weeks off. Unfortunately, it takes about three days to get from there to here, which eats into my time off."

"I guess it would." She took a bite of her sandwich and continued to watch him as if she were observing an exotic animal in the zoo. He took the opportunity to wolf down a few spoonfuls of the rich chowder.

She took a sip of coffee. "How long have you known Chris?"

He swallowed. "Let's see. I was in my senior year at the University of Alaska Fairbanks when we met, so seventeen years. I had a part-time job at a pizza restaurant, and he started working there as a cook. We've been friends ever since."

"And he never mentioned he had a sister?"

"No." He watched her face, looking for signs of distress, but she seemed more puzzled than anything. "Chris doesn't talk about his family."

"Don't you think that's strange?"

"Not especially. Sometimes people come to Alaska to get away from something or someone. If people don't volunteer information, you learn not to ask."

"Oh." She bit into her sandwich.

"So, I gather this is your first time in Alaska?"

"Yes. It's beautiful. I love the mountains."

"What brings you here after all this time?"

She didn't meet his eyes. "My father died. He and Chris had some sort of falling out. I don't know what it was all about, but Chris left when I was sixteen. I needed to find him and let him know Dad left him something in his will."

"Good for Chris. Did you get a chance to tell him before he left?"

"Yes." She bit her lip. "But he didn't seem too happy about it."

Sam swallowed a spoonful of soup. "I can understand that."

"Really? Because I don't." Dana leaned a little closer. "Obviously, Dad left him the money to try to make it up to him. Why won't Chris accept it?"

Sam shrugged. "Maybe he doesn't want to make up. Maybe it's too little, too late. You don't know what was said."

"I know my father was a good man. How bad could it have been?"

Sam considered while he chewed another bite of sandwich. "Bad enough to make your brother leave home and never go back. If Chris takes the money, it gives your father all the power. Maybe Chris doesn't want to be beholden to the man who kicked him out."

"How do you know he kicked him out?"

"I don't. But I know Chris. He's not the type to hold a grudge over something minor. Besides, if he doesn't want the money, why should it matter to you?"

"Because, well, it's my responsibility." Her cheeks were growing pinker. "Chris is my brother. My dad left it to me to set things right."

That seemed like a pretty big burden for one person. Sam's jaw clenched, but he reminded himself Dana's family dynamics were none of his business. Still, his sympathies were with Chris. "Why you? If he really wanted to patch up things with Chris, he could have come himself, not sent you after he died. It seems to me he took the coward's way out."

She narrowed her eyes and sat up straighter. "You didn't even know him."

"You're right." Sam held up his hand. "I'm sorry. I mean no disrespect. I'm sure your father was a fine man."

She raised her chin. "He was."

"I believe you. He raised my best friend, so he can't be all bad."

The corners of her bow-shaped mouth quirked upward. "Your best friend, huh?"

"Absolutely. Chris is the closest thing I have to a brother."

She gave a little laugh. "So, if my brother is like your brother, does that make me your sister?"

The idea of Dana as a sister didn't appeal to Sam. Maybe it was because of the way her eyes softened when she talked about Alaska. Or because of that cute mouth of hers that seemed to naturally curve into the shape of a kiss. Not that he had any intention of following through on any impulse to kiss Chris's sister. That would be a bad idea for so many reasons. Although he couldn't think of any at that precise moment.

Instead of answering, he rose and carried his dishes to the sink. "That was a wonderful meal, Dana. Since you cooked, I'll clean up." He glanced out the living room window at the mountains. "Then what do you say we get outside? It's an exceptionally beautiful day. Would you like to go kayaking?"

"Kayaking?"

"You can use Chris's boat. He won't mind."

"I've never been kayaking." Her voice sounded doubtful, but her eyes sparkled.

"They're small lake kayaks. It's easy. Go change into some pants or shorts while I take care of the dishes and then we'll go."

She caught the edge of her lip between her teeth. "You don't have to entertain me. I don't want to be any trouble."

Sam shrugged. "I'm going kayaking. You can come or not. It doesn't matter to me." But to his surprise, it did. He needed to get outside, to loosen up the kinks, but he didn't want to just leave her alone. Besides, he wanted to show her his favorite lake, a jewel of nature tucked away in a city neighborhood.

Her face cleared. "Okay, if you're sure. Thank you."

"You're welcome. Go get ready." Sam smiled to himself as he loaded the bowls into the dishwasher. The sun was shining and he was going kayaking. It was good to be home.

SAM HAD PULLED his truck from the garage and loaded two plastic boats onto the roof rack by the time Dana got changed. She climbed into the truck, and he backed out of the driveway. When they reached the speed bump, Sam slowed but still had to grab his coffee cup before it spilled. He muttered something under his breath that sounded like "Reynolds."

"Who's Reynolds?"

Sam grimaced. "Martin Reynolds. City assemblyman. He lives at the back of this neighborhood." They reached the corner of the cul-de-sac and Sam stopped, waiting for a car to pass. "The couple in that house—" he nodded toward the corner lot "—were concerned that people drove too fast through the neighborhood, so they complained to Reynolds. He got a speed bump installed, but instead of putting it on the main street, where there's actually a problem, he put it in the middle of our cul-de-sac. That way he wouldn't have to go over it on his way home."

Dana laughed. "Your government in action."

"Exactly."

He drove from the neighborhood and down a couple of main streets before turning into another neighborhood and pulling into a parking lot near a playground. Only then did Dana notice the small lake behind a row of town houses. Still water reflected the mixed greens of spruce and birch around most of the perimeter, except for a grassy area at one end with a dock.

It only took seconds before Sam was out of the truck, reaching up to remove a kayak from the roof rack. Dana tried to help, but she couldn't reach that high. Sam lifted the second one down and then effortlessly picked up a boat in each hand and started toward the dock.

Dana followed. "I can carry one."

"I've got them. If you want to grab the paddles and the PFDs from the back, that would help."

"PFD?"

"Personal Flotation Device. Life jackets."

"Oh." She gathered the equipment and hurried after him. Before they got to the dock, they reached a low, muddy spot. Sam walked through it without hesitation, but Dana carefully picked her way around.

Sam dropped the boats on the dock and looked back to see her circling. Laugh lines gathered at the corners of his eyes. "A little mud won't hurt you."

Dana shrugged. "I should have worn my other sneakers."

"I thought Kansas was farm country. Aren't you used to mud?"

"I live in town. Streets, sidewalks, grass. Minimal mud."

When they reached the dock, a group of mallards followed by rows of ducklings cut vees through the water, racing each other toward the dock.

Dana smiled at the fuzzy babies. "Cute. But they're not very wild, are they?"

"No. City ducks. They're used to people." He dropped a boat into the water next to the dock with a splash. The ducks quacked in protest and swam farther away. Sam tied a rope from the boat to a post on the dock. "Put your life jacket on and I'll help you in."

Dana buckled the jacket in place, but it hung loose around her body. Sam shook his head. "You need to adjust the size. Unbuckle and turn around." He tugged on something on the back of the life jacket and then reached around her to snap the buckles closed. His breath stirred the hair on top of her head.

He was close enough for her to detect the scent of his bodywash, mingling pleasantly with the underlying scent of man. She closed her eyes for a moment before she realized what she was doing and stepped away. "I can get it now. Thanks."

He nodded, pulled on his own PFD and stepped closer to the edge of the dock. "Ready?"

"Sure." The small boat didn't look too intimidating. She put one foot into the well in the center and the kayak rocked. She would have fallen if Sam hadn't grasped her arm.

"Easy." He squatted down to hold the boat with his free hand without letting go. She managed to slide her legs forward into the boat until she settled in and he released her.

He handed her a two-bladed paddle, untied the boat from the dock and gave it a shove. She went scooting across the water, sending the ducks that had congregated in all directions. A breeze caught her and pushed her farther into the lake. "Wait. What do I do now?"

"Paddle."

She dipped the end of the paddle into the water and her boat curved toward it, slowing her and eventually bringing her around so she was facing the dock just in time to watch Sam slide into his kayak in one easy motion.

As he pushed off from the dock and dipped his paddle into the water, his face changed. Happy lines formed at the corners of his dark eyes. He seemed relaxed, at home on the water. He worked the double-ended paddle with practiced ease.

He paddled closer and rotated his boat

so he was next to her and facing the same direction. Once he showed her a couple of basic strokes, she found handling the kayak surprisingly simple. In no time, they were circling the lake, easing into the scalloped edges.

Sam pointed toward a tiny island across the water, covered with grass and a patch of purple irises. "There's a loon's nest. Don't get too close."

Dana stopped and held up her hand to shade her eyes. Sure enough, she could make out a black-headed bird, with an intricate pattern of black and white across its body and wings, nestled among the grass on the very edge of the island. "How did you spot it?"

"I saw the nest last year, so I was looking for it. Loons like to use the same nest again. Look. Here comes the male. Must be time for shift change."

As they watched, another similar bird swam closer and rubbed bills with the bird on the nest. After a moment, the first bird wrenched herself off the nest and flopped awkwardly into the water. Once there, though, she was remarkably graceful. The other bird waddled onto the nest. He took a moment to arrange something with his long, pointed bill before settling down.

Sam resumed paddling and she followed him farther around the lake. On the shore, a fat robin watched them, a worm hanging from his mouth. He flew into a tree, greeted by a chorus of chirping from the baby birds in the nest. A sound carried across the water, a haunting three-note call. "What's that? A coyote?"

Sam smiled and shook his head. "The loons. Look." He pointed at a tall spruce with a dead top on the shore near the loon's nest. A huge bird with a white head perched there.

"Is that an eagle?"

"Yes. The loon is calling her mate to warn him."

A moment later, the eagle spread his wings and lifted off, soaring into the sky. Dana gasped at the sight. "Beautiful."

"I know."

She watched Sam's face. "You love this, don't you?"

"What?"

"This place. Alaska."

A slow smile stretched across his face. "It's home."

"It must be hard to leave for so long at a time."

He shrugged. "That's my job." He paddled forward. She watched him for a moment as he pulled away, how his arms flexed under his shirt, the confident way he handled the small boat.

What would drive someone to leave a home he loved for such long stretches? Did he have family? Dana had only been gone a day when her mother started calling. Didn't Sam have anyone who counted on him?

Dana gave herself a little shake. Sam's personal life wasn't any of her business. She was here to follow up on Dad's estate, not to make a friend. It was nice of Sam to include her on this outing, but she needed to focus on her goal and then get back to Kansas, to her life. She picked up her paddle and propelled herself across the sparkling water. Maybe Chris would be back from his fishing trip tonight.

Sam narrowed his eyes at something over at the shoreline. "Wait here a minute."

Dana watched as he worked his kayak through a tangle of vegetation to a place where a spruce tree leaned over the water, casting a shadow. He eased up to the bank, his movements almost languid and yet precise. He parted some weeds and something flashed green. His hand reached in to extract a fishing lure attached to a snarl of line, which he tucked in his kayak before paddling back to her.

"How did you know that was there?"

He shrugged. "It caught the light. Wouldn't want the ducks getting tangled up."

They paddled around the lake for another half hour before Sam led her back to the dock. Her shoulders ached from the unaccustomed exercise, but the sense of peace she felt after her time on the lake made up for it.

Sam climbed up on the dock and tied his boat to a post. Dana paddled alongside and he reached for her hand. She felt a moment of panic as the boat rocked while she tried to climb out, but he just smiled and pulled her onto the dock.

He lifted her boat from the water. "You did well for your first time in a kayak. Did you have fun?"

"I loved it. I've never seen a loon or a bald eagle before."

Sam removed the mess of tangled fishing line from his kayak and deposited it into a garbage receptacle near the dock. "Whenever I get back from a rotation, I come here.

I like to see the ducks growing up, the seasons changing."

"It's a special place. Thanks for bringing me along today."

He flashed her a smile. "Anytime."

CHAPTER THREE

THE NEXT MORNING, Sam checked his watch as he hurried across the office parking lot. He was barely going to make the meeting on time. Ordinarily he came in early to prepare, but Dana cooked him French toast for breakfast and it would have been rude not to eat it. Then he got caught up in a conversation advising her what sights she might want to see in Anchorage. Before he knew it, he'd lingered too long.

He smiled to himself. Having a houseguest wasn't turning out to be nearly as much of a bother as he'd feared. On the contrary, he'd thoroughly enjoyed kayaking with Dana yesterday, watching those eyes of hers light up when she saw the loons and the eagle. And the fact that she kept cooking for him didn't hurt. It was tempting to play hooky today and go be a tourist with her instead. But he resisted.

He pushed through the glass doors leading

to the office atrium and started toward the secured area near the elevators. He'd sent in his reports, so technically he didn't have to attend the meeting during his days off, but his boss, Ethan, liked to have him there for questions. Besides, face time with the big-wigs was always a good career move.

"Excuse me, sir. Do you have a badge?" An unfamiliar man stepped from behind the security desk and blocked his way. His short hair and determined stance marked him as ex-military. Must be a new guy.

"Yeah." Sam reached for his shirt pocket, but the ID badge wasn't clipped on as usual. He patted the pockets of his pants. "Darn. I must have left it in the car. I'll go get it."

"Sam, you're here. Good." Ethan slapped his shoulder. "On your way up?"

"Yes, I just need to go get my badge from the car."

"No need for that. Jake, Sam is one of our best engineers. He works a rotation in Russia, so you might not have met him before. He's with me."

"Yes, sir." The security guard almost saluted before returning to his desk. Ethan swiped his badge and Sam followed him to the elevators.

Ethan pushed the button for the top floor. "I hope you have good news for us."

Sam nodded. "It's coming along. Slowly."

"But you're making progress?"

"Yes. We got the number fourteen spudded, finally. It's not like Prudhoe Bay. Everything takes at least twice as long."

"Hard to work with those guys?"

"That's not it. They're excellent engineers. It's logistics. The equipment is old and not easy to come by, and there's so much red tape."

"Any problem with the language barrier?"

Sam grinned. "Haven't you heard? Everybody in the world understands English if you speak it slowly and clearly enough. Seriously, I have a great assistant who speaks four languages. Puts me to shame." His assistant was also convinced Sam might be a long-lost relative, but that was another story. "It's just frustrating to plod through the bureaucracy."

"Well, keep it up a little longer. I can't tell you about it yet, but there might be an exciting opportunity opening up before long. Are you married, Sam?"

"No." Sam's heart rate kicked up a notch. Maybe this was the break he was looking for, a step closer to upper management.

"Engaged, committed, whatever?"

"No, none of those things."

"So whenever we need you to travel, you're free to go?"

"I am."

"Good." Ethan nodded in satisfaction. "Just keep that passport current, okay?"

"I will." The elevator opened and they walked down the hallway to the conference room. He knew Ethan well enough to recognize the futility of asking for more information, but that passport comment sounded like another overseas assignment. While Sam would have welcomed a job in Alaska, everyone said overseas was the way to move up in the company, and Sam fully intended to move up. No matter what it took.

DANA DROPPED BY the log cabin visitor's center downtown and picked up a few tips for sights to see in Anchorage from the friendly woman behind the desk. But after stepping outside into the sunshine, Dana ignored her suggestions of shopping and museums and instead took Sam's advice to grab a reindeer dog from the stand in front of the courthouse and hike along the coastal trail.

Most of the people in line for hot dogs

seemed to be locals on their lunch breaks. She collected her hot dog with onions and peppers and strolled along the street, pausing under an enormous hanging basket of blue and gold flowers as she took the first bite. Sam wasn't kidding—it was one of the best hot dogs she'd ever eaten. She found a bench and stopped to savor her lunch.

Once she'd finished, Dana started walking. Past the courthouse and down the hill, a blue Alaska train pulled into the depot. Not far beyond, fishermen lined up along a creek. As she watched, a woman's pole pulled into an arc. A man nearby brought a net and helped her land a salmon. She did a little happy dance and hugged him. All this practically in the shadow of twenty-story buildings downtown.

The coastal trail overlooked the ocean, as promised, but it wound through forest and behind homes with bloom-filled gardens along the way. Across the inlet, a row of mountains rose from shaggy spruce trees, parallel to the range that stretched behind the town. Dog walkers, bicyclists and skaters shared the trail, and she saw geese, ducks, seagulls and possibly a ptarmigan. At least it looked like the picture of the state bird on the pamphlet she'd picked up. The short walk Dana planned extended on until she realized if she didn't head back, it would be evening before she made it to her car. Green and gorgeous. She could see why Chris had remained here all these years. But it didn't explain why he never contacted her or why he changed his name.

Ahead of her, a couple strolled along the pathway, holding hands. A puppy trotted along beside them on a leash. When the woman turned to point at a cluster of wildflowers, Dana saw that she was pregnant. Her husband smiled at her and touched her back as he listened to what she was saying. They looked happy.

Dana smiled at them as she walked by. She used to wish for a husband and children and a waggly tailed dog, a normal family that ate dinner together and played board games and talked. But it didn't happen. A few boyfriends came and went, but never anyone she could see making a life with. Not that she spent a lot of time worrying about it. Between working for her dad and watching after her mother, there wasn't a whole lot of time to cry over might-have-beens. Although, sometimes she wondered what it would have been like if Chris hadn't gone away.

Maybe he'd be back tonight. Surely, once she'd explained the whole situation to him, Chris would agree to accept his place in the family. It wasn't as if she was demanding much from him. She just wanted the truth. After that, she would look for this Petrov person. Her father was an honorable man. He wouldn't want any unpaid debts lingering. Once she'd determined whether or not that claim had any validity, she could head home and get on with her life.

At least one good thing came of Dad making Jerry manager. Now that Dana had quit her job at the equipment and tool rental, she was free to follow her original plan to teach. She loved teaching, loved watching the kids' eyes light up when they grasped a concept. She'd have to do a semester or two to get her credentials up to speed first, though, so her inheritance would come in handy in the meantime.

Once she had her teaching certificate, she could find a job at the high school in her hometown. And, of course, do her other job of making sure her mother's house didn't become so packed with junk as to become dangerous. When Dad was alive, he'd insisted all Mom's stuff had to hide in the spare bedrooms or in the basement. The living room, kitchen and garage were off-limits as storage areas. But over the last month or two, Dana had been seeing an ominous number of bags and boxes starting to gather in the main rooms, faster than she could return them.

She shook her head. One problem at a time. First Chris. Then this Petrov guy. Once all that was straight, she could worry about her mother.

On her way back to the car, Dana strolled through the flower gardens in the town square. She loved flowers. Her yard in Kansas overflowed with perennials like coneflowers, irises and yarrow, but they seemed understated compared to the vivid flowers here. Who would have thought they'd bloom so well this far north? Dahlias as big as her head sprung up behind colorful clusters of snapdragons, edged with some sort of flowering cabbage and carpets of tiny blue flowers.

The people downtown seemed to be an interesting combination of tourists, office workers and shoppers. They all looked purposeful and happy. Did any of them have crazy mothers and uncooperative runaway brothers? Or was that just her?

She shrugged. It was a beautiful day. She couldn't do anything until Chris came back, anyway, so she might as well put it out of her mind and enjoy her time in Anchorage. She pulled out her phone to snap a selfie in front of the fountain surrounded with magenta geraniums. Someday she might want it to remember the time she went to Alaska.

SAM TRANSFERRED A load of clothes from the washer to the dryer. The house was oddly silent without Chris or Kimmik rummaging around. It didn't usually bother Sam to be alone, but for some reason, today was different. It was after five. Wonder where Dana had gotten to? Hopefully she wasn't lost or anything.

He frowned. Dana wasn't helpless. In fact, two days ago, she'd threatened to shoot him. It was highly unlikely she'd come to any harm on a nice day downtown, surrounded by people. And yet here he was, worrying about her. Maybe Chris was right—Sam hadn't been out with a woman for too long. He needed to get a grip.

He was pulling the warm clothes from the

dryer when he heard the garage door opening. He carried the basket upstairs, reaching the living room just as Dana bounced into the kitchen. Her bright smile assured him his worries were groundless.

"Hi. How was your meeting?" She reached into the basket and started folding a towel as if folding clothes together was something they did every day.

"Fine. How was your day?" He pulled a pair of jeans from the basket.

"Great. You were right. I loved the coastal trail and the hot dog was excellent." She set down the towel and reached for what had once been a white T-shirt but was now faintly gray. "You really shouldn't wash darks and lights together."

Sam shrugged. "Probably not, but I just want to get it done. I hate laundry."

"Really?" She smoothed the T and folded it into a neat square. "I like folding laundry." She held up the shirt and sniffed. "I may be mildly addicted to the smell of dryer sheets."

Sam couldn't help a little smile. Dana chattered on about the wildlife and scenery she'd seen during her hike as they worked, and before he knew it, the entire load lay neatly stacked in the basket. He had to admit, folding laundry wasn't nearly as boring with good company.

"Thanks. So, how about dinner at Moose's Tooth?"

"Moose's Tooth? What's that?"

"A mountain." He grinned. "More importantly, a pizza brewpub named after the mountain."

"Sounds great."

As usual, Moose's Tooth had a long line of folks waiting for a table, so he and Dana sat at the bar temporarily. The waiter gave Sam a calculating look before he delivered their drink orders. Dana took a sip of her raspberry wheat microbrew. "Nice." She set the glass down and leaned forward. "So, tell me what you do in Siberia."

"I supervise a drilling program."

"Okay, but what does that mean?"

Sam tried to explain the job as briefly as possible, but she kept asking questions and he found himself telling her more details about his work than he'd ever told anyone. When a table finally opened up for them, he realized he'd been doing all the talking.

"Sorry. I usually don't monopolize the conversation like this. I'm sure I'm boring you."

"No, you're not. I had no idea how much engineering went into drilling oil wells. What happens after the well test?"

"If it's good, we put the well on production. If not, we try to figure out why and fix it. But that's enough about my work. Tell me what you do."

"I worked in the office for my dad's business, an equipment and tool rental company."

"Worked?"

She shrugged. "I don't work there anymore. I have my degree in math, as a teacher. I really loved being in the classroom during my student teaching, but Dad wanted me in the business, so I did that instead. It was okay, but I plan to teach now."

So, her father insisted on choosing her career. Controlling. Maybe that's what drove Chris away. The waiter came to take their order. "Another beer?"

Dana shook her head. "I'm still on this one."

"I'll have a root beer." Once the waiter left, Sam turned back to Dana. "So, do you have a teaching job lined up?"

She gave a little head shake. "I'll need to take some courses to get recertified. But tell me more about Alaska. Did you grow up in Anchorage?"

Sam nodded. "I was born in Fairbanks, but we moved here when I was in elementary school."

"What is Fairbanks like?"

"Smaller than Anchorage. Inland, on the Chena River, so warmer in summer, much colder in the winter. I went to the University of Alaska there."

"Is it as green as Anchorage?"

"It's nice, at least when the temperature's above zero. Lots of cottonwoods growing along the river. It looks like a summer snow there sometimes when the trees are shedding."

"We have cottonwoods in Kansas, too, but it's not this green and rugged. You're so lucky to be a Native Alaskan."

"I am, although, it comes with its own set of challenges. Sometimes people make assumptions."

"Challenges." She looked puzzled, but then her eyes widened. "Oh, because you're Native American... I only meant you were born in Alaska."

"Oh." Sam looked down at the table. "Sorry."

"No, don't be. So you're an Alaska Native?"

"One-quarter Inupiat." At her blank expression, he grinned. "Eskimo."

"Eskimo, really?" A slow smile spread across her face. "I think that's pretty cool. Do you have a lot of special traditions or food or anything?"

He shook his head. "Not me, personally. It was on my dad's side and I never knew him. My mom wasn't Native, so I don't know much about it."

The waiter returned with his root beer. He noticed Dana looking at it thoughtfully. Fine. She might as well know up front he limited himself to one alcoholic drink a day. Living with his mother's alcoholism had prompted him to set strict boundaries for himself.

"I get that about people's assumptions." Dana sighed. "Some of the people I worked with assumed the boss's daughter was just doing some make-work job and didn't know anything about the business. When Dad got sick, I noticed the manager wasn't keeping the parts inventory up-to-date, but he wouldn't listen to me. I had to have Dad call him to get him moving."

"That must have been frustrating. At least

in my job I have the authority to get things done." Sam took a swig of his root beer. How did the conversation get so personal? He never whined like this. Time to lighten up.

He smiled at Dana. "So, I've never been to Kansas. What's it like there?"

She told him about the town where she lived, mostly funny stories about her and Chris growing up together. It sounded like a television-worthy childhood, growing up in an old Victorian home with a big lawn.

"It was about ninety-five that day, and Chris decided he didn't want to mow the grass. He tied a rope onto a tree in the yard and hitched up the lawn mower to it. Then he strapped the levers down and went in the house for a drink while the lawn mowed itself. His theory was that the rope would wind around the tree getting shorter at each pass until it reached the tree, and he would just have to do the edges."

From the twinkle in her eyes, Sam could see disaster written all over this story. "So what happened?"

"Somehow, the mower ran over the rope and cut it. By the time Chris came outside to check on it, it was halfway down the block and had mowed through six neighbors' flower beds. He was grounded for a month."

Sam laughed. "I'm guessing he wasn't too popular with the neighbors, either."

"Not so much."

The Thai chicken pizza arrived. Dana told him a few more stories while they ate. It was obvious she'd adored her older brother when they were growing up. What could have gone so wrong with his father that Chris would completely abandon his life and his sister? Sam had never pried into Chris's previous life, but he was starting to wish he had. If he'd been lucky enough to have a sister, he couldn't imagine leaving her behind.

A familiar face appeared behind Dana's shoulder. Marge Hansen, Ursula's closest neighbor and best friend. She waved and came over to their table. "Hello, Sam."

"Hi, Marge. Dana, this is Marge Hansen. Marge, you remember my roommate, Chris? This is his sister, Dana Allen."

"Of course I remember Chris. The two of you thawed my pipes when we had that early cold snap winter before last. I'm glad to meet you, Dana."

"You, too. Actually, I'm Dana Raynott." Sam blinked. Did he hear correctly? Dana extended her hand and smiled at Marge. They chatted for a few minutes, fortunately not noticing that Sam had lapsed into stunned silence.

Marge turned back to Sam. "Goodbye, Sam. I'll tell your auntie I saw you."

Once Marge left, Dana turned back and helped herself to another slice of pizza. "She seems nice."

"Your last name is Raynott?" Sam had to be sure.

"Yes." She raised her eyebrows at his tone.

"*R-A-Y-N-O-T-T?*"

"Right."

"But you're Chris's sister. His name is Allen." He knew he sounded like a simpleton, but he couldn't seem to grasp what was happening.

"Allen was Chris's middle name. Apparently, he changed it legally somewhere along the way. I don't know why."

"So Chris was a Raynott, too?"

She laughed. "Yeah. Why is that so unbelievable?"

"It's an unusual name."

"I know. I've never met anyone else with the same name. Why? Do you know another Raynott?"

Sam shook his head. "No. Just caught me by surprise, I guess. So tell me the rest of the story about Chris's football career."

Dana laughed. "It was over in the fifth grade. The first day of practice, Chris played receiver. He caught the ball, but when he turned around this two-hundred-pound twelve-year-old caught him and…"

Sam nodded and smiled in all the right places, but his head was spinning. Raynott. There had to be a connection. But he'd known Chris for years and years. If anyone had asked him yesterday, he'd have said he would trust Chris with his life. And all that time, Chris had never let on that he was one of the dreaded Raynotts. It couldn't be an accident.

Dana kept chatting away. Whatever the big secret was, he'd lay odds she wasn't in on it. Her panic when he arrived in the middle of the night was no act, and she was perfectly straightforward when she introduced herself to Marge. No, Dana didn't know. But once Chris got home, he was going to have some major explaining to do.

She trailed off as she finished the story. "Sam, is everything all right?"

"Huh? Oh, fine. Sorry. I was just thinking of something I need to check into."

"Anything I can help you with?"

"I don't think so, but thank you." He smiled. "So, are you ready to go?"

"Sure, I guess so." She set the half-eaten slice of pizza back onto her plate. "We can get a to-go box for the rest."

"Okay." Sam signaled the waiter for the check. He knew he was being rude, rushing her out of there before she'd even had time to finish, but he needed to get home, where he could be alone and think.

Raynott, the name his mother used to curse, the name on the check she'd torn to shreds. Who were these Raynotts and what did they have to do with his mother? And with him?

CHAPTER FOUR

DANA SLID A muffin tin into the hot oven. She'd picked up the pan, as well as the ingredients, yesterday on the way back from hiking. Blueberry muffins used to be Chris's favorite breakfast, and she'd hoped to surprise him this morning, to put him in a good mood and get him talking. But Chris still wasn't back from his fishing trip. Hopefully Sam would enjoy the muffins.

What was up with him? Last night, they'd been having a great time. He obviously loved his job, and she found it fascinating to listen to him talk about how he did it. It would be wonderful to have a job she could feel passionate about like that. He seemed to enjoy her stories about Chris growing up. But at the end of the evening, Sam had suddenly withdrawn into himself, and she had no idea why.

Not that it was really any of her business. She needed to remember she was in Alaska to get the answers she needed, not for a vacation. Her phone beeped and she found a text from Ginny. When r u coming home?

A problem with Mom? Dana bit her lip and typed a reply. Not sure. Still working.

OK. Will handle. Handle what? Dana found she really didn't want to know. Whatever it was, either Ginny would take care of it or Dana would deal with it when she got home. She had enough on her plate here. Which reminded her—she needed to call the women's shelter where she volunteered.

"Hi, Jane. It's Dana. How are things there?"

"Not bad. We got in a new family with three kids in elementary school who could probably use your help."

"Ooh, sorry. I was actually calling to let you know I'm out of town and won't make it in for tutoring next week and possibly the week after."

"That's too bad, but I'm sure Melinda and I can muddle through. Good thing we don't have any kids in high school right now because I've forgotten everything I ever knew about algebra."

"Maybe you can sit in on my next lesson. I'll let you know when I get home. Bye, Jane." Dana smiled as she hung up the phone. She loved tutoring the kids at the shelter. So many of them thought they hated math, but really they were just struggling with some basic concept. A little individual attention did wonders for their confidence.

While she had her phone out, she checked her voice mail. A message from the lawyers asked if she'd located Chris and gotten his signature. She called and left a message of her own.

"Hi, it's Dana Raynott. I got your message. I did locate Chris, but he's temporarily away from home. I expect him back anytime now, and I will certainly get that signature and send it to you ASAP. Then I'll concentrate on locating that other party." She ended the call. The lawyers didn't seem too worried, but she wouldn't feel right if she didn't at least try to locate this Petrov guy and check out his story.

"Did I hear you say Chris would be back soon?"

Dana jumped at Sam's voice and turned. "Oh, hi. I didn't realize you were up. I was just leaving a message with the lawyers. They were checking up on my progress."

"You know he's fishing, right?"

Dana nodded. "Yes, but I expected him to be home by now. How long does it take to catch a fish?"

He gave her an odd look. "Chris is a commercial fisherman. He's on a shrimp trawler. They won't be back to shore until they fill the hold or the season ends. It might be a few weeks."

"Weeks?" Dana's voice squeaked.

"I thought you knew."

"Chris just said he was going fishing. I didn't realize…" A commercial fisherman? Okay, he had a job, which explained how he paid for the sports car in the garage. That was a good thing, she supposed, but now what? She shook her head. "Do you have his cell number?"

Sam smirked. "There are no cell towers in the middle of the ocean."

"No, I guess there wouldn't be." This whole plan was falling apart. She looked up at Sam. "There's really no way to reach him?"

"There's ship-to-shore radio for emergencies. Is this an emergency?"

Maybe. Well, no. She could call from Kansas if she had to, but she wanted to talk with him face-to-face. "I guess not." Okay. New plan. "How long is he usually gone for?"

Sam shrugged. "Depends. I believe the season closes in mid-August, but I doubt they'll be out for more than a month, sooner if they're having a good catch. Once they fill the hold, they'll come to shore to unload and refuel, and Chris will probably check in and maybe stop by for a day."

One month. Plus however long it took to convince Chris to see it her way. She would probably get better results face-to-face than on the phone. Ginny could handle her mother in the meantime. She hoped. "I'll wait for him."

Sam raised his eyebrows. "You're going to wait for Chris? Here?"

"Oh." She hadn't thought about where she would wait. "No, of course not. I'll get a hotel."

"That's not what I meant. You can stay here as long as you want. I just thought you'd need to get back to Kansas. I can call you if Chris shows up."

She shook her head. "This is more important. I don't want to take a chance on missing him. Besides, I have another task about my dad's estate to handle in the meantime." The timer went off and she pulled the muffins from the oven, all the while preparing a mental checklist of items to accomplish. "But I will find a hotel or something. You never signed on to have me here for a few days, much less a month."

"I don't want you to move out." His declaration sounded surprisingly firm.

She cocked her head and studied his face. "I can't keep imposing on you. You don't even know me."

His shoulders twitched. "You're Chris's sister. I want you to stay." He eyed the pan cooling on the counter and the corners of his mouth tugged upward. "Assuming, of course, that you're going to offer me one of those muffins."

Dana laughed. "You can have all the muffins you want." She pulled out a plate, plopped a warm muffin on top and set it on the counter in front of him.

"Then I believe we have a deal." Sam poured himself a cup of coffee and settled at the bar. He broke off a bit of steaming muffin and popped it in his mouth. "Delicious." He took a sip of coffee and eyed her. "So, what's this other task you need to handle?"

"It's possible my dad owed money to someone, and I want to check it out before they settle the estate. I need to get into public records in Fairbanks. Are they online, do you think?"

"Probably. Although I don't know how far back they would go."

"I'll find out." Dana dried the batter bowl and utensils and put them into the kitchen cabinets. "I brought my laptop."

Sam nodded. "The password for Wi-Fi is in the top drawer of the desk in your room. Good luck."

SAM SPENT THE morning going through his mail and generally catching up. Dana had disappeared into her bedroom right after breakfast and he hadn't seen her since. Was he crazy, inviting a Raynott to stay in his house? Apparently, he'd been living with one for years and never knew it.

Maybe it was a coincidence. Maybe the Raynott his mother blamed for everything bad that had happened to them wasn't related to Chris and Dana. Yeah, right. Sure, it was just a coincidence that his best friend happened to have been born with the same unusual name as this person his mother hated. The whole situation was fishy, and while Dana sure didn't seem like the type to be running some sort of scam, the whole point of a con was to appear trustworthy. Still, he couldn't see what she had to gain by hanging around him.

Just out of curiosity, Sam did an internet search on his phone for Raynott. Dana had a couple of mentions in fund-raising articles for a women's shelter. A business article about a chain of equipment and tool rental stores mentioned a Wayne Raynott as owner. And a newspaper in Kansas showed an obituary for Wayne Raynott from three months ago. That was all he found.

Wayne Raynott. Sam couldn't be positive, but he was fairly certain that had been the name on the check his mother tore up. And now Dana was here in Alaska, trying to talk Chris into taking an inheritance and looking for some mysterious person her father owed money to. He couldn't see the whole picture yet, but he was starting to collect a big stack of puzzle pieces.

His phone rang. Ursula. He smiled. "How's it going, Auntie?"

"It would be better if a certain someone would check in with me like he's supposed to when he gets in from his rotation."

He settled on the barstool. "Sorry about

that. I only got home on Wednesday and I've been a little busy."

"So Marge tells me. Gallivanting around town with your pretty new girlfriend instead of calling your auntie Ursula. Tsk-tsk." Laughter bubbled through her words.

Ursula was worse than Chris. Chris just thought Sam needed some female company. Ursula was determined he needed a wife. Better shut her down before she started making wedding plans. "She's not my girlfriend. She's Chris's sister."

"Really?" She paused. "I didn't know Chris had a sister."

"I didn't, either."

"He didn't mention her when he came by to drop off the dog."

"Odd, huh?"

"You've been roommates for years. What does he have to say about this?"

"So far, nothing. He went out fishing and left her here. I haven't talked with him since I got home."

"Huh. Well, bring her along for the weekend. I had a cancellation."

"This weekend?"

"That's right. I need you to make me a new gate on the vegetable garden. A moose smashed it. You can come down this afternoon."

"You want me to build a gate?"

"That's right, Mr. Landlord."

"Why didn't you just call a carpenter?"

"There's no need to waste money on something you can do yourself. Didn't Tommy teach you anything? Surely someone with a fancy engineering degree can build a gate." Tommy, Ursula's husband, had been a gifted handyman and a patient teacher to twelve-year-old Sam after he moved in with them. And yes, he could probably build a gate. "Besides, this dog of yours is eating me out of house and home."

Not likely. "Didn't Chris bring his dog food?"

"Kimmik prefers real food."

Sam was sure he did. "Dog food is better for him."

"Well, then, get over here and pick him up, and you can feed him however you see fit. And bring Chris's sister along. I want to meet her."

Not a bad idea, actually. Ursula had good instincts about people. He'd like her read on Dana. "I'll see. She's working on some things of her own."

"It's the weekend. Tell her all work and no play will give her wrinkles."

Sam laughed. "Says the woman who never sits down."

"It's not work if you love it. I'll make chili for dinner. Don't be late."

Sam smiled as he pocketed the phone. Ursula and Tommy were the best things that ever happened to him. Now he just needed to check out the internet for gate designs.

Sam knocked on the open door of Dana's room and stuck his head in. "Sorry to bother you, but I need to get my laptop from the drawer there."

"Sure." She got up from her chair at the desk and stretched.

He extracted the computer. "Having any luck?"

She shook her head. "I can't seem to find anything except current property tax records. I think I'm going to have to drive to Fairbanks. How long does it take to get there?"

"About six hours."

"So if I leave after lunch today, I could get there by sundown."

"No problem." Sam grinned. "Sundown is after midnight in Fairbanks this time of year. But today is Friday. Government offices won't be open until Monday."

Her shoulders sagged. "That's right. I lost track of the days. So, no Chris and no public records."

"I do have an alternative plan for the weekend. I have to go repair a gate for my auntie Ursula. She runs a B and B down on the Kenai Peninsula. You could come along."

Her face brightened, but then she frowned. "Does she have room for an extra person?"

"She had a cancellation, so yes."

"I'd like that." She studied his hands as if taking his measure. "You know about carpentry?"

"Not as much as Ursula thinks I do. That's why I need my laptop. To bone up. You can come along and laugh at me. You game?"

Dana grinned. "I wouldn't miss it for the world."

DANA GAZED ACROSS the water, the glassy surface reflecting the snowcapped mountains on the other side of the arm. She was happy to gawk while Sam did the driving, his truck winding along the road, hugging cliffs on one side and the ocean on the other. "So beautiful. Does the snow stay all year?"

"It will gradually melt, all but a few shady spots. It's already gone on the south-facing slopes."

They passed a small waterfall spilling from the rock on the left side of the road and trickling underneath to the ocean. "What ocean is this?"

"This is Turnagain Arm, on Cook Inlet, on the Gulf of Alaska, on the Pacific Ocean."

"Turnagain? Odd name."

"It was named by Captain Bligh, Captain Cook's sailing master. They were exploring Cook Inlet and looking for the Northwest Passage. They followed Knik Arm first, but reached a dead end and turned back. Then they followed this arm, and when they found it was also a dead end, the captain ordered the ship to turn again."

"Makes sense. Captain Bligh." Dana thought for a moment. "Why do I know that name?"

"Did you ever see the movie *Mutiny on the Bounty*? That was Captain Bligh."

"Yes, I watched that movie on TV once. I thought it was fiction."

"Nope, it was a real incident and Captain Bligh was a real person."

"Not a very nice person, if the movie was any indication."

Sam laughed. "Aren't you glad you don't work under him?"

"I am. The last boss I had was bad enough." Dana continued to watch the water. A seagull swooped down and snatched something from the surface. Eventually, the road left the shoreline and began to climb. They passed through birch and spruce forests until they reached a fork in the highway.

Sam went left. "We'll be at Ursula's in another ten minutes or so."

Dana suddenly felt shy, wondering if she should have tagged along on a family visit. She pictured a fussy old lady with a houseful of doilies and knickknacks. Or maybe it was a family business. "Will you have cousins, too, or is it only your aunt?"

Sam didn't answer immediately. His eyes remained on the road. Dana was about to repeat the question when he spoke. "Ursula doesn't have any kids." He paused. "And she isn't really my aunt."

"Family friend?"

"More than that. If it weren't for Ursula and her husband, Tommy…well, I don't know what I'd be, but it wouldn't be who I am today. They took me in when I was twelve and raised me."

"What happened to your mother?"

He shrugged. "I don't know."

Wow. She hadn't seen that coming. Dana started to ask for more information, but something in his closed expression stopped her. Instead, she just nodded.

A few minutes later, they pulled into a graveled parking area in front of a tall cedar building. A scent of smoke and fish greeted Dana when she climbed out of the truck. Sam came around to stand beside her and took a deep breath. A smile crossed his face. "Ursula must have been fishing."

A familiar brown dog rushed up to Sam, wagging his whole rear end. Sam crouched down and fondled the dog's ears. "That's a good dog. Did you miss me?"

The dog pressed his body against Sam but scooted closer so he could rub his head against Dana's jeans, obviously inviting more affection. She stroked along his broad crown. "Hi, Kimmik."

Sam looked up at her. "You know Kimmik?"

"We met, briefly. How did he get his name?"

"Kimmik is an Inupiat word."

"What does it mean?"

Sam grinned. "Dog."

Dana laughed. "Original."

"So here's the prodigal son. Did you get lumber?" A woman with cropped gray hair emerged from an opening in a fenced area beside the house. She carried a basket on her arm. A smile of delight lit up her face.

"I did." Sam held out his arms and the woman wrapped him in a big hug, the basket of greens bumping against his back. Seeing the obvious affection between Sam and Ursula, Dana felt almost jealous. Neither of her parents had ever greeted her with such enthusiasm.

"Good boy." She reached up to run her hand over his jaw as if inspecting him. "Tommy would never have believed you'd grow up to be so tall. I guess I fed you well." She turned a smiling face toward Dana. "And you must be Chris's sister."

"Yes. I'm Dana."

"Welcome." Dana got a friendly hug, too, if not quite as exuberant as the one Ursula gave Sam. Ursula looked her over. "You don't look much like your brother."

"No. I take after my mother, and Chris—well, I don't know who Chris takes after.

Must be a recessive Viking gene or something."

Ursula smiled. "Well, any sister of Chris's is a friend of mine."

"You know Chris well?"

"Oh, yes. He stops by to see me every time he's up or back." She changed her voice to a stage whisper. "Between you and me, I think he really comes for the scones."

Dana laughed. "He does have a sweet tooth."

Sam took a deep breath. "I smell fish smoking. Did you get some reds?"

Ursula smiled. "A king."

"How big?"

"Twenty-two pounds."

"Excellent. When will it be ready?"

She chuckled. "Not until tomorrow. I have chili for tonight."

"I suppose that will have to do." From the laugh lines at the corners of Sam's eyes, Dana suspected chili must be a favorite of his.

Ursula turned toward the building. "Well, come on in."

While Sam grabbed their bags, Dana followed Ursula into the inn, Kimmik trailing behind them. They crossed a large deck and entered into a room with a soaring ceiling. A stone fireplace dominated the room along the back wall, with a chimney reaching up to the crown. Flanking the fireplace, floor-to-ceiling windows overlooked a spruce-covered mountain, even greener than the ones in Anchorage. Two stained glass inserts depicting small blue flowers were set high in the windows, tinting the light that fell on the wood floor.

Four dining tables of various sizes clustered at one end of the room. At the other end, comfortable chairs and sofas gathered in front of the fireplace. Two armchairs with table lamps snuggled in the corners, creating cozy reading nooks. Kimmik plopped down on a rug in front of the fireplace.

"This is gorgeous." Dana turned to Ursula. "I love the windows."

"Thank you. That's why we call it the Forget-me-not Inn."

Sam carried in the bags and kicked the door shut behind him. "Where do you want us?"

"The west wing. You can get to work on that gate first thing in the morning. We have three couples in the main bedrooms tonight. Try to keep your language within bounds."

Sam laughed. "If you don't want salty language, you shouldn't draft me for building projects."

"Watch it, buddy. You're not too old to feed the curse jar." She made a shooing motion. "Go put those bags away. Put Dana in Rose. Dana, would you like a tour?"

"I would love that."

They started in the kitchen. The scent of meat, onions and chili wafted from a slow cooker. Ursula set the basket on the counter. "Lettuce thinnings for the salad tonight, along with chili and cornbread."

"Yum." Two ovens, a six-burner range and a commercial dishwasher identified the room as a working kitchen, but the baskets on the wall and crocks of utensils on the countertops gave it a homey feel. Behind the kitchen, a bookshelf-lined sitting room and cozy bedroom made up Ursula's private quarters.

"I've already cleaned and made the beds, but come with me and I'll show you the guest rooms." Ursula handed her a jar of foil-covered candies. "You can help me with the mints."

Continuing the wildflower theme, each room had a different blossom painted on the door. The furniture was simple but elegant, with soft duvets or patchwork quilts on all the beds. Not a doily in sight. At Ursula's direction, Dana left a piece of candy on each nightstand.

Ursula led her back to the main room and to another hallway. "You'll have the Wild Rose room and Sam is across the hall in Lupine. I'll let you freshen up while I make tea. Today we have wild blueberry scones."

Dana opened the painted door and walked into the room. A quilt in muted shades of rose, amber and green covered the bed. Through an open doorway, she could see a shower curtain with a large-scale print of wild roses framing a huge tub. A beveled mirror reflected sunshine from the window and projected a rainbow on the wall above the bed.

She reached into her suitcase for her toiletry kit. Pausing in front of the mirror, she brushed her hair and put on lip gloss before she hurried back to the gathering room. She wouldn't want to be late for tea.

THAT EVENING, SAM and Dana sat with Ursula in front of the big fireplace. The three couples staying at the inn had turned in early after a full day of offshore fishing in Seward. Sam watched Dana struggling with a hook and a ball of yarn. Poor kid—she'd made the mistake of admiring Ursula's crocheted afghans, not realizing it would lead to a crochet lesson.

Or maybe she did. She seemed to be trying to get it right. "So, down, loop, back through and another loop, right?"

"That's perfect. Now just keep doing that until you come to the end of the row and I'll show you how to turn."

Sam had purposely chosen not to reveal Dana's last name yet. He wanted Ursula's unbiased evaluation of her character first. And while he hadn't talked to Ursula alone, it was obvious the two women clicked. It may have been when Dana offered to make the cornbread, or possibly when she complimented one of Tommy's whirligigs, but at some point today, Dana had won Ursula over. He wondered if it would stay that way once Ursula knew her last name.

Dana held up the somewhat irregular row of stitches. "Look, Sam. A whole row."

He nodded. "Looking good. Some mouse with a cold neck is going to love that scarf."

She gave a little giggle, the sound almost like the tinkle of the wind chimes on Ursula's deck. "I think I'll keep going until it's a pot holder."

Kimmik repositioned himself on the rug

and laid his head on top of Sam's foot. The sun had shifted far to the northwest, peeping through the small upper windows along the west wall to paint diagonal stripes across the room. Sam leaned back in his chair and closed his eyes. A stomachful of moose chili, a good dog at his feet and the sound of soft laughter as Ursula and Dana put their heads together over their project—tonight, Sam was content.

CHAPTER FIVE

THE NEXT MORNING, after a decadent breakfast in the gathering room, Sam went outside to take some measurements. To his relief, all the guests had gone out sightseeing after breakfast, so he didn't have to worry about disturbing them with his hammering.

Dana followed him out. He caught her eye. "I was kidding about watching me. I'm sure you can find something more interesting to do. You can take my truck into Seward if you want."

She shook her head. "You're not getting rid of me that easily. You said I could watch, and I'm holding you to it. Besides, I think you need an assistant."

"Suit yourself." Sam had been hoping enough of the original gate would remain to take measurements, but the moose had done a thorough job of smashing it apart. According to Ursula, he'd done a nice job of gobbling up most of her cabbage plants, as well, but a few blasts from an air horn convinced him to move along before he'd completely wrecked the garden.

Sam pulled out a measuring tape, and Dana jotted the figures on a scrap of paper as he called them out. They unloaded the lumber from the back of his truck and Sam fetched Tommy's old miter saw from the shed and set it on his tailgate.

The first two cuts were simple, just straight braces the width of the gate. He pulled out his phone and opened the calculator. "Let's see. If the braces are thirty-six inches long and forty-eight inches apart, the crosspiece would need to be—"

"Just under seventy inches." Dana reached for a two-by-six.

Sam looked up from his phone. "You're right. Sixty-nine point nine seven."

"I know." She spoke as though calculating the Pythagorean theorem in her head was a common skill.

Interesting. Sam decided to test her further. "But we need to cut it at an angle."

"Yes. Approximately thirty-two degrees."

Sam punched it out. "I get thirty-seven."

"But you forgot to subtract the width of the board when you calculated the triangle."

"You're right." He laughed. "You would have made a good engineer."

"I hope I'm going to make a good math teacher."

"You absolutely will. So do you solve simultaneous equations just for fun?"

She gave a little smirk. "Sometimes."

"Too bad you weren't around when I was slogging my way through calculus in college. I could have used a math genius."

With Dana's help, they soon had the pieces cut and the gate nailed together and installed on its hinges. Dana held the latch in place while Sam drove in the screws. He opened the gate and pushed it closed. It swung easily into place and latched.

After putting away the tools, they found Ursula in the kitchen, chopping green onions. "How's it going?"

"Done," Sam said. "I used extra-heavy framing, so hopefully it will discourage the moose in the future."

Ursula pinched his cheek. "See? I knew you could do it, and I didn't even hear any cussing."

Sam smiled at Dana and turned back to Ursula. "Fortunately, I brought in a ringer. She calculated all the angles for me."

"Well, thank you, Dana. I knew there was a reason I liked you." Ursula dumped the onion bits into a mixing bowl. "What are your plans for the afternoon?"

"I was thinking of taking Dana into Seward." Actually, the idea had just occurred to him, but she deserved a reward for helping him with the gate. And the idea of an afternoon kicking around the pretty little town with Dana held a certain appeal. "If she wants to go."

"Um, okay." She seemed hesitant, but her eyes sparkled.

"Good idea," Ursula said. "But first I want your opinion of this salmon dip." She arranged a tray of crackers and two bowls. "One is the king—the other is some red I smoked earlier. See what you think."

Dana scooped up a generous dollop on a cracker. She closed her eyes, her expression blissful. "This is so good."

"Now try the other."

Dana repeated her actions. "Honestly, I love them both. I can taste a little difference, but I'm not sure one is better than the other. Sam, what do you think?"

He'd stuffed his mouth full. He could never get enough of Ursula's salmon dip. "Mmm."

He swallowed. "I like the king. But maybe I'd better have some more of that red, just to make sure."

Ursula laughed. "You do that."

THAT EVENING AFTER DINNER, Ursula put them to work stuffing envelopes. After a full day of carpentry and then strolling through Seward, Sam was happy to sit. He'd had fun, though, showing Dana the town nestled between the mountains and the blue ocean. It drizzled all afternoon, but she'd borrowed a rain jacket from Ursula and didn't seem to mind. She loved the sea otter they spotted in the bay.

"I just had these flyers and envelopes printed." Ursula's voice intruded on his thoughts. "What do you think of the new logo?"

"I like it." Dana reached for another flyer with an abstract tree and moose flanking the inn's name. "Does the B and B have a web page?"

"We sure do. I took a course at the community school on web design and made my own. We're tied into several booking sites, too. I try to keep up with technology."

"Ursula stays pretty full all summer, and she's starting to pick up more winter business, mostly skiers and snowshoers." She'd only been innkeeping for five years now, but Ursula's reputation was growing. Sam was proud of her.

"The equipment and tool rental business I worked for had good luck with those daily deal coupon sites. We offered a discount and pulled in quite a few people who'd never heard of us before. Many of them turned into repeat customers. Have you tried that for your off-season?"

"Now that sounds like a good idea. Can you send me the information?"

"Sure."

Once they had enough envelopes stuffed, Dana stretched. "I believe I'll go try out that big tub in my room with a nice soak. I'll see you in the morning."

"Breakfast is at nine, church at ten."

"Church? I'm afraid I didn't bring a dress."

Ursula laughed. "Wear your jeans and you'll fit right in. Enjoy your bath. Oh, and before I forget, I want you to sign the guest book."

"Okay." Dana signed her name in the leather book on the table near the front door and disappeared down the hall.

Ursula watched her go and then turned to Sam. "How's work?"

"Good. Spudded another well on my last hitch. Ethan's hinting at another overseas assignment."

"Really? Where?"

"He's not saying. I heard they might be looking for people in Dubai."

"Dubai? We almost moved there once. They were recruiting experienced people for a new drilling program."

Sam frowned. "You did? Tommy never mentioned that."

Ursula paused while she fiddled with the crochet hook in her hand. "Do you remember the first time you ever wandered into the garage and met Tommy? What he was working on?"

"Sure. He was using a power sander to refinish a door that had gotten gouged."

"That door had been scratched for years. You know why he'd decided to fix it then?"

Sam shook his head.

"Because we were thinking of putting the house on the market. Tommy knew people who had gotten jobs in Dubai, and the money was great. We were considering selling the house so he could take one of those jobs."

"What happened?"

"There was this kid who kept hanging around. Tommy said he had a mind like a sponge." She smiled. "Tommy loved talking to you, teaching you how to do things. So he dragged his feet about looking for another job because he didn't want to leave you. Then you came to live with us, and that settled it. You know we wouldn't have been able to get a passport or visa for you. We weren't your official guardians."

An icy fist gripped Sam's heart. "Tommy gave up a great job opportunity for me?"

Ursula chuckled and shook her head. "Tommy didn't give up anything. You gave him the opportunity he'd always wanted. We'd tried for years to get pregnant. Eventually Tommy got tested and found out he was sterile. Broke his heart, but instead of getting depressed, he put that energy into his oil field job on the North Slope, and he did it very well. He made good money, but when this Dubai idea came along, he wanted it. You see, everyone knew only the best and brightest got overseas jobs. Tommy wanted to prove he was one of the best."

"He was one of the best. Everyone who worked with Tommy respected him. He's practically a legend in the oil field at Prudhoe Bay, up on the slope."

"I know. And after you came along, he realized he didn't need to move across the ocean to get the respect he craved. You looked up to him, and that was more important to him than any overseas assignment."

"I never realized—"

"He loved you, Sam. You made him happy. A whole lot happier than moving to Dubai ever would have. Everything worked out just like it was supposed to." She picked up the rather sad-looking potholder Dana had been working on. "I like Dana."

"I can tell."

Lines of amusement fanned from the corners of her eyes. "You like her, too."

"She's Chris's sister."

"Oh, but that's not why. You like like her."

"Maybe. But I have a few reservations." He got up, fetched the guest book and set it down before Ursula. "Take a look."

"At what?" Ursula pulled her glasses from the top of her head and peered at Dana's signature. Her eyebrows drew together. Slowly, she turned her head to look at Sam. "Raynott?"

"That's her name."

"Your mother hated him."

"I know."

"But that's not Chris's name. Is Dana married? Or divorced?"

"No. She says Chris changed his name. He grew up a Raynott."

She drew back. "Chris lied?"

"Technically, no. I've never asked him if he changed his name. He just never volunteered the information."

She paused. "It can't only be a coincidence."

"I don't think so, either. What exactly did my mother tell you about him?"

Ursula thought for a moment. "She said a man named Wayne Raynott had your father's blood on his hands."

"What does that mean?"

"I don't know. Your mother could be a little…dramatic sometimes."

"Yeah."

"You've known Chris for years. You trust him. What do you know about this sister? Why did she suddenly show up after all this time? Maybe she's lying."

Sam shrugged. "She says she's here to persuade Chris to accept an inheritance according to her father's will. And apparently to find someone he owed money to."

"Someone he owed?"

"That's what she said."

"Hmm." Ursula tapped her finger against her chin. "Do we even know for sure she is Chris's sister?"

"She knows a lot about him and he gave her the keys to the house and his car. He apparently trusts her. You know how he feels about that car."

"Still, can we trust a Raynott?"

"Trust a Raynott about what?" Dana stepped into the room. Her brown eyes reflected the hurt her voice didn't. She picked up her cell phone from the table where she'd signed the guest book and crossed to stand in front of them. "What's this all about?"

Sam and Ursula looked at each other before Sam spoke. "According to what my mother told Ursula, she held a man named Wayne Raynott responsible for my father's death."

Dana frowned. "My father's name is Wayne Raynott."

"I assumed so."

"That can't be right. My father was an honest, upstanding man. He built a business in Kansas and established a reputation for fair dealings. As far as I know, he was never even in Alaska."

"Then why are you here?"

"To find Chris."

"But you were searching public records in Fairbanks."

"Well, yes, for this other person I need to find— Oh, you think if he owed money to someone in Fairbanks, Dad must have been there."

"It seems a reasonable assumption."

She nodded slowly. "Maybe so. But just because he was there doesn't make him guilty of anything."

"No, it doesn't. And the fact that Chris never told me his father's name was Raynott doesn't make Chris guilty of anything, either. But you have to admit, it's odd."

Dana put her hands on her hips. "Did you ever mention your mother's accusations to Chris?"

Sam thought about it. He tried to avoid thinking about his childhood at all, much less discussing it with anyone. "No, I don't think so."

"Then why is it odd he wouldn't mention it to you?"

"Fair enough."

Ursula spoke up. "What about this other person you're trying to find? What money?"

Dana shrugged. "There were some letters in with my father's personal papers, claiming he owed money to a man who died, and that the money should go to the man's son. The letters didn't mention the son's name. I'm going to Fairbanks Monday morning to search the birth records."

"Will they just give you someone else's birth certificate?"

"I hope so, once I show them the legal papers and explain why I'm trying to find him. The lawyers seemed to think they would." Tiny lines formed between her eyebrows. "As long as I'm there, I'll look into the other records, see if I can find out if there's any record of my father being there or his relationship to this man."

"What's the man's name?"

"Roy Petrov."

Ursula stared at her. Sam jumped up, almost knocking the chair over in his haste. "Say that name again."

Dana took a step backward. "Roy Petrov. I have to find his son."

Sam moved closer. "I can save you time looking for that birth certificate."

"How's that?"

"I happen to have a copy at home."

"What? Why would you have it?"

He blew out a breath. "Because I'm the son of Roy Petrov."

CHAPTER SIX

EARLY MONDAY MORNING, Dana repacked her bag for the trip to Fairbanks. The birth certificate Sam showed her raised more questions than it answered. Sam had been born in Fairbanks about a year before Dad started the tool rental business in Kansas, so Dad could have been in Fairbanks during that time. But what was the relationship between Roy Petrov and her father? Friends? Enemies? She felt compelled to find out.

She'd just stowed away her computer and was about to unplug her phone from the charger when it rang. She looked at the screen. Reliable Equipment and Tool Rental. Jerry certainly wasn't likely to be checking in with her. She could still picture the smug look on his face when she had resigned.

"This is Dana."

"Dana, it's Heather." Her voice was almost a whisper.

"Hi, Heather. How are you?"

"I'm fine, but the business isn't." Dana could almost see her cupping her hand over the phone.

"What's wrong?"

"Everything is completely screwed up. Jerry won't let the service guys do the scheduled maintenance until the machines break down. And he won't let me keep the parts in inventory, so when they do break, they're out of commission until we get the parts in. Customers are starting to complain because they can't get the tools they need."

"Did you tell Jerry?"

"I said we were out of the parts we need. He blew it off, said to order more."

The man was totally incompetent. Why did her dad ever hire him, much less put him in charge? "I'm not sure what I can do about it. The trustees decided to keep him as manager, not me."

"I don't know, either. I just thought I should tell someone. I can't argue with him."

"Yeah, I know." Jerry was big on loyalty, which translated into expecting everyone else to be a yes-man. He wouldn't hesitate to terminate an employee who wasn't what he considered a team player. Heather was a single mom. She couldn't afford to risk her job. But that business was Mom's main source of income. "Maybe I can talk to him. Thanks for the heads-up, Heather."

"No problem. Bye, Dana."

Dana set the phone on the counter. The business her dad had worked so hard to build was going down the tubes, and she couldn't stop it. That stupid will putting everything in the trustees' care had tied her hands. How could her father have been so blind?

Two years ago, when Dad had the first heart attack and mentioned transitioning to retirement, Dana thought he was leading up to putting her in as manager. But since she was taking time off to run him to doctor's appointments and therapy, he put his golf buddy in charge instead. Dad said Jerry had a degree in business and would know how to run things. Dana suspected Jerry's college career had centered more on frat parties than business theory, but what could she say?

Jerry might be a scratch golfer, but he was a lousy manager, and maybe it was her fault Dad hadn't realized that. As Dad spent less time working and Jerry started to take charge, Dana had quietly worked around him, keeping everything running smoothly despite Jerry's mistakes and bad decisions, and she let him take the credit so Dad wouldn't worry. How was she to know Dad's will would put the business in the trustees' hands instead of hers?

Once he died, it was too late. The trustees who managed the trust for Mom saw no reason to upset the management that Dad had put in place. As far as they could see, Dana was just a part-time employee there.

It was tempting to let Jerry crash, but for Mom's sake as well as all the employees who worked there, Dana couldn't just stand by and watch the business flounder. She picked up her phone and dialed the direct number to the office.

"Reliable Equipment and Tool Rental."

"Hi, Haley, it's Dana. Is Jerry in?"

"Yeah, he's here." Haley dropped her voice. "Do you want to disturb his putting practice?"

He hated that. Dana grinned. "I'll risk it."

A minute later, he picked up the phone. "Dana. This is a surprise. I hope you're well."

"I am, thanks. How is everything going there?"

"Just fine."

"Say, I've heard customers aren't always

finding the tools they need. Is there a problem with inventory?"

"Where did you hear that?" His voice was sharp.

She couldn't throw Heather under the bus. "A friend, wife of one of the local contractors."

"Well, everything's fine. I have a system. It's called just-in-time inventory control. All the big companies are using it."

Yeah, she could read business articles, too. Jerry liked to throw around buzzwords, but he'd missed the whole point. Just-in-time didn't mean two weeks late. The only reason his system ever worked was that she'd ignored it and ordered parts on her own authority. Heather couldn't risk going around him like that.

"Maybe you could tweak the system a little, just to make sure."

"Now, Dana. Your father put me in charge for a reason. I understand these things. It all has to do with cash flow."

Dana silently counted to ten before she said something to make it worse. Her pretty little head could comprehend cash flow, and she knew if the tools and equipment they needed weren't available, their customers' cash would flow right to their competitors. And they might never come back. How could she make him understand?

"You know, I read an article on the plane that due to various labor problems, shipping times are increasing. I think it was in *Wall Street Weekly*. It said businesses needed to double their lead time."

"The *Weekly* said that?"

"I'm pretty sure it was them." Actually, she hadn't seen any such article, but Jerry held the *WSW* in such reverence it was worth the gamble. Besides, he seldom actually read it.

"Hmm." He paused. "Oh, my appointment's here. Nice talking with you, but I need to go."

"Okay, Jerry. Thanks for listening."

She ended the call and stared at the wall. Appointment. Right. He just didn't want to have to defend his strategy. Not that she could throw stones. She'd just told a blatant lie to manipulate Jerry into doing his job. Did that make her a bad person? That business supported her mother and thirty employees, so she felt somewhat justified. Not that she really expected her suggestions to carry a lot of weight with Jerry.

Should she be making this trip to Fairbanks? Maybe she should be at home, keeping an eye on Mom and the business. She shook her head. The business wasn't her problem anymore.

No, her problem was to try to figure out if her father legitimately owed Sam's father money. The woman who wrote the letters, signed Ruth, turned out to have been Sam's mother. From what little Ursula and Sam said, her credibility sounded a little questionable, but Dana was willing to look into it. After all, Dad would have wanted to pay off any legitimate debts.

Besides, she wanted to prove to Sam and Ursula that Raynotts were not the sort of people that had "blood on their hands." It was all probably a misunderstanding of some sort. Hopefully, she would find something in Fairbanks that would clear her family's name.

She carried her suitcase to the garage, only to find Sam already there. He picked up her bag and set it in the back of his pickup. Dana frowned. "I planned to take Chris's car. He said I could use it."

Sam shook his head and closed the door on the topper. "That car is Chris's baby. I don't want to get dog hair all over the seats."

"Dog hair?"

"Yeah. I could put Kimmik in a kennel, but it's easier to take him with us."

"You're coming?"

"Of course. I made us reservations in a two-bedroom cabin where they allow dogs."

O-kay. She'd planned on doing the research herself and presenting it to him when she returned, but maybe this was better. Sam knew his way around Fairbanks and she didn't. And this way, there could be no question of her tampering with evidence or hiding anything. Not that there would be anything to hide. Reputation was everything to her father. He would never have done anything that might damage his standing in the community.

Maybe that's what the fight with Chris was all about. Maybe Chris had done something Dad thought reflected badly on him. It was hard to imagine Chris doing anything that unforgivable, but he could be a little impulsive. Her eye fell on his car, gleaming under the florescent lights of the garage. Perfect example. "How practical is a convertible in Alaska, anyway?"

Sam smiled in amusement. "Not practical at all. The clearance is too low for snow. He only drives it in the summer, and only on sunny days. That's what I meant about it being his baby."

An extra car just for sunny summer days. Imagine. "Fishing must pay well."

"It does, but that's not Chris's main job. He owns a business clearing snow from parking lots. I believe he has six trucks and ten seasonal employees now."

"I didn't realize Chris was an entrepreneur. Dad was always trying to get him involved in his business, but Chris was never interested. Dad made him major in business, but he minored in history."

"Well, he must have inherited some business skills because he's been quite successful. Still, given his schedule it makes sense for him to just rent a room from me." Sam closed the back of the topper and turned toward her. "Ready to go?"

Dana cocked her head and studied him. "Are you sure you want to come?"

"I'm sure. It will be easier to find the information if two of us are looking." He opened the door to the house and called the dog. "And I need answers."

"That makes two of us." Since so far, all she'd managed to uncover were questions.

At Sam's whistle, Kimmik jumped into the

back seat and the two of them settled into the front. Sam growled as they crossed the speed bump, and Dana hid a grin. Ten minutes later, they were cruising on the highway. It was only seven in the morning, but the sun peeped through a break in the clouds well up over the mountains. For the first hour or so, Sam didn't speak, just sipped his coffee as he drove.

Dana opened the folder in her lap and skimmed over the legal papers, trying to read between the lines, but of course she didn't find anything new. She looked over the copy of the birth certificate Sam had given her. Samuel Roy MacKettrick. Mother: Mary Ruth MacKettrick. Father: Roy Petrov.

Finally, Dana couldn't keep the questions bouncing around in her head quiet any longer. "So, if your name is MacKettrick, I gather your parents weren't married."

He flashed a look from the corner of his eye. "You gather correctly."

She flushed. "I didn't mean that as an insult. I'm just trying to understand the situation."

"My mother said they had plans to get married but he died. That was before I was born."

"So it was just you and your mother." Dana

tried to imagine what life would have been like without her father's stability and common sense. Would her mother have been less flaky if she were solely responsible for two children? Or would that just have pushed her over the edge?

"Yes, just us." Sam kept his eyes straight ahead.

"So how did you end up with Ursula?"

He glanced toward her. "Nosy, aren't you?"

"I'm sorry. You don't have to answer. It's none of my business." She settled back in her seat. "I was just trying to understand the situation."

Sam shrugged. "I don't know what happened to my mother."

"How can you not know?"

He drove on, apparently at the end of his patience as far as her questioning went, but after a few minutes, he let out a long sigh. "My mom wasn't exactly Mother of the Year material. She drank. Sometimes a little, sometimes a lot. We moved from Fairbanks to Anchorage when I was in fourth grade."

Dana nodded encouragement. After a moment, Sam continued, "We were staying with someone she knew for a while, but eventually they kicked us out. Probably tired of her excuses. We wound up in a shelter."

Thank goodness they had a shelter. Dana shuddered to think what would have happened if a ten-year-old and his mother had to live on the streets. She'd heard stories from some of the shelter kids. She just hadn't realized Sam had been one of those kids. "What happened after that?"

His shoulders twitched. "We got by okay for a couple of years. Some agency set us up in an apartment and my mom had a job. I liked my school. Ursula and Tommy lived a couple of houses down from the apartment building and I'd walk past their house on my way home from school every day. Tommy worked on the North Slope of Alaska at Prudhoe Bay. His rotation was two weeks on, two weeks off, and when he was home he was always building something in the garage." Sam gave a little smile. "The sound of power tools is hard for a boy to resist."

"I'll bet."

"I'm sure I was a nuisance, but Tommy let me hang around, anyway. It didn't take long before Ursula was feeding me a snack after school every afternoon and checking over my homework. When Tommy was working on the slope, he'd leave me a project to keep me busy until he got home."

"Like what?"

"Oh, a couple of times he cut out pieces for a birdhouse I could assemble and paint, and when he came back we'd hang it in the yard together. I wasn't allowed to use his power tools without supervision, of course, but he had a set of hand tools set aside for me and encouraged me to use his scraps to build things. Or he'd ask me to spade the garden or help Ursula clean out the basement. There were a couple of boys who lived in my apartment building Tommy didn't approve of. Minor troublemakers. He made sure I kept too busy to hang out with them."

"Wise man."

"He was. I got so comfortable with them that one day I let it slip to Ursula that my mom had left me alone all night. I was scared to death someone would take me away and put me in a foster home. That's what my mom said would happen if I told anybody."

Poor kid. "What did Ursula do?"

"She made a point of befriending her. After that, when my mom would go out, she'd let me stay over at their house."

"Ursula is really something, isn't she?"

"Yeah. She and Tommy were both great to me. Mom stuck it out for a while, but the overnights got more frequent, and sometimes it stretched over into two nights. And then one day, she didn't come back."

"What do you think happened to her?"

He shrugged. "Massive bender? Left town? I don't know. Not sure I care."

"Didn't someone investigate?"

"Ursula and Tommy decided not to report me. I know that sounds sketchy, but you have to understand, they weren't approved as foster parents. They didn't want to risk someone taking me away from them. We told the school I was staying with them for the time being. It may have been implied they were my aunt and uncle."

"What happened to Tommy?"

"He died when I was in high school. Heart attack."

"Rough. I'm sure it was a comfort to Ursula to have you there."

"I hope so."

"And you never saw your mother again?"

"She's probably dead by now." His mouth tightened. "Doesn't matter, anyway, as far as I'm concerned. She made her choice."

"I guess she did." Dana was silent, lost in

her thoughts. This was the woman who wrote the letters demanding money? Were they just a scam? Or maybe she just imagined someone owed her something. Dana had a hard time feeling any compassion for the woman. How could anyone just abandon a twelve-year-old? How must Sam have felt when he realized she wasn't coming back?

Her thought must have shown on her face because Sam frowned. "Hey, don't you feel sorry for me. I'm not into pity parties. I'm fine. I'm more than fine. I have a good job, a good life."

"I don't feel sorry for you." Dana gave a wry smile. Maybe she did feel bad for that boy whose mother deserted him, but not for the man he'd grown into. "In fact, if I'm honest, this weekend when I saw you and Ursula hug, I was a little jealous. I'd love to have someone in my life who was that glad to see me show up."

He shot her a questioning look. "What about your mom?"

Dana shrugged. "She's kind of lost in her own little world of retail therapy. Dad never paid much attention. I thought once we started working together..." She trailed off before turning toward Sam. "Chris was the only one I ever felt close to."

"Until he left?"

"Yeah. I missed him so much." She gave him a tight smile. "But you're right. No pity parties. Moving on."

He nodded. After a few moments, he spoke in a quiet voice. "That's the only way, you know. Moving on. Life moves forward, and you can either paddle your own boat, or you can throw up your hands and let the current carry you wherever it will. But you can't stay where you are. It doesn't work that way."

"You're quite a philosopher."

"That's me." He grinned. "After my shift, I go to the gym and work out on the rowing machine for a while. Gives me time to think."

"I suppose it would." They rode in silence. Time to think. Maybe that's what had been missing in her life. Between work and babysitting her mother and volunteering at the shelter, not to mention caring for Dad and then chasing after this will, Dana hadn't taken the time to stop and think for a long while. Maybe she'd done it on purpose, kept herself busy so she wouldn't have to think about where she was going, why she was doing what she did. "I believe you're right."

Sam glanced at her. "About what?"

"About moving forward. Maybe it's time I did a little paddling of my own."

SAM DROVE ONWARD, the only sound the hum of his tires over the highway. The day had started out overcast, but as they drove north through the tunnel of trees lining both sides of the highway, blue sky appeared overhead. Dana had been quiet for the last thirty miles or so, to his relief. He didn't talk about his childhood. None of the people he worked with knew, and yet, once Dana had started asking questions, the story seemed to pour out. And she hadn't judged him.

More importantly, she didn't pity him, not really. There seemed to be a connection between them, a certain empathy that allowed her to understand. Maybe because she had those same empty places inside.

Her phone rang. She checked the screen and made a face before answering. "Hi, Mom."

There was a long pause. Dana rubbed her forehead while she listened. Finally, she spoke. "No, she's right." Another pause. "If you let the account overdraw, there will be huge fees and you'll have that much less next month."

Beside the road, Sam spotted the sign for a scenic overlook. On a clear day like this, it was worth stopping. He never got tired of this view.

Dana continued to listen, tapping her free hand against her knee. She was obviously agitated, but she kept her voice gentle and matter-of-fact. "You'll either have to wait until the first of the month, or return something. That's just the way it is. Yes, well, that's her job. Goodbye. I'll talk with you soon."

She closed her eyes and flung her head back against the seat just as Sam pulled into the overlook. He turned off the engine.

"Why…" Dana opened her eyes and looked through the windshield. "Ooh." The word whooshed out in a long breath, almost a sigh. The mountain rose before them in all its glory, the sun glistening off the snow-covered peaks against the blue sky. "It's beautiful."

"We're lucky. Denali is so high it makes its own weather. Most days we wouldn't be able to see the peak."

"I had no idea mountains like that existed."

"Denali. The Great One."

"We don't have anything like that in Kansas."

He laughed. "Well, we don't have cornfields, so maybe it all evens out."

She just shook her head and climbed out of the truck without ever taking her eyes off the mountain. Eventually, he coaxed her into turning so he could take her picture with Denali and Foraker in the background. "Ready to go?"

"Just a few more minutes?"

"Take your time." He came to stand beside her, feeling oddly proud, as if he were somehow responsible for arranging the weather so that she could see Denali at its best. He gazed at the mountain for a few minutes and then turned to watch Dana. Happiness and wonder transformed her face from simply pretty to beautiful.

"Sam." She reached for his hand and gave it a squeeze. "Thank you."

BY THE TIME they arrived in Fairbanks and checked into a cabin so they could leave Kimmik, Dana was starving. Sam must have felt the same way. "I know a little sandwich shop near the campus. They have great homemade soups."

"Sounds perfect."

A few minutes later, they were sitting at a pine table, chowing down on turkey sandwiches. Dana took a spoonful of soup, savoring the mushrooms blended with the nutty taste of barley. "Yum."

"Sam?" A man with a thick head of gray hair crossed to their table.

Sam stood and offered his hand. "Professor."

"Good to see you. I wasn't sure you were still working in Alaska."

"I'm actually doing a rotation in Siberia now, infill drilling."

"Excellent. And this must be your wife?"

Dana wondered if she imagined the smile that flashed across Sam's face for just a moment. "No, a friend. Dana Raynott, this is Dr. Higgins. He performed the miracle of pounding the principles of thermodynamics into my head."

The man chuckled. "Don't let that modest act fool you. Sam was one of my most gifted engineering students."

"I'm sure." Dana smiled. "Nice to meet you, Doctor." She shook his hand.

"Well, I just wanted to say hello. I'll let you get back to your lunch."

Dana watched him go. She'd been out of college for thirteen years. She doubted any of her professors would remember her. Sam must have been an exceptional student. All around her, young people were settled at tables with open laptops. This seemed to be one of those places that let customers nurse a cup of coffee all day while they studied.

She could picture a younger Sam at one of these tables, immersed in a book, with that line across his forehead that appeared whenever he concentrated. Getting top grades would have been important to him, part of paddling his own boat. He'd come a long way from that little boy with no father and an alcoholic mother.

And how did her own father fit into that picture? There must have been some relationship between him and Sam's father. How else would Sam's mother have known to write him? Once they finished lunch, they would go to the city clerk's office to see if public records gave them any clue as to what that relationship could be.

Part of her was eager to find more, but at the same time, she worried. What if they found something awful? She set her sandwich on her plate. Her father was a good man.

Maybe he wasn't the most hands-on father, but he had built a reputation for honesty and fairness in all his business dealings. She had nothing to worry about. So why did her stomach feel as if she'd swallowed a rock?

Sam had cleaned his plate and was eying hers. "Are you going to finish your sandwich?"

She shook her head. "I'm full. You can have it if you like."

"Thanks." She smiled as she watched him wolf down the sandwich as if he wasn't sure where his next meal might be coming from. He saw her noticing and gave a sheepish smile, but that didn't stop him from eating every last crumb.

Once their plates were empty, Sam gathered their dishes onto a tray and bussed it to a cart near the kitchen. "Ready to get some answers?"

She stood up straight and nodded. "Ready."

TEN MINUTES LATER, they found the city clerk's office and walked up to the desk. Dana smiled at the clerk. "Excuse me. We're trying to find information on two men that may have lived in Fairbanks in the late seventies. How can we access the census records?"

"Census records are federal. This is city."

"Oh. How would we go about finding the federal records?"

"I don't know, but it doesn't matter." The clerk shook her head. "Federal census records are sealed for seventy-two years."

Dana looked at Sam in dismay. He stepped forward. "Are there any public records from that time we can see?"

"Well, there are property tax records. Did either of them own a house?"

"Possibly."

"If you know when, you can search the records."

"Okay. Can you help us with that?"

"Oh, no. That's not city, that's borough. You'll need to go to the assessor's office." She gave them directions.

They found the assessor's office without much difficulty but had to wait in line. The white-haired woman in front of them was there to complain about the assessment on her home, but although the clerk repeatedly explained to her that the appeal process had expired months ago, she continued to argue that the taxes were much too high and she wasn't going to pay them. The discussion went in circles for almost half an hour before she managed to pacify the woman with the mailing address for the review board.

Finally, the harried clerk turned to them with an obviously forced smile. "How may I help you?"

"We need to find out if either of two men owned property in Fairbanks."

"That information is available online." She looked past them to the next customer.

"Yes, but this would have been in the late seventies."

"Oh. If it's that old, it wouldn't be on the computer. You'll have to go over to the Fairbanks North Star Borough office, where the old records are stored. They close in thirty minutes, though." She handed them a flyer listing the addresses of all government offices and turned to the next person in line. "How may I help you?"

They walked into the sunshine. Sam gave a wry smile. "Well, that wasn't too productive."

"We'll try the borough office tomorrow." Dana felt a certain relief that they hadn't found anything yet to tie their fathers together. In spite of the frustration of trying to cut through the red tape, she felt comfortable working with Sam. Once they knew the whole story, it would most likely prove either

her father or his mother a liar, and things might never feel comfortable between them again.

He yawned. "I need some air. Let's take a walk."

"Sounds good to me."

As they strolled toward their parking spot, they passed a consignment store. A pillow in the window caught Dana's eye and she stopped.

Sam peered at the jumble of items in the window. "What are you looking at?"

"This needlepoint pillow with the wild rose pattern. It would be perfect in Ursula's Rose room." She leaned closer, trying to read the price on the handwritten tag. "I'm going to get it for her, as a thank-you for her hospitality."

Sam followed her into the store. "I suspect she would say fixing the gate was more than enough thank you."

Dana picked up the pillow to examine it. "You did that."

"Are you kidding me? If you hadn't caught that math error before I cut it, I'd have had to drive to town for another board. It wouldn't be the first time."

She laughed. "Why was Ursula so insistent

you fix it instead of hiring someone, any-way?"

"Tommy was an amazing handyman, and he taught me a few things, so she tends to overestimate my abilities. Besides, she's al-ways trying to save my money for me."

Dana looked up from the pillow. "For you? Do you pay all the maintenance for her?"

"I have to. I'm the landlord."

"The B and B is yours?"

"Yes. Or at least it will be in twenty-five years when the mortgage is paid off. The place only has six guest rooms, but it brings in enough income to make it worth Ursula's while and cover the mortgage payments."

"Sweet. What made you decide to buy an inn, of all things?"

"Self-defense." Sam gave a low chuckle. "Ursula used to work part-time at a store downtown, but it closed about six years ago. That left her at loose ends, and Ursula with time on her hands is a dangerous thing. I was in Seward one weekend and happened to see the For Sale sign when I drove by. I remem-ber thinking how much energy and organi-zation it would take to run an inn. When I came home, I found Ursula alphabetizing my pantry and decided it was a sign. I bought the place and she runs it."

He bought an inn to make his foster mother happy. Wow. "It's a beautiful building, and the guests seemed thrilled to be there."

"Ursula is a born hostess and a great cook."

"She certainly is. That caramel French toast we had for breakfast was outstanding." Dana carried the pillow to the cash register. Once she'd completed the transaction, she smiled at Sam. "I'll get the address from you and mail it to her. I think she'll like it."

"I know she will, but why don't you just bring it next time you visit?"

If only she could. She felt more welcome there than she had anywhere except her own home, at least until Ursula found out her name. But she wasn't in Alaska for a vacation. She had two tasks to finish, and then she was going back to Kansas. "I don't know how long I'll be here. It all depends on Chris."

"Of course." The look of disappointment on his face mirrored her own feelings. Or maybe she imagined it.

She tried for a cheerful voice. "So, where are we walking?"

"I know just the place." He passed a table

of assorted footwear and stopped. "What size shoe do you wear?"

"Five and a half. Why?"

Sam reached below the table and picked up a pair of bright yellow rubber boots with black polka dots. "Size six. Close enough." He took the boots toward the register.

Dana trotted after him. "Why do I need boots?"

"You'll see." Sam insisted on paying the ten dollars for the boots, drove to the cabin to pick up Kimmik and then drove out on a road that ended near an old log cabin with a sagging roof.

Sam parked, let Kimmik out, and grabbed a tennis ball from the back of the truck. "We'll exercise him first, then take our walk."

"He can't come with us?"

"It's better if he doesn't." Kimmik barked at Sam to throw the ball. Sam obliged and Kimmik galloped after it, snagging it on the fly and proudly returning it to Sam for another turn. After twenty minutes, the dog was still wagging his tail and begging for more play, even as he panted. Sam poured him a bowl of water and shut him in a wire crate in the shade of the truck.

He handed Dana the boots. "Ready for our walk?"

"I really need boots?"

Sam looked down at her feet. "We wouldn't want to ruin those pretty pink sneakers."

True. She hadn't brought a backup pair. Dana accepted the boots and slipped them on. She probably looked like a duck with these ridiculous yellow feet. Sam pulled on a pair of black boots, making her feel better. He wasn't just teasing her about her aversion to mud. He pulled a pair of binoculars from his glove compartment.

"Where are we going?"

"You'll see."

They walked past a field of grain. This was the first sign of farming Dana had come across in Alaska. On the other side of the field, a variety of ducks swam on a shallow pond. "So pretty. What are the ones with the feathers sticking out the backs of their heads?"

"Wood ducks. Come on. I have something to show you, if it's still there. I'm afraid it might not be, but I think it's worth checking out."

The path ran past an old cottonwood. Sam held some branches back so she could push through the brush and follow a narrow and largely overgrown trail beside the creek that fed the pond.

They marched single file along the trail, which was getting fainter and wetter with every step. The mud clutched at their boots, making a squelching sound as they pulled their feet free. Dana stepped on a slick spot and would have fallen if Sam hadn't caught her arm.

"You okay?"

"I'm fine, but this better be good."

He looked at the mud caked well up over her ankles. "You want to turn back?"

She weighed the muddy trail against the eager expression on his face. "I'm already muddy. Might as well go on."

"Good. I only hope it's there still." They continued to follow the creek, sometimes wading in the water when the trail became too overgrown to use. Eventually, the creek started to widen. Sam pointed. "See that old beaver dam? What we're looking for should be just behind that bush. Try to be quiet."

She tiptoed after Sam, coming closer to the pile of sticks and logs partially damming the creek and creating a calm pool behind it. Something white caught the light behind the bush. A few more steps and she was able to see the black beak and long neck of a swan.

She grasped Sam's arm in excitement. He smiled at her and handed her the binoculars. Through them, she could see all the details of the white swan resting there. As she watched, a second swan came into view. The nesting swan stood and five fuzzy babies spilled out from underneath her. She stepped into the water and swam closer to the second one until the two of them touched beaks, their curving necks forming a heart. The babies swam behind her, all in a row.

The sheer beauty brought tears to Dana's eyes. "Aww." It was a whisper, but the swans must have heard. They looked toward her and one of them herded the babies farther away. Sam took her hand and tugged her back down the path.

"We'd better go. We don't want to disturb them while they're nesting."

"They're so beautiful. How did you know they were there?"

"I used to come out here sometimes when I was in college, just to get away from people. Swans mate for life and tend to come back to the same nests. To be honest, I didn't expect to find them. Swans live for a long time, but not that long. I suspect this might be one of their cygnets and his mate."

"I'm so glad you brought me. I've never seen wild swans before."

He looked at her feet. "I'll clean your boots for you."

Dana laughed. "Not necessary. Seeing those swans was worth every bit of mud. When was the last time you came here?"

He thought about it. "The day after I graduated. I was packing up, getting ready to move back to Anchorage, and I decided to visit one last time before I left. The swans were here, getting their nest in order." He met her eyes. "I've never brought anyone with me before."

Dana reached for his hand. "I'm honored."

He held her gaze for several moments before he stepped closer and slowly lowered his head. Her lips parted in a tiny gasp just before he pressed his mouth against hers. She closed her eyes and let her entire focus shift to the sensation of their lips meeting. His hands settled around her waist, and her arms automatically reached up around his neck. She pushed her fingers into his thick hair and pulled him closer. He responded, tilting his head and deepening the kiss.

He didn't rush, simply kissed her as though

it was the one and only purpose of his life. Dana wasn't completely inexperienced. She'd had a boyfriend in college, dated a few other men, and yet somehow, she'd never truly been kissed. Not like this.

The sun may well have moved several degrees across the sky before he lifted his head and looked into her eyes once again. He stroked her cheek with one finger, setting the nerve endings in her skin vibrating.

After a few minutes, he took her hand and led the way along the path. He didn't let go until they reached a tangle where he had to hold the brush out of the way so she could squeeze by. She shivered, suddenly cold without his touch.

When they returned to the truck, Kimmik greeted them as though they'd been gone for months. Sam rubbed his head before commanding him to jump into the cab. Sam climbed into the driver's seat and looked over at Dana, holding her gaze for several long moments before he started the engine, and he drove back toward town without a word. Dana didn't speak, either, afraid words would break the spell.

They pulled up in front of the cabin. Sam

turned off the engine but made no move to get out. "About that kiss—"

"Don't." She didn't want to hear how it was a mistake, or didn't mean anything, or couldn't happen again. She knew all those things, knew she was going home soon and would most likely never see Sam again. But she couldn't be sorry that kiss happened when it did. Because tomorrow, everything might be different.

He took a deep breath and looked at her. She could see some emotion deep in his eyes, a struggle taking place before his self-discipline won out and he was once again in control. He nodded and climbed out of the truck. "Let's get changed, and then we can go to dinner. All that exercise must have stimulated my appetite."

CHAPTER SEVEN

THE OFFICE OPENED the next morning promptly at nine. Sam held the door for Dana. They were the first customers, having waited outside the office door for the borough office to open. He was tempted to suggest something else this morning, some touristy thing to give Dana and him an excuse to put this off until afternoon. But they needed to know the truth, even though he had a good idea that in this case, the truth wouldn't set them free.

Today was more productive. The clerk, a smiling middle-aged woman who introduced herself as Linda, wrote down the names and invited them to have a cup of coffee while she looked through the files. Within an hour, she handed a sheet of paper to Dana. "I found this one."

Sam looked over her shoulder. "Wayne Raynott. So he was in Fairbanks."

"Yes." Dana eyes roamed over the paper. "Looks like he owned a commercial property on Zelda Street named The Nugget. The note says also residential. Wonder what that means."

"It may have been a business with an apartment above." Linda looked at the address on the record. "Or maybe there was a house on the lot as well as a business. That's way out on the edge of town."

"Zelda Street." Sam shook his head. "I don't think I've ever been to that part of town. Did you find anything about Roy Petrov?"

"Not yet. I'll keep looking." Linda disappeared into the file room once again.

Dana paced around the room, studying the paper in her hand. "Okay, so we know my dad owned property. What does that tell us?" She rotated her shoulders as if she were trying to shrug off her misgivings. "The Nugget doesn't sound like any sort of tool or construction business."

Sam put his hands on her shoulders and massaged them. He could feel the tight ribbons of muscle beneath his fingers. "I've been thinking. If your father owned a commercial property, he probably ran a business from it, right?"

She looked up at him, her eyes brightening. "So he would have had to have a license."

"Right. Let's check on business licenses."

After another thirty minutes, the clerk returned, admitting defeat. She found no indication that Roy Petrov had ever owned property in the Fairbanks borough.

"We appreciate your help," Sam said. "Where would we check on business licenses from that time?"

"Well, that might be a problem."

Now what? "Were the records lost in a fire or something?"

The clerk shook her head. "No, Fairbanks didn't require a business license before 2005."

Dana let out a sigh. "So there's no way of finding out what kind of business it was?"

"Well, there's the state business license."

"Where are those filed?"

Linda gave a wry smile. "Juneau."

Dana let her chin fall to her chest. Linda laughed and wrote something on a notepad. "Here. Go to the library and ask for my friend Gretchen. She's big into genealogy, knows her way around the state computer system. She'll help you."

"Thanks."

Gretchen turned out to be a tiny woman with unnaturally black hair scraped back from her face and wrapped into a knot on top of her head. She set down the book she was reading and listened with rapt attention while they explained what they were trying to find and where they'd looked so far.

"State business license division." She tapped on her computer for a few moments. "Hmm, computer records don't go back that far." She picked up the phone and punched in some buttons. "Helen? This is Gretchen."

Dana leaned closer to Sam and spoke in a low voice. "Sounds like another dead end. How long to drive to Juneau from here?"

"You can't drive to Juneau. You have to fly or take the ferry."

"You're kidding. You can't drive to the state capital?" Before Dana could ask more questions, Gretchen hung up the phone, a smile on her face. "She found it. She's emailing it to me right now."

"Wow, just like that?"

Gretchen's eyes twinkled. "I'm that good." A minute later, she printed out a copy of the business license and handed it to Sam.

Sam skimmed it. "Pay dirt. Wayne Raynott and Roy Petrov were business partners in— what's this code mean? Oh, a drinking establishment—alcoholic beverages."

"Partners?" Dana leaned closer to read it. "They ran a bar?"

"That's what it looks like. Business name is The Nugget, and the address is the same as the one your father owned." He looked up at Gretchen. "This is exactly what we needed. Thank you."

"My pleasure." Gretchen picked up her book.

Sam and Dana made their way to a relatively private corner of the library. She shook her head. "This is so strange. My dad didn't even like bars. He always said nothing good ever comes from hanging out with drunks." She looked at Sam. "Sorry. I didn't mean…"

"Don't apologize. I tend to agree with him. But whether that was an opinion he formed after being in the business or just decided a drunk's money was a green as anyone else's, he obviously did own a bar. And ran it with my father."

Dana worried at her lip as she stared at the paper. "I'm surprised to find my father had a partner. He didn't tend to trust other people. I wonder…" She stopped talking.

It seemed to Sam that Raynott was the one who couldn't be trusted. But seeing the concern in Dana's eyes, his own melted away.

None of this was her fault. "Hey, we're trying to get at the truth here. I don't want you holding back information to avoid hurting my feelings. According to the State of Alaska, they were business partners, so maybe your father developed his attitude because of whatever happened to end the partnership."

Dana studied the printout. "I guess they must have been successful. I never asked Dad how he got enough money to start the equipment and tool rental business, but it wouldn't have been cheap. I've never seen any records of bank loans or other investors."

"That would have been during the time they were building the Trans-Alaska Pipeline. From what I understand, money was flowing like water in those days, and there would have been a lot of thirsty men in Fairbanks with a wallet full of cash and not many options on how to spend it. But where did he get the money to buy the bar in the first place?"

Dana shrugged. "I don't know. He didn't talk much about his childhood, but I doubt his family had a spare dime. He sometimes mentioned he'd been working full-time since he was sixteen. I gathered he must have dropped out of high school."

"How old would he have been when he bought the property?"

She did the math. "Maybe twenty-six?"

"So he probably worked for someone else for a few years first."

"Something about working for a cousin who paved parking lots. I think he drove some of the work vehicles."

"The Alaska pipeline would have needed drivers. At the rates they were paying, a frugal man could have saved up enough to pay cash on a modest property in a few years."

"He was frugal—" Dana gave a wry smile "—especially when it came to business matters. But how does your father fit into the equation? He's on the business license but not listed on the property."

"I don't know. From what my mother said, my father grew up in a village quite a ways north of here. I don't think he had a lot of spare cash, either. So how would they have met, much less become partners?"

They looked at each other for a few moments before Sam shrugged. "I'm stumped. Let's go see this property."

As they reached the parking lot, Dana's cell phone rang. She glanced at the screen and grimaced. "It's my mom. I need to take this."

"Okay. I'll wait here." Sam sat in the truck and watched her pace along the sidewalk in front of the library. She mostly seemed to be listening, shaking her head. Occasionally she would stop moving and say something, but whatever she said didn't seem to be going over well because the pacing would start again.

Sam wasn't sure what to make of the conversation he'd overheard in the car yesterday. Dana sounded more as if she were dealing with a spoiled teenager than her mother. Not that Sam was any sort of expert when it came to mothers, but he was beginning to suspect Dana hadn't been on the receiving end of a lot of nurturing when she was growing up, from either of her parents.

Eventually, she ended the call. She dialed another number on her phone and spoke briefly before sliding the phone into her pocket. She seemed to give herself a little shake before she turned toward the truck. "Sorry about that."

"No problem. Is everything okay at home?"

Dana rubbed her forehead. "Nothing I haven't handled a million times before. I left a message with the person who's helping out while I'm away. She'll take care of it." She gave him a tight smile. "So, you ready to go see the bar?"

"I'm ready."

They drove across town to a run-down area. Dana tried to find numbers over the doorways of the strip malls, but the signs were old and faded. They came to a block with even older-looking businesses. A nail salon and a tobacco shop filled the two halves of a sagging wooden building originally painted mustard yellow but now mostly faded to a nondescript tan. Next door sat a cinder block pawnshop with iron bars covering the windows. At the other end of the parking lot, two cars were parked in front of a Vietnamese restaurant.

They passed a vacant lot, and then a house with a pile of bicycles in the yard and a few more scattered houses until the road ended abruptly in front of an abandoned building that looked like it might have been a small church at one time. The street number on the mailbox in front of the small house next door indicated that they had come too far. Sam turned around and they crept back along the road, checking for addresses. Finally, Dana spotted a number on a filling station. "Eight forty-seven. It should be the block we just passed."

Sam turned the car around. Silvery leaves of birches fluttered in the breeze of the vacant lot where the business should have been. Sam pulled to the side of the rode and parked. "You think this is the place?"

"I think so."

They got out of the car and walked into the woods. Sam kicked at a crumbling stone foundation sticking up from the ground. "Whatever was here has been gone a long time." He followed the scars and rubble to trace the foundation of a long, narrow building. Toward the back of the lot, almost hidden among the trees, the walls of a long-abandoned frame house still stood, a spruce growing through what had been the roof. Cushions of green moss lined the boards of the sagging front steps. "Maybe this was the residence mentioned."

Dana wandered back to the crumbling foundation, her face a picture of confusion. "What do you think happened to the bar?"

"Let's see if we can find out." Sam took her hand and led her across the street. After considering the four businesses there, he chose the pawnshop, based on outdated lettering on the faded sign. The shop looked like it had been there since statehood. Of course, that didn't guarantee the employees had.

A cowbell clanged when they pushed open the door. A gray-muzzled Rottweiler sleeping in a cracked leather chair beside the door opened one hazy eye. They must not have looked like a threat because he closed it again and let out a snore.

Sam put a hand on Dana's back and guided her farther into the store, where he leaned over to inspect the jewelry displayed underneath glass cases. The shop appeared to be empty, but they heard sounds from behind a curtain. Soon, the curtain was pushed aside and Sam was gratified to see a white-haired man with a cane hobble into the store. "Can I help you?"

"We're just looking right now. You have some nice things." Sam let his eyes wander over the jewelry. "Been here long?"

"Long enough. Looking for an engagement ring, maybe?"

A pink blush painted Dana's cheeks. "No. How long have you worked here?"

The man's eyes narrowed in suspicion. "Why do you want to know?"

Sam nudged her gently. "Her dad used to

live in Fairbanks a long time ago and we were looking at the old neighborhood. Didn't there use to be a bar across the street?"

"Yep." The man's expression didn't change.

Sam's gaze fell on a tray of silver rings. "Could we see that ring, the one with the feather?" The curved plume shape of the ring reminded Sam of the swans they'd seen yesterday.

The man nodded, pulled out the tray and selected the ring. "This is a nice one. Got it from an estate. You don't find quality like this anymore."

He handed it to Sam. Sam inspected the heavy silver carving. "Nice. Here, honey. Try it on."

Dana shot him a skeptical look out of the corner of her eye before allowing him to slip the ring on her finger. It fit as though it had been crafted just for her.

"That looks real nice," the old man said.

"It does. Dana, do you see any others you like better?" He let his arm rest across her shoulders and squeezed. If they wanted the old man to open up, she was going to have to play her part. Dana stepped closer to inspect the rings in the tray.

Sam kept his voice casual. "So what happened to the bar?"

"The Nugget? It burned down ages ago." He looked at Dana. "Any more you wanna try, missy?"

"Um, I might take a look at that blue one. The bar caught fire, you say?"

He nodded. "Yeah. Real sad story. Two people died in the fire. Some folks said it was arson. I ain't sure if it's true or not. But the owner, once he collected the insurance money, he went and skipped town so fast it set tongues to wagging. Rumor is, with his partner gone, he didn't want to take no chances on ole Roy's relations showing up and staking a claim. You know how them families can be. Don't pay no mind unless there's money to be had. Or maybe he didn't want nobody askin' questions about what the two of them was doin' there together in the middle of the night."

"The two of whom?" Dana's voice was sharp, but when Sam bumped his foot against hers, she softened the question with a forced smile and pretended to inspect the ring with the blue stone.

"Why his partner, Roy, and his wife. Some folks figure maybe they was up to no good, and maybe the owner fellow—can't think of his name—he didn't much like it, and set the fire hisself."

A fire. That's how his father died. But what was this about a wife? Or did they mean Mom? But obviously his mother didn't die in a fire. Maybe that was why his parents weren't married, if Roy already had a wife. Of course, it could be that the old man was just confused.

Dana's breathing grew faster. She dropped the blue ring onto the countertop and glared at the man. Obviously not a fan of gossip when it involved her father. Fortunately, the pawnshop owner was still bent over the tray of rings instead of watching her. Sam could see the anger building inside of her, waiting for a spark. Better get her out of there now and worry about this later. They might want more information from the man at some point.

Sam stepped between them. "Well, I think she's chosen the ring she wants. How much?"

The old man squinted at some markings on the box and named a sum. Sam could almost feel Dana breathing fire behind his back, but he smiled and pulled some cash from his wallet for the ring. "Sounds fair. Thank you."

"Nice doin' business with ya. Come again."

Dana's arm trembled beneath his hand as Sam led her out the door. To her credit, she said nothing until they reached the truck. She slammed the door and turned on him. "That man is a liar."

"I don't think so. He may not know all the facts, but I doubt he was deliberately lying."

"Spreading rumors, just as bad. Accusing my father of arson. I can't believe you gave him money."

"It worked. We got the information we were looking for."

"Information? Or hearsay? You've just wasted your cash."

Sam grinned. "It was a reasonable price for the ring. Why? Don't you like it?"

"The ring is fine." She looked down at her hand and her face softened. "It's gorgeous, in fact. It's the information I object to."

"Ah."

She raised that strong yet sweet chin in a stubborn gesture. "I know my father."

Well, that made one of them. Sam didn't know his father at all, and yet he shied away from the idea that Roy might have been married to someone else when Sam was conceived. He could understand why Dana was upset. Still… "You knew him when he was your father, but he had a whole other life before that. Maybe there's a reason he never mentioned his time here."

"I'll never believe he was a cheat, much less an arsonist."

She sounded so sure. Sam had his doubts, but there was no use upsetting her. "I don't recall that our informant said he was. Only that there was speculation to that effect."

Dana thought for a moment. "So, who were the two people who died? He said Roy and his wife."

"Yeah, I noticed that."

"Do you think he meant—"

"I don't know who he meant, but I do know where we can get more information."

"Where's that?"

"The newspaper. We need to check out the back issues from that time."

"Good idea." She pulled the silver band from her finger. "Here's your ring."

He shook his head. "Keep it. I got it for you."

The look she gave him was a mixture of suspicion and puzzlement. "You believe my father may have set a fire that killed yours, and yet you bought me a ring?"

"I don't believe anything yet. I'm just gathering information. But even if I did think so, it has nothing to do with you. I don't see why I can't buy you a souvenir of your first trumpeter swan sighting."

A small smile tugged at her bottom lip. "Seeing those swans was pretty awesome."

"Yes, it was."

She slid the ring back onto her hand and studied it. "It's a beautiful ring. Thank you, Sam."

"You're welcome."

She took a deep breath and straightened her shoulders. "Okay, then. Let's go find out what the newspaper had to say."

DANA PEERED INTO the microfiche machine. Now that they knew when her dad owned the Fairbanks property and the year he started the business in Kansas, it didn't take long to find the article and print it out. The burning of The Nugget had been front-page news. Two pictures accompanied the write-up. The before picture was an interior shot of a bar decorated in a gold rush theme, with gold pans and pickaxes on the walls and kerosene lamps on the tables. Only a pile of black-ened rubble remained in the second photo. Even the small cabin behind the bar sported a singed wall.

Two died when local drinking estab-lishment The Nugget burned to the ground Wednesday night. According to Fire Chief Mike Barlow, the fire started in the public area, pos-sibly from a kerosene lantern left unattended. Fiona Raynott, age 25, wife of bar owner Wayne Raynott, perished in the fire, along with co-owner Roy Petrov.

A wife? Her father had been married be-fore and never bothered to mention it? Worse, a wife who had died under suspicious circum-stances. Dana's shoulders sagged. So that was what the old man at the pawnshop meant. Not Roy's wife. Dad's wife. She read on.

Raynott, who resides in the house adjacent to the popular bar, re-ported the fire at 3:52 a.m. His report states he woke, and finding his wife missing, went searching for her and observed the fire, at which time he called the fire department.

"It was a tinderbox; all that old wood just went up like kindling," Chief Barlow stated. "We were lucky to keep it from spreading through the whole town."

The article went on to get quotes from locals about what a popular place it was and how much they would miss it.

A bystander, who declined to give his name, said, "That Roy, he was a good guy. He'd give you the shirt off his back. And Miss Fiona, I don't care what people are saying about her. She was a fine lady. It's a crying shame."

Much as she hated to, Dana could read between the lines. A missing wife, alone with Dad's business partner in the wee hours of the morning. A convenient fire that took both their lives. Motive and opportunity screamed in capital letters.

Sam laid a comforting hand on her shoulder, but she shrugged it off.

"I know it looks bad…"

Sam shrugged. "We still don't know the whole story."

"But the more we find out, the worse it seems. A wife he never mentioned—"

"How old is Chris?"

"He's— Oh. Wow. I didn't think about that. This woman who died. She must be…"

Sam finished her thought. "His mother."

How could Dana not have realized? She, the math nerd, hadn't added up the years until this moment. Looking back, she realized her parents didn't dwell on or talk much about how long they'd been married. They never made a big deal out of anniversaries or birthdays, anyway, so she hadn't noticed.

"You had no idea Chris was your half-brother?"

"No. The thought never entered my mind." She tried to think if there had ever been any indication, but she couldn't remember anything. "This might be what Chris and my dad fought over."

"Could be."

"Let's see if we can find her obituary."

They found it in the following week's paper. A grainy photo topped the column, leaving no doubt as to Chris's DNA. The same nose, the same wide, generous mouth, curly hair. The obituary itself was generic. Died suddenly, age twenty-five. Memorial service tomorrow. Down at the bottom, Dana found her suspicions spelled out in black-and-white: Fiona is survived by her husband, Wayne Raynott, and their infant son, Christopher.

Roy Petrov's obituary in the same issue was even more brief. Died suddenly in tragic fire. Family unknown. No photograph.

Dana reached for Sam's hand. "I'm sorry about your father."

He nodded, his face almost expressionless, but a muscle in his jaw twitched. He squeezed her hand. After a long moment, he spoke. "I always knew he died. It just seems wrong that there was no family to mourn him."

"What about your mother?"

"Good question. I don't see anything about her here. Of course, if he was cheating on her…" Sam stared down at the newspaper as if he could change history by the sheer force of his will.

"With his partner's wife." Dana shook her head. "It's all so sad."

"Yeah." Sam looked up. "Let's get out of here."

CHAPTER EIGHT

DANA SAT IN the passenger seat beside Sam as they retraced their route along the highway back to Anchorage. He hadn't said a word for hours now, his face expressionless as he drove. Kimmik stirred in the back seat and gave a mighty yawn. Next, he rested his front paws on the back of their seat and snuffled his nose against Dana's hair. It tickled.

Her giggle finally brought a little smile to Sam's face. "Kimmik, get down. What are you doing?"

Dana twisted around so she could rub the dog's ears. He thumped his tail against the seat. "I bet he just wanted to make sure we were still breathing up here."

"Probably."

She watched Sam's face for a moment. "You okay?"

"Sure. I mean, nothing's really changed, right?"

"Not really. I guess if they were partners, I

can see why your mother thought he owed her money and wrote those letters. Apparently he disagreed, since he never paid."

Sam rubbed his chin. "I know for sure my mother received a check from him at least once, but she tore it up."

"What? When?"

"When I was a kid. I remember her getting a check, and it made her angry. She tore it to shreds."

"How old were you?"

"About nine."

Dana did the math. "One of the letters we found was dated a couple of years after that. So why did she tear up a check and then turn around and demand payment?"

He shrugged. "Maybe she thought the check was a way to buy her off instead of giving her what she thought he owed."

"So obviously she didn't trust him."

"Maybe she had a good reason not to trust him."

"Your mother wasn't a rational person. You said so."

"I said she drank. When she wasn't drinking, she was quite rational. And she said she wouldn't accept blood money from Wayne Raynott."

Blood money? Dana almost pointed out that rational people didn't abandon their twelve-year-olds, but she bit her tongue. Sam knew better than anyone what his mother had done. So why would he trust her judgment in anything? The official reports were on her dad's side. They'd gone back to the paper this morning to get copies of follow-up articles, including when the insurance settled the investigation and paid the claim. "The investigation cleared him of arson."

"They failed to find evidence of arson."

"Same thing."

"Not exactly." He glanced at her. "Inability to prove guilt isn't proof of innocence."

"Well, it sure isn't proof of guilt."

"True." At least Sam gave her that. "But if he sent money—"

"Maybe he just felt sorry for her. You have to admit, the facts support him."

"No." He raised his chin. "I don't."

She crossed her arms and stared straight ahead. After a minute, Sam glanced her way. "Sorry. I didn't mean to snap at you."

She shrugged.

Sam reached across the seat and touched her arm. "I need some time to think about this before I come to any conclusions."

"You can have all the time you want. I'm just here to determine if you, as Roy Petrov's son, have a legitimate claim on my father's estate, not whether he burned down a bar. Because I'll never believe he was an arsonist."

"Well, then, let me check off that agenda item for you. I don't want anything to do with Wayne Raynott or his money. You can tell the lawyers that."

Her mouth dropped open. "You think he did it."

"I. Don't. Know." From the back seat, Kimmik whined, upset by Sam's tone. He continued in a softer voice. "I never met him. You tell me he was an honorable man. But that doesn't quite jibe with Chris cutting ties with him. I'd like to hear what Chris has to say about this." They came around a bend and found themselves in some tiny town. "I need to get gas. Would you mind going inside and getting me a cup of coffee?"

"Fine." Dana went in, used the ladies' room and bought two cups of coffee. She carried them to the truck and handed one to Sam. "Black, right?"

"Thank you." Sam took a sip and set it in the cup holder. He turned to face her. "Really. Thank you."

Dana nodded. By unspoken agreement, they didn't discuss anything they'd learned in Fairbanks for the rest of the drive home. Sam pointed out a few sights along the way, but his heart obviously wasn't in it. They had lapsed back into silence by the time they reached the outskirts of Anchorage.

Sam made a left into his neighborhood. "Hungry?"

Dana agreed. "A little."

"How does pizza sound?"

"Fine."

He pulled into the garage. "I'll call in the order. What do you like on it?"

She shrugged. "I like everything."

"Good, because that's exactly how I like it. With everything." They grabbed their bags and he followed her up the stairs, Kimmik bounding on ahead.

Dana opened the refrigerator door and checked the contents. "I'll make a salad to go with it."

"Sounds good."

Sam pulled his phone from his pocket and disappeared into his bedroom. Dana allowed herself to shoot an imaginary dagger into his back before she went to work slicing a carrot and a tomato. She was tossing them with the salad greens when Kimmik ran toward the front door, wagging his tail. Steps sounded on the stairs outside. That was fast. Dana stepped over to grab her purse for a tip.

The door flew open and she spun around, startled. But not as startled as Chris looked when he spotted her.

"You're still here?" There was a note of panic in his voice.

"Obviously."

"Then you've met—"

"Yes, she has." Sam strode in from the hallway. "I can't tell you how surprised I was to discover you have a sister. And that was only the first surprise of many."

Chris looked back and forth between them like he was expecting an attack from both sides. He held up his hands. "I can explain."

"You better make it good." Sam came to stand beside Dana. "Because right now I'm not sure if I believe anything that comes out of your mouth."

BEFORE ANYONE COULD explain anything, the pizza arrived. Sam decided the discussion might go better on a full stomach, anyway. He tipped the delivery guy and carried the pizza to the bar.

"Let's eat first." He looked pointedly at Chris. "And then you can tell us exactly what's been going through that so-called mind of yours."

Chris gave a smirk, probably assuming that if Sam was ribbing him, he wasn't about to blow a gasket at him. Which was true. Nevertheless, Sam didn't intend to let him get away with anything short of full disclosure.

Dana set out plates, dropping the one in front of Chris with more force than necessary. Sam was amused to see the look of trepidation on Chris's face when he realized how angry Dana was. Good. They could work together to get the truth out of Chris.

Chris opened the pizza box and wrinkled his nose. "Mushrooms?" At Dana's withering gaze, he set a slice on his plate. "I'll pick them off."

"Good plan."

Sam took some of the salad Dana had made and passed it to her. She caught his eye and, for a moment, he felt they were on the same side. Then he remembered their argument in the car. She must have remembered, too, because she broke eye contact and served herself some salad.

Once the pizza was gone, they moved to

the living room. Chris settled on the couch. Dana perched on the other end, and Sam sat in a nearby chair. He leaned forward, resting his elbows on his knees, and stared into Chris's face. "Okay, talk."

"I don't know what you know—"

"Then why don't you tell us everything? From the beginning. Starting with why you came to Alaska."

Sam glanced at Dana. She was staring at Chris, her usually soft brown eyes focused like a laser on her brother. "Yeah. Let's start with the day you left home."

Chris looked toward the ceiling and sighed. "Okay. But first, I need to show you something. Wait here."

Chris trotted down the stairs to his bedroom. After a few minutes, he returned carrying a metal box. He unlocked it and, after shuffling through a few papers, pulled out a yellowed envelope. "I was up in the attic, putting away some stuff, and I happened to see an old trunk I thought I could use in my apartment at school. When I opened it, I found these."

He spread the contents of the envelope on the coffee table. Dana leaned forward to examine them. Even upside down, Sam could

read Chris's State of Alaska birth certificate listing his mother as Fiona McCarthy
Raynott. A yellowed clipping of the article
they had seen about the fire rested beside it
on the table. Dana picked up the two card-
board photograph folders and opened the top
one. She examined it, a trace of a smile cross-
ing her face, and then she handed it to Sam.

The man on the right could have almost
been Sam, if he'd grown his hair into a
shaggy mullet and dressed in a really loud
polyester shirt. The grin on his father's face
indicated a day of celebration, as did his arm
around the shoulders of the man Sam could
only assume was Wayne Raynott. Each of
the men held a full mug of beer.

As he looked closer, he could see some
resemblance to Chris: the stubborn jaw, the
broad shoulders. Raynott seemed happy, too.
Behind them, Sam recognized the gold pans
and pickaxes from the photos in the newspaper. Carefully, he slipped the photo from the
folder and found a handwritten note on the
back. *Wayne Raynott and Roy Petrov. Opening Day at The Nugget.*

He looked up to see Dana staring hard at
the other picture. She finally closed the folder
and set it on the table. She turned to Chris.

"So I gather you were as much in the dark as me that we didn't have the same mother?"

"Before that day in the attic, I had no idea. Although looking back, I seldom got a lot of warm fuzzies from Mom. On the other hand, neither did you."

Dana nodded as if that was old news. "So what did you do?"

"I confronted Wayne. He wouldn't tell me anything, even confirm that the birth certificate was genuine. He told me to forget what I'd seen and mind my own business. Eventually, I said if he wouldn't tell me what I wanted to know, I was going to Alaska to get the truth. He said if I did, he wouldn't welcome me back. I decided I could live with that."

"And you drove off without saying goodbye." Dana's voice was small, the hurt of the teenager coming through.

"I'm sorry, Dana. I didn't have a choice."

"You could have contacted me later, told me what happened and where you were."

"I didn't want to get you in trouble with the old man. You know he never backs down."

Dana closed her eyes and balled her hands into fists, as though trying to keep some violent emotion in check. Sam fought the urge to thump Chris on the head. Did he realize when he ran away how much he would be hurting his sister? Sam had to believe he didn't. Chris could be a bit clueless, but he was never deliberately cruel.

Dana blew out a long breath and opened her eyes. Her features were once again calm and in control. "What happened next?"

"I went to Fairbanks. Actually, it took me more than a year to earn enough money to make the trip, but I arrived in late summer. I changed my name in the meantime. I figured if I didn't have a father anymore, I didn't need his name. Once I made it to Fairbanks, I asked around, did some digging and finally found a group of old-timers in a bar who remembered the whole scandal."

Chris opened the photo folder Dana had inspected to display what was obviously a wedding picture. Almost as tall as her husband but slender and delicate, Fiona wore a gauzy white dress and had a wreath of daisies nested in auburn curls. Wayne wore a rust-colored suit and lizard cowboy boots. They smiled at each other, looking happy and very much in love.

Chris squirmed and looked at the table. "Most of the town seemed to be of the opinion that Wayne caught his partner and his wife in a compromising situation and started a fire that burned down the bar."

"But the investigation didn't find arson," Dana piped up.

Frown lines formed on Chris's forehead. "So you know about the fire?"

"We read the newspaper article," Sam said. "What else did you hear?"

"Some of the group used to be regulars at The Nugget. They said Fiona and Roy both worked in the bar and had never shown the slightest romantic interest in one another. In fact, they said Roy was in love with another girl, but kept it quiet because—" he darted a glance of apology at Sam "—Wayne didn't like her."

Raynott sounded like a real prize. Sam raised an eyebrow. "My mother, I assume?"

Chris nodded. "They said after Roy died, Wayne skipped off with all the insurance money. Roy was supposed to be an equal partner, but with him dead, who was left to question the settlement? By that time, Roy's girlfriend had her baby. After Wayne skipped town, she kept asking around, trying to find him. Eventually she found somebody who remembered where he moved. She said she was going to make him pay, but nothing ever came of it, as far as anybody knew."

Sam sat back and crossed his arms. "Okay, this makes a nice story, but you're not going to sell me on the idea that you just happened to meet me and had no idea who I was."

"No." Chris shook his head. "They remembered your name. I found you easily enough through newspaper articles." Chris turned to Dana. "There were several pieces in the Anchorage paper. Sam had earned quite a few scholarships when he graduated high school and told the reporter he planned to major in mechanical engineering at UAF." He shifted his attention back to Sam. "It wasn't hard. I hung around the engineering dorm, got somebody to point you out and followed you. The place you were working had a Help Wanted sign in the window, so that seemed like the easiest way to meet you."

"Why did you go to all that trouble?"

Chris shrugged. "I don't know. The guys in the bar seemed to think your dad's death kinda knocked your mother off-balance. If my father was responsible for you not having a father, I wanted to make sure you were okay."

"I was fine," Sam barked. It was true, thanks to Ursula and Tommy.

Chris gave him that crooked grin. "You were fine. In fact, you had your life together a lot more than I did."

"So why'd you stick around?"

"Honestly? I liked you."

"Not enough to tell me the truth."

Chris had the grace to look embarrassed. "Fair enough. But put yourself in my position. As far as you knew, I was just a guy who ran off to Alaska on a lark. I had no influence with Wayne, no access to his money. I couldn't actually do anything to right past wrongs. All I could do was keep an eye on you, watch your back. If I told you who my father was, would you have let me hang around?"

"Maybe." Sam thought about it. "Probably not."

It was true. Chris did watch his back. In college, he'd shown up in time to throw a few punches and help run off a drunken mob yelling slurs at Sam when he was walking home from his job late one night. Years later, Chris warned him away from a girl he was considering dating. A coworker got involved with her instead. That woman was drama 24/7 and still making the man's life miserable. Sam had never had a reason to doubt Chris's loyalty. Not until his sister showed up and spilled his secret.

Sam looked over at Dana. She sat very still, her eyes on Chris, but as Sam watched, a tear escaped and slid down her cheek. Sam wasn't sure why she was crying: for her father, for the years she'd lost with her brother or for some other reason, but he couldn't stand to sit and watch her cry, and Chris was oblivious. Sam moved to the couch beside her and pulled her against his shoulder.

"Hey, it's okay. Don't cry." He wiped the tear with his thumb. "Everything's going to be fine."

"B-but you both think that my father… That he—"

"It doesn't matter. We can't change things that happened before we were born."

Dana shook her head and sniffed. She wiped away any trace of tears and sat up, drawing away from him.

Sam turned to see Chris eyeing them, his expression indicating he'd just added up two and two and wasn't altogether pleased with the answer. He met Sam's eyes and held them. "Does that answer all your questions?"

"For now." Sam's gaze didn't falter. He wasn't the one in the wrong here.

"Good. Because I may have a few of my own tomorrow. Right now, I'm going to bed."

CHAPTER NINE

SAM HAD A restless night. At about five, he finally abandoned his tangled sheets and went looking for coffee. Light leaked over the mountains and into the kitchen window, allowing him to make out a shape at the bar. He stumbled into the kitchen and flipped on the light. Chris sat hunched on one of the barstools, a cup half-filled with dark liquid in front of him beside a jar of instant coffee granules.

Sam grimaced and put a filter into the coffee maker. "I don't know how you drink that stuff."

Chris shrugged. "You do what you gotta do."

Whatever that meant. Sam spooned the Colombian blend Dana had chosen into the coffee maker and flipped the switch. "I'm surprised you're still here. Isn't your boat going back out today?"

"Yeah. I found a guy to take my place. I'll

hire on with one of the salmon boats tomorrow."

"How come?"

"I thought I'd better come up and make sure everything was back to normal. I'm glad I did." Chris picked up his mug and took a sip. "What's going on with you and my sister?"

Sam turned his back to reach into the cabinet for a mug. "You mean the sister you never mentioned you had? The one you haven't seen in nineteen years?"

"Yeah, that one. What are your intentions?"

Sam gave a wry laugh. "My intentions? Are we in the twenty-first century or what?" He filled his cup with the fragrant brew.

Chris set his mug onto the bar with a bang. "I know your five-year plan, Sam, and it doesn't include a wife. Don't play around with my sister's heart."

"I don't think you should be throwing stones. Do you have any idea how upset she was when you abandoned her without a word?"

"Abandoned? She was sixteen. It's not like I left her to be raised by wolves."

"You left her with a father who ignored her and a mother I haven't quite figured out yet but obviously isn't the nurturing type. She needed you to look after her."

"Well, I'm here now and I'm not sure I like what I'm seeing. Are you sleeping with her?"

Sam gave Chris a look of disgust. "No, I'm not sleeping with her. No, I haven't promised her a ring or a white picket fence. I have a lot of respect for your sister, Chris. She's strong, and determined, and generous. And she came all the way here to find you because, for some reason, she thinks you deserve your share of the inheritance."

"Yeah, well, I'm not going to take it."

"Why not?"

Chris shrugged. "It's dirty money."

"Maybe."

"No maybe about it." Chris's jaw tightened. "In spite of the way he ignored her, Dana always acted like our father was some sort of white knight. Okay, he kept his nose clean and maintained a good reputation for the store, but he used the moral high ground like a club. He fired an employee for taking off early twice in a week because her kid got sick at school. He took advantage of a mistake on a price sheet to gouge his suppliers on a huge order. He once grounded me for a month because I didn't rat out my mother for going to an estate auction without telling him."

"An estate auction?"

"Don't ask. The point is, Wayne Raynott might have morphed into a scrupulously honest pillar of society, but he wasn't a good man. Half of that insurance settlement should have been yours. You know it. I know it. And he knew it."

Sam tended to agree but tried to see if from the man's perspective. After all, Dana had faith in him. "Maybe he tried to make things right. He sent a check."

"What check?"

"To my mom. She tore it up."

"How much?"

"Five hundred, I think."

Chris snorted. "That was chickenfeed compared to his net worth, and he made that fortune with your money."

"Not my money."

"Your father's money. They were partners. Roy's share should have gone to his son. Per stirpes and all that."

"Per stirpes?" Sam raised an eyebrow.

"Latin. By branch. Meaning passed through the branches to the next generation."

Sam let out a snort.

Chris grinned. "I read, you know."

Sam sipped his coffee and turned over the situation in his mind. "The only name on the property tax record was Raynott. Maybe Roy wasn't an owner of the building itself and that's why he didn't collect insurance."

"It was common knowledge they were equal partners. My father wouldn't have taken on a partner who didn't bring in at least an equal investment, believe me." He eyed Sam with suspicion. "Why are you defending him?"

Sam shrugged. "I try not to let my own self-interest color my perceptions. Besides, Dana seems convinced her father wasn't a cheat."

"When I left, Dana's number one goal was trying to please Wayne. From what she said when she showed up on our doorstep, nothing's changed. The man is dead, and she's running around Alaska, settling his affairs. His image is important to her. If it turns out he's not the man she thought he was, what does that say about her?"

"That she's loyal to her family? Not such a bad trait."

"Blind loyalty can be."

Sam took another swig of coffee, hoping

the caffeine would clear the cobwebs that were preventing him from seeing things objectively. But all he could see was the fury on Dana's face after they talked to the man in the pawnshop. If he took Chris's side, she might never forgive him.

He pulled out a skillet and opened the refrigerator. Soon the sizzle and irresistible aroma of bacon filled the room. He slipped slices of bread into the toaster, adding the scent of fresh toast to the bacon. Within minutes, the door to Dana's bedroom opened and she stumbled into the kitchen to the coffeepot.

"Why is everybody up so early?" She poured a mug and settled onto the stool beside Chris.

"Healthy, wealthy and wise, like Ben Franklin said." Chris tousled her hair, and she swatted his hand away, but the corners of her mouth turned up.

"Cut it out."

Sam put the bacon to drain on a paper towel and pulled out some eggs. "Fried or scrambled?"

"Fried," Chris and Dana answered at the same moment.

Dana laughed. "If you can flip them without breaking the yolks. Chris never could."

"Ah, but he didn't have my patented technique." Sam broke several eggs into the hot bacon fat and covered the skillet with a lid.

Dana grabbed a slice of bacon off the plate and nibbled on the end. "Mmm, bacon."

"So." Chris took another sip of coffee and turned to Dana. "I was thinking."

"Did it hurt?"

"Only a little." His smirk indicated it was an old joke between them. "Anyway, I have to go back to work tomorrow, but we should spend today together."

"That would be great." The expression on her face touched Sam's heart. It took so little to please her. The slightest attention from her brother and those amazing eyes lit up like a Christmas tree. It was as though she were starved for the smallest scraps of affection from her family. Once again, he considered how lucky he'd been to have Tommy and Ursula in his life.

Chris gave her that lopsided smile women always swooned over. "I know just where we should go. It's something you always wanted to do, but Dad would never let me take you."

Dana grinned. "Really? They have them here?"

"I've never been, but I've driven by lots of times. I think they're open all summer."

"What are we talking about?" Sam transferred the eggs to plates and passed them around.

"Go-carts. Wanna come?" She looked as excited as any ten-year-old.

A momentary shadow passed over Chris's face, but Sam didn't care. Maybe Chris didn't want him there, but Dana did, and just then, he wasn't overly concerned about Chris's feelings. Dana deserved a happy day with her brother, and after hearing Chris's opinions of his father, Sam wanted to go along and keep the conversation away from touchy subjects. "I'd love to race go-carts with you."

"Great." Dana smiled and took a bite. "Good eggs, Sam."

The amusement complex didn't open until noon, so they spent the morning hiking through the forest adjacent to their neighborhood. Kimmik ran ahead of them, snuffling the trees and bushes along the path. Dana seemed to have a permanent smile on her face, excitedly pointing out squirrels and Steller's jays as though they were something exotic. When Sam showed her a set of bear tracks, you'd have thought he'd discovered gold. She must have taken a dozen photos.

They stopped by Chris's favorite burger place for lunch and then headed to the go-cart track. The attendant gave them an odd look when the three of them showed up with no children in tow, but soon they were buzzing around the track along with a birthday boy and his rowdy friends.

Sam took the outside lane, testing the speed and control of the little car. Dana flew by him and waved. Even over the roar of the engines, he thought he could hear her happy laugh as she passed. Chris was right on her heels and gained on the corner, but Dana pushed forward and beat him into the finish. Sam grinned, watching her raise her clenched hands in victory.

After they'd had their fill of go-carts, they had a round of mini golf at the adjacent course. Dana's putting skills were truly terrible. Almost all of her shots either stopped halfway to the green or shot out the other side, but she never stopped smiling.

At least that was Sam's impression, until he watched her high-five Chris after he sunk his putt, and he moved to the next hole. When

Chris's back was turned, Dana's expression turned pensive. What was she thinking? Sam brushed a hand against her back, and she flashed a smile at him.

"Having fun?"

"Sure." Sam sunk his putt. "I haven't done anything like this in years."

"Chris used to take me to movies or bumper boats sometimes when he was in high school."

"Sounds like he was a good brother."

"The best."

"Hey, I'm waiting." Chris stood at the next hole, his putter in hand. "Chop, chop." Dana hurried on ahead and Sam watched as Chris explained his strategy for the hole, and Dana promptly disregarded his advice and putted right over the middle to leave her ball stranded in a puddle in the center of the fairway.

They had dinner at a popular seafood restaurant. Chris joked that he wanted to keep demand high so they could get better prices for the fish he caught. Sam needn't have worried—none of them brought up the will or the information they'd uncovered in Fairbanks. Instead, Chris told Dana stories about life in Alaska, of the moose that got drunk on fermented crab apples and staggered around town, and a neighborhood woman's ongoing quest to try to find a way to hang a bird feeder so she could fill it but the bears couldn't reach it.

"She ran a cable on a pulley to the middle of her yard, but one morning she looked outside and a black bear cub hung upside down from the cable, batting at the bird feeder until he knocked it to the ground. Bears love sunflower seeds."

"So, they're not just after pic-a-nic baskets, I guess. Do you get a lot of bears?"

Sam nodded. "Because we're next to the park, we get quite a few. The tracks this morning were from a black bear, but once the salmon spawn, the grizzlies will be around."

"I'd like to see a grizzly," Dana said. "From a distance. And preferably through a window."

They returned home and Sam made an excuse to leave Dana and Chris alone in the living room. Dana'd had her day of fun, but now she and Chris needed to finish their business. Sam still wasn't sure if she had a prayer of convincing Chris to take the money, but he wasn't ruling it out. Chris's sister had a way of getting under your skin.

DANA WATCHED SAM disappear down the hall. It was nice of him to come along today. He was clearly annoyed with Chris, but they had been friends for a long time and that wasn't going to change. She was glad, for both of them.

Chris opened the door to the refrigerator. "Want a beer?"

"I'm fine, thanks."

He opened the bottle and returned to the living room to sit in the chair across from her. After a long pull on the bottle, he wiped his mouth with his sleeve. "So, you and Sam went to Fairbanks together."

"Uh-huh. We found out about the bar and the fire."

"And that's all you did there?"

She frowned. "Pretty much. I mean, we ate a couple of meals and went for a walk. Why?"

"No reason. Just making conversation. How's Mom?"

Dana shook her head. "Worse than ever, I think. Without Dad to rein her in..."

"How is she taking care of everything? I mean bills and money and all the stuff he did?"

"I was doing it. Before I came up here, I hired somebody to pay the bills and balance the checkbook, and I showed Mom how to write a check." She sighed. "That may have been a mistake."

"What do you mean?"

"She apparently almost emptied the checking account. I had to make her promise not to write any more until the first of the month, and transferred enough from my savings to pay the utility bills until then."

"This has to stop."

"It's a sickness. She can't stop."

Chris leaned toward her. "Wayne should have done something a long time ago. Instead, we all pretended it was a normal thing. She needs help, Dana."

"She doesn't see a problem."

"You have to make her see."

Dana stared at him. "You don't know how hard I've tried. You haven't been there. Once Dad had his heart attack, he couldn't handle her anymore and it all fell to me. I had to keep her under control, and the business under control, and the whole stupid system under control, but nobody gave me the authority to do any of it. I'm tired of being the one with all the responsibility and no power, of trying to coax everybody into doing the right thing."

He gawked at her. "That's the first time I've ever heard you complain. You always did exactly what Dad told you to do without question."

Dana shrugged and looked away.

"No, really. Other teenage girls threw fits because their parents gave them a curfew. You worked at the store on weekends and cleaned up after Mom, and half the time you made dinner because Mom was still out shopping and you didn't want her to get in trouble with Dad when he got home, and I never heard a word of complaint."

"Somebody had to do it."

"What do you mean about keeping the business under control?"

She rolled her eyes. "When he got sick, Dad hired Jerry Brinkman as manager."

"Not good-time Jerry."

"Yeah. He's completely incompetent, but since Dad hired him, the trust managers left him in charge. When I was in the office, I could work around him to make sure everything got done, but I understand there have been some problems since I've been gone."

"I didn't realize you were under so much pressure. I'm sorry I said what I did."

Dana nodded. After a few minutes, she spoke. "Chris, about that inheritance."

He paused, obviously torn. "Dana, I don't know. It doesn't feel right."

"You're his son. My brother. We're family. We should share equally."

"But it was money Wayne was never entitled to. I can't accept it and keep my hands clean. That's why I cut ties."

Cut ties. Exactly what she didn't want now that she'd found him again. She tossed out the first argument she could come up with. "You don't know for sure. And it's clear Dad was entitled to half the money at least. Maybe your part of the estate was earned with that half."

He shook his head. "You're splitting hairs. He couldn't have started the same business with half the money. It's all built on a lie, and I can't be a part of it."

Which meant he still wouldn't be a part of the family. She closed her eyes and her shoulders sagged. Finally, she opened her eyes and locked onto his. "Is that your final decision?"

He looked into her face for a long while, and eventually shook his head. "Can you give me time to think it over?"

"Sure." Maybe there was still hope. "The

lawyers do need an answer before they'll distribute, though, and if I expect to get the classes I need this fall, I need to make a tuition payment soon. But didn't you say you're leaving tomorrow?"

"Yes, but I'll be on a salmon boat in the bay. We'll come to shore at night, so you can reach me on my cell phone." He gave her the number.

A spark of hope surged. He planned to stay in contact. Dana entered it into her phone and texted him back her number. His phone chimed.

"Got it. I'll give you a call in the next couple of weeks, once I make up my mind. All right?"

Dana nodded slowly.

Chris scooted closer. "So you found what you came for. There's really no reason for you to stay in Alaska any longer. Just leave the papers, and if I decide to sign, I'll overnight you a notarized copy. Would that work?"

Leave Alaska? Why did the idea startle her so much? Of course she was going to leave Alaska. She'd come here to locate Chris and investigate the possible claim on her father's estate, and she had. But something felt unfinished. "I still don't know for sure what happened in Fairbanks."

"You know as much as you're going to know." Chris gave her a searching look. "It is just business, isn't it? This thing with Sam?"

"Well, yeah. I mean, uh, I'd like to think he and I are friends, too."

"Friends is okay. But, Dana, Sam is married to his job. He has a plan to move into upper management within five years, and that's his entire focus. He doesn't have a lot of extra time for friends and family."

"What about Ursula?"

"She understands what drives him. So do I. We don't get in the way of his career." He patted her knee. "Sam's a great guy, but he is who he is. I don't want you hurt."

Dana tried for a laugh. "You're imagining things. I have no illusions about Sam. Besides, you're right. I have to get back to Kansas before Mom digs herself any deeper."

"Good. Well, I'll need to leave in the wee hours of the morning to make it to the boat on time. So I guess this is goodbye."

Dana blinked back the stupid tears that suddenly filled her eyes. "It was good to see you again, Chris."

"Hey." He pulled her into a hug. "It's not

forever. Now that Dad isn't standing between us, we don't have to be strangers anymore. You can call me, you know, just to talk.
Maybe I can come see you in Kansas one of
these days."

"You'd do that?" Did he mean it? That they
could be family again?

"Sure. I have some downtime between
fishing and snow seasons."

"You can stay with me. I have a guest
room."

"You live in an apartment?"

"No. I own a two-bedroom cottage, yellow
with white shutters. Do you remember those
houses over by the park, on Redbud Street?"

"Oh, right. Cute little houses with big
lawns and gardens. It's settled then. I'll come
visit in a few months."

The lump in Dana's throat made it hard
to speak, but she managed to squeak out a
reply. "Okay."

Chris stood, and Dana scrambled up to
face him. He patted her on top of the head.
"Good night, Dana. Take care of yourself.
And whenever you need your big brother,
call me."

Her brother was back. She still wanted
him to take the inheritance, to reconcile with

their father's memory, but this was what she wanted most of all. "I will. Goodbye, Chris."

Dana went to bed, but sleep eluded her. Instead, she stared at the ceiling as if the answers to her questions might be hidden there in the grain of the cedar planks. Chris was right. Her business here was done. Whether Chris took the inheritance or not wasn't important. The important thing was that he was back in her life. Sam said he didn't want to pursue any claim to the inheritance, so there was no need to chase that thread any further. There was no reason to stay in Alaska, and every reason to get home to Kansas.

So why did it feel so wrong? Why did the idea of saying goodbye to Sam cause an ache inside her chest? She twisted the silver feather ring on her finger. So Sam kissed her. Once. And yes, it was the most amazing kiss she'd ever experienced. So what? Sam was a good kisser. It didn't necessarily follow that the kiss meant anything to Sam, or that she meant anything to Sam.

They had very different lives, in very different places. Sam had dreams and hopes she couldn't comprehend. She had responsibilities. Her time with Sam was a diversion, an experience she would draw on and remember fondly when she needed a boost. It wasn't real, just an illusion, and any feelings she might have for Sam were part of that illusion. When her real life resumed, they would disappear.

She almost believed it.

CHAPTER TEN

ANOTHER EARLY MORNING. Sam looked through the front window to check the driveway. As expected, the spot where Chris's truck had been parked was empty. He hoped Chris had a chance to set things right with his sister before he left.

Kimmik came to greet him, and Sam rubbed his ears and let him outside before returning to the kitchen. He pulled the package from the cabinet and set it on the counter, but instead of starting the coffee, he stared blindly at the countertop. Chris lied to him. A few weeks ago, Sam would have laughed at the very suggestion. Chris, his best friend for so many years, had lied about who he was from the very beginning.

Oh, Sam understood. It started off innocently enough, just curiosity to see how the boy left after the tragedy had faired. In the same circumstances, Sam might have even done the same thing, and he could see how, as more time passed, it became more and more difficult for Chris to confess. But somehow, it shook Sam's foundation to know that this enormous lie stood between them all these years and he'd never suspected.

Dana could never have gotten away with it. Those big brown eyes of hers would have given her away in an instant if she tried to lie about something so important. But was it important? Maybe who Chris used to be before he met Sam didn't really matter. He'd been nothing but a loyal friend ever since. Really, wasn't that what counted?

Chris and Dana seemed so different, but they were alike in one important way. They did the right thing. In spite of his shady history, their father must have instilled a moral compass that pointed them in the right direction.

The trouble was, to Chris the right thing was to reject his father and all wealth associated with him. To Dana, the right thing was to defend her father's reputation. Sam wasn't sure which side he was rooting for.

He needed some time to think about all this, to let it settle in his mind, and he always thought better outdoors. Preferably far from civilization.

"Hey, are you going to make coffee or just look at it?" Dana smiled as she reached into the cupboard for a filter.

"You mean I can't just absorb the caffeine telepathically?"

"Afraid not. Believe me, I've tried. So, Chris is gone?"

"Yeah. Did you get a chance to talk to him about the will?"

She nodded. "He's still on the fence. He'll let me know within a couple of weeks. Are you sure you don't want to make a claim?"

"I'm sure. I don't need Wayne Raynott's money." Sam spooned coffee into the filter she had placed in the basket and started the drip. When he turned, she was watching him, her face pensive. "Isn't that what you want?"

"I don't want you to regret your decision down the road."

She wouldn't say it, but Sam knew what she wanted. She wanted him to believe in her version of her father, the man who could do no wrong. Never mind she'd admitted he wasn't much of a father. Or that he'd lied to them about Chris's mother. She was still hanging on to her fantasy. Her bottom lip trembled a little. What harm would it do to indulge her? "Don't worry about those letters from Ruth. He was your father. He built a successful business, which isn't easy, and he left money to the family he loved. That's the way it should be. I want you to take the inheritance. Get your teaching credentials. Be happy."

She threw her arms around him and pressed her cheek against his chest. "Thank you, Sam. It means a lot to me."

He chuckled and rubbed his hands up and down her back. Her undisguised gratitude made it hard to deny her anything. She looked up at him, that pink mouth of hers curved in joy. He wanted to kiss her the way he had in Fairbanks, to taste the joy that bubbled up from inside her like champagne, but he didn't. He couldn't.

Chris was right. Sam had a five-year plan, and Dana wasn't on it. Kissing her again would only send the wrong signals. Instead, Sam stepped back and reached into the cupboard for mugs. When he handed one to Dana, he thought he saw a small droop of disappointment in her lower lip, but he probably imagined it.

She licked her lip. "So, I guess now that I've talked to you and Chris, I'm pretty much done here."

A cold shiver went through Sam's chest. He took a drink from his cup to cover his confusion and burned his tongue. He set the cup down on the counter with a thump and splashed the liquid over the rim.

Done. So she was leaving. Of course she was leaving. She lived in Kansas. That's what people who lived in other states did. They left. Sam was an engineer, logical and rational. Why were his thoughts running in crazy circles?

Dana handed him a paper towel. He wiped the spill from the counter. "So when do you leave?"

She shrugged. "I'll go online and see what flights are available. What are you doing today?"

"I don't know." What did he do with himself on his off time when Dana wasn't there? It took a minute to remember. "I might take a fly-in float trip in the next day or two. I'll probably spend the day getting my gear together and inspect my raft."

She cocked her head. "What do you do on a float trip?"

"This one is a mix of white water and fishing. It takes me about five days to get down Brazzle Creek."

"Brazzle Creek? I've never heard that name before."

"Brazzle is an old name for pyrite, fool's gold. There was once a mini gold rush on that river. Someone in a saloon in Anchorage had too much to drink and bragged to everyone in sight about the gold he'd found there. The next day, he discovered it was pyrite, but the rumor had already started. There were a lot of disappointed goldpanners, but the fishermen love it."

"You have to fly to get there?"

"A floatplane drops me off on a little lake upriver and picks me up at another lake five days later."

Her eyes widened. "So you're all by yourself for that whole time?"

"I usually take a buddy along. Occasionally, I'll go on a short trip alone. That's kind of the point. To get away from people and into the wild."

"Wow. It sounds amazing."

"It really is."

She set down her cup and opened the refrigerator. "Well, before we each get started, how about if I make us mushroom omelets?"

"Yum." His mouth watered.

After breakfast, Dana departed for her

room, presumably to look for flights. Sam dug his raft from the corner of the garage and inflated it in the backyard, checking carefully for leaks or cracks. He got out his checklist and went through all his gear, making sure tent poles, waders and life jackets were all present and accounted for.

He thought about who he might ask along. He knew a couple of guys who worked the slope and would be off this rotation. Jeffrey just got married in May, so probably wouldn't be inclined to spend his time off away from his new bride. Graham was always game for a fishing trip, but he was a talker, and Sam wasn't in the mood to listen to his views on the state of the world for five days. Chris was out, obviously.

Maybe Sam should just go by himself. He'd never done more than a two-day float alone, but he needed time to think, to get his bearings. He'd floated Brazzle Creek a dozen times, so there shouldn't be anything unexpected he couldn't handle. Yeah, a few days alone on the creek might be just what he needed.

Dana wandered outside and stood with her hands on her hips, looking over the blue inflatable. "So, this is your raft."

"This is it."

"How do you get it inside the plane?"

Sam laughed. "I let the air out of it. I pump it up again once I get there."

"By hand? It's what, about sixteen feet long? That must take a while."

"It's a big pump." He tightened a clamp on his oar frame. "Did you find a flight?"

"I found a couple. With so little notice, I'll have to fly at about two in the morning."

"You'll find the airport surprisingly busy then. Did you book it?"

"Not yet. I wanted to see if it mattered to you whether I went tonight or tomorrow."

Frankly, he didn't want her to go at all, but he couldn't tell her that. "Either is fine."

"Okay." She turned toward the house.

"Dana?"

She looked back over her shoulder. "Yes?"

"Want to come on the float trip with me?" As soon as the words were out of his mouth, he regretted them. She had zero experience with primitive camping. She would probably be miserable if she did come, and make him miserable, too. And yet, a part of him still hoped she'd say yes.

She blinked. "Your fly-in five-day trip down Brazzle Creek?"

"Yeah, that one."

"You're serious?"

"Sure, if you want to." But he had to be honest with her about the conditions. "But there will be mud. And mosquitoes. And no toilets or showers for a week. And the water's cold. But if you want, you can come."

Dana laughed. "Sam, it's a good thing you don't sell used cars for a living. Yes, I'd love to see your wild river."

In spite of himself, his mouth stretched into a grin. "You can take another week before you go home?"

"I shouldn't, but I'm going to. When will I ever have another opportunity like this?"

"Well, okay, then. Ursula has some stuff stored in the downstairs closet. You might want to take a look and see if it fits you. If not, we'll go shopping and get you kitted out."

"I'll go look." She started toward the house, but looked back, and the sparkle in her eyes made him glad he'd offered his impulsive invitation. "Sam?"

"Yes?"

"Thank you." She almost skipped into the house.

This was probably a big mistake, but maybe it would be exactly what he needed:

a cold splash of reality. He could take her to the wild parts of Alaska, the parts he loved best, and she'd hate it. At the end of the week, she would be glad to get back to civilization, he would be glad to see her go and that feeling deep inside him that whispered that Dana might have a place in his life would finally shut up.

FROM THE BACK of Sam's pickup, Dana grabbed a duffel filled with fleece, wading boots and wool socks. She wore waders and a slicker over thermal underwear and river sandals. Until yesterday, she hadn't known there were such a thing as river sandals and thought waders were another name for cropped pants. A light drizzle fell from scattered clouds, but that didn't seem to bother anyone.

Sam and the bush pilot loaded the raft into the floatplane. They seemed to be old friends, chatting as they worked. Deflated, the tubes rolled into a surprisingly small package. A teenage boy helped ferry everything from the truck to the dock.

Dana gazed across the calm water of Lake Hood. According to Sam, this was the world's busiest seaplane base. As Dana watched, a blue plane took off across the lake, tilting to lift one float out of the water and then clearing the water and rising into the sky. Within a couple of minutes, it was a dot on the horizon. Once they had everything loaded, that would be them taking off in a tiny plane.

Was she crazy? Her mother certainly seemed to think so when Dana called her yesterday to say she'd be out of cell phone range for a few days. In fact, she pleaded with Dana to return immediately because Ginny dared tell her she had no more money to spend for the month. That nagging angel of guilt Dana knew so well stomped on her shoulder and tried to force her home to Kansas, but for once she ignored its demands. Mom and her problems would still be there next week, but she might never have a chance like this again.

Dana set the duffel beside the piles of equipment on the dock. Back in the truck, Kimmik stuck his nose through the window crack and gave a little woof to make sure they didn't forget him.

Sam reached for the ice chest. "Dana, could you get the dog and lock up the truck, please?"

"Sure." She hurried to comply, while Sam and the pilot arranged the rest of the gear in the plane. She returned with Kimmik on a leash.

"Bear spray?" the pilot asked Sam.

Sam handed him a bag and he put it into a hatch in one of the floats.

"Guns unloaded?"

"Yes."

Guns? They had guns? She'd helped Sam pack but hadn't seen everything that went into the various bags. Hopefully, they wouldn't need them. Dana had never fired a gun in her life.

The pilot turned to Dana and looked her over. "What do you weigh, about one-ten?"

"Uh, about." Was guessing her weight his idea of a conversation starter?

"Okay. You ride beside me." He turned to Sam. "You and the dog go in the back."

Oh, he was balancing the load. She stepped closer to the plane. Sam stood on the dock beside the open door and reached for her hand. He leaned closer and whispered in her ear, "Last chance to back out."

Dana's stomach threatened to abandon her body, but she managed a smile and shook her heard before she climbed into the plane. Sam made sure her harness was securely buckled and then loaded Kimmik into the back seat and strapped him in. The dog's tail thumped against the seat.

Dana forced herself to take slow breaths in and out. Hey, Kimmik had done this before and he was wagging his tail. If the dog didn't mind, how bad could it be?

Sam and the pilot climbed in. Before he buckled, Sam leaned forward to pat her on the shoulder. She gave him a thumbs-up, and he rewarded her with a grin. The pilot handed them each a set of headphones.

After completing his checklist, the pilot taxied away from the dock and moved into place. Dana dug her fingernails into her palms as the engines revved and the plane skimmed across the water. Sucking in her breath, she stared determinedly at her lap as the plane lifted from the lake and rose into the sky. Once it was clear they were flying, she found the courage to look up. The pilot tossed her an amused glance.

She looked through the windshield, or whatever you call it on an airplane. Across the inlet, a sprinkling of white windmills rose from a dark carpet of spruce. The tall buildings of downtown grew smaller, and then they crossed some mountains and the city was gone.

From the air, Alaska was even greener, with wide swathes of deep loden interspersed with blue lakes and rivers. Mountain peaks above the tree line still held patches of snow. Two big mountains rose in the distance, and they seemed to be flying right toward them. They looked familiar.

"That's Foraker on the left, Denali on the right." The pilot's voice came through her headphones. The mountains grew as they came closer. She'd thought Denali was spectacular from the ground, but it was even more amazing from up here. The peaks still rose far above them, and she was beginning to wonder if they shouldn't fly higher to avoid crashing into the side of the mountain. Instead, they started descending toward a smallish lake. A gravel shoreline gradually came into focus.

Dana's stomach clenched once again as the plane seemed to drop precipitously, but they glided onto the water as smoothly as a duck. The plane slowed and turned, eventually pulling up beside a gravel spit and stopping. Sam jumped from the plane.

He opened the door and released Kimmik, who leaped joyfully onto the gravel and immediately started to sniff around and mark his territory. Sam reached across and helped her unbuckle. Dana tried to climb from the plane but found her legs were unsteady. Sam caught her and set her firmly on the gravel bar, keeping his hands on her waist.

"Okay?"

She willed her legs to work and, hallelujah, they did. "I'm fine." Now that she was on solid ground once again, she was better than fine. She felt elated. Along the way, they'd flown out of the clouds and the sun warmed her shoulders and glinted off the water. She pulled the visor of her baseball cap lower over her eyes.

It only took about thirty minutes to unload the floatplane. The pilot climbed into the plane. "You should have the river all to yourselves for now. The next group we have scheduled is in three days, and I'll pick you up at the lower lake in five. Right?"

"Sounds good. See you then." Sam came to put his arm around Dana's shoulders while they watched him take off across the lake. The noise of the engines faded into a distant whine, and then the plane was gone, and they were alone.

The silence after the roar of the plane highlighted just how alone they were, but as she listened, Dana started to hear other noises. Birds chirped in the trees at the edge of the lake, Kimmik rustled through the leaves of the reeds growing in the edge of the water and a familiar and unwelcome hum whined near her ear.

Sam slapped his hand against her neck and drew it back with a splatter of blood across it. "I'll find the mosquito repellant."

Once they had both applied a generous coating of the helpful liquid, Sam unrolled the raft tubes and set up the pump. It looked like the one Chris used to fill up his basketball when they were kids, except bigger. Both Sam and Dana shed their jackets in the sunshine. She watched him pump up the tubes, his movements smooth and efficient. His biceps flexed with each stroke against the sleeves of his T-shirt.

He stopped to catch his breath.

Dana handed him a water bottle. "Do you want me to take a turn?"

He grinned. "Sure, go ahead."

Dana stepped on the protrusions on the bottom as she had seen Sam do, pulled out the plunger and pushed it down. It had a lot more resistance than she expected. After ten strokes, she was panting. By fifteen, she had to stop and rest.

Sam finished his drink and set the bottle down. "My turn."

Dana stepped out of the way and tried to think of how to be helpful. "Maybe I should, I don't know, gather firewood or something?" That's what people did when they camped, right?

"We can pick up firewood when we camp, but go ahead and explore. There are some interesting burled trees just over that rise. Don't wander far, though." Sam winked. "I may need you to do another round of pumping."

"No problem. I figure at the rate I pump, we'll be done by Christmas at the latest." She started to walk toward the forest.

"Dana."

She turned back. "What?"

He tossed a small pouch her way. "Bear spray."

"There are bears here?"

"Possibly. Take Kimmik, too."

"Can he fight off a bear?"

Sam grinned. "No, but if he takes off running, you'd better run, too."

Sam was kidding. Right? There were bears in Alaska, of course, but they wouldn't be here. On this river. Where there were salmon coming to spawn. Duh. Of course there would be bears. She was starting to understand about the guns.

"Actually, wait a second." Sam fumbled in a bag, pulled out a whistle on a lanyard and hung it around her neck.

"What's this for?"

"Just a good idea in case you get lost or anything. Three blasts is the standard distress call."

"Three blasts. Okay, then."

She carefully read the instructions on the bear spray before attaching it to her belt. Feeling armed and dangerous, she hiked into the woods. She found the trees he'd mentioned, with odd swellings on the trunk. One looked almost like an apple-cheeked grandmother. Dana was considering fetching her cell phone to snap a picture when she heard something moving in the brush beside her.

Kimmik froze, staring into the bushes. They rustled again, and Kimmik barked and launched himself into the woods.

"No, Kimmik. Come back." Dana grabbed the bear spray from the holster and followed. Kimmik barked again, and she saw a flash of movement in the tree above him. A squirrel sat on a limb barely out of his reach, scolding the dog. Dana let out a huge breath and re-holstered her bear spray.

Before long, Kimmik lost interest in the squirrel and followed her willingly back to the raft, where Sam had made noticeable strides in inflating the tubes.

He smiled at her. "Find anything interesting?"

"Those trees. They look like something from an enchanted forest. And Kimmik treed a militant squirrel."

"I'm sure he enjoyed that. Why don't you pull up a campstool and relax?"

"Okay, but let me know if you want me to take a turn pumping." She found the aluminum tripod stools in the heap and perched a little up the gravel bar, out of Sam's way. A duck, followed by a row of fuzzy ducklings, appeared from the reeds, and Kimmik jumped to his feet, sending the mother duck scooting back toward cover.

"Down, Kimmik." At Sam's command, the dog dropped to the ground, but his quivering muscles made it clear it went against all his Labrador instincts.

Behind the lake, the slopes of Denali rose into the sky, broken patches of clouds clinging to the mountain like lint, even though the rest of the sky remained clear. The raft tubes looked full to her, but Sam continued to work the pump. She half-heartedly offered to take a turn, but he waved her away. Finally, he pressed on the tubes and seemed satisfied with their firmness. "Done." Sam wiped his forehead with the tail of his T-shirt.

"That was a lot of work. What happens now?"

"Now I assemble the frame, load the raft and we raft for a few miles to our first night's camp."

Dana stood. "Can I help?"

"Sure. Can you find the screwdriver in that green bag?"

She scurried over and found the tool he asked for. He assembled a bunch of metal pipes and tightened the clamps holding them together with the screwdriver. Dana handed him parts as he asked for them. Two horseshoe-shaped pieces flanked a low seat in the center of the frame. He strapped the frame to the raft tube and pushed the raft to the edge of the water before loading in the ice chest and strapping it down.

They formed a team, with Dana bringing the various bags and equipment and Sam securing them to the raft or the frame. It didn't take her long to realize everything that went into the raft except for the three of them had to be strapped in. She tried not to think about what they might be facing that would require this kind of secured attachment.

Sam handed her a PFD and pulled one on himself, and even one on the dog. From the big bag that had been on the floor of her closet, he pulled out two helmets and handed her one.

"What's this for?"

Sam grinned. "What do you think? To protect that valuable brain of yours."

"From what?"

"Hopefully nothing, but in case you decide to take a swim, I don't want your head coming in contact with any rocks." His face turned more serious. "If you should ever end up in the water, keep your head up and try to keep your feet downriver with your knees bent in case you need to push off from sweepers or boulders."

"Sweepers?"

"Fallen trees." Her fear must have shown on her face because he stepped closer and touched her cheek. "It's okay. I've never flipped a boat yet. This is just a precaution.

You don't need to put it on until we get to the white water later this afternoon. It's nothing too scary, just some mild rapids."

"This afternoon?"

He nodded. "Tomorrow, we'll go through a rock garden with some class-four rapids."

Class four. Whatever that meant. Better not think about it yet. She looked at him for reassurance. "But not today?"

"Nope. Today's class three at the most." He reached for both her hands and held them in his. "Are you ready to get started?"

If she wasn't, it was going to be a very long week. "I'm ready."

"Good." He gave her hands a squeeze and released them. "Let's go."

CHAPTER ELEVEN

SAM GOT KIMMIK settled into the back of the raft with the gear and Dana in the front, facing him. He pushed off the gravel bar and climbed in, arranged himself in the seat and reached for his oars. A good long stroke and they launched into the current.

Dana's knuckles were pale from her grip on the grab lines running around the perimeter of the boat, but when he smiled at her, she smiled back. Funny girl, scared of bears, scared of the river, and yet she'd still chosen to come with him. Tommy once told him courage was being afraid and acting, anyway. If so, she had it in spades.

The river ran slow here. Sam rotated the raft, turning his back downstream, and established an easy rhythm rowing to ferry them toward tonight's campsite. His mind automatically noted obstacles and danger points, and he avoided them. He'd made this trip a dozen times and knew the river as well as he knew his own name, and yet every trip was unique. Differences in water levels due to heavy snows or early thaws could expose or hide boulders. Floods and storms could drop trees across the river. It was good to stay alert, even in this relatively gentle section of water.

The soothing sound of water lapping against the boat, of the oars splashing, was starting to have a relaxing effect on Dana. One hand still gripped the rope, but the other brushed a loose strand of hair from her eyes as she took in the scenery. Something in the distance caught her attention. Sam glanced up to see a pair of ravens playing in the wind on the edge of a bluff. As Dana watched them tumble and surf in the wind, a slow smile lit her face. She saw it: the sheer joy of the birds playing together, testing themselves against the wind. Most people never noticed, much less appreciated, things like that, but Dana did.

Sam had always felt drawn to birds, to the huge variety in the way they looked and the way they moved. Eagles soared for hours, hardly moving their wings at all, as they swept the sky in circles. Hummingbirds beat their wings faster than the eye could see.

Puffins, awkward on land, cut through water like fish-seeking missiles, with no extraneous movement or wasted effort. Each bird had found their niche.

When Sam rowed or paddled a boat, he felt like the loons he loved so much, skimming across the water. His arms, his back, his whole body worked together to control the craft, instinctively making tiny adjustments in course and speed. It felt natural.

He was going to miss this when he got that promotion Ethan had hinted at. It could be anywhere from Trinidad to Azerbaijan, but one thing was for sure—it would be a long way from Brazzle Creek. But taking the position would move him up in the company, just like Tommy said. Sam hoped Tommy somehow knew he'd earned that engineering degree they talked about, had worked his way into management, because Sam owed it all to him. Tommy had believed in him, and Sam was determined to make him proud.

Being on the river always reminded him of Tommy, who taught Sam everything he knew about rafting, fishing and camping. Even more important were the things he taught indirectly. By following Tommy's example, Sam learned how to deal with people, how to inspire confidence, how to be a man. He hoped he was half the man Tommy had been. It was a shame Dana and Tommy would never have the chance to meet. They would have liked each other.

A warm breeze stirred Dana's hair. She tilted back her head and closed her eyes, letting the sunshine warm her face. That didn't take long. She was drinking it in, feeling the natural energy of the river. In spite of the puffy, orange life preserver she wore, she'd never looked more beautiful. He watched her as he rowed, watched the way the corners of her mouth twitched. Whatever she was thinking about, it made her happy.

He hated to disturb her, but he could hear the sound of rushing water up ahead. The first set of rapids was coming. "Dana."

She opened her eyes. "Yes."

"We're coming up to a little boulder field. Put on your helmet."

She scrambled to snap the helmet in place and grabbed the rope, her mouth in a grim line. Sam almost laughed out loud, but managed to school his face into a neutral expression while he buckled his own helmet. With a quick double-oar turn, he reversed the raft so that he was facing the river. Dana half turned to watch the water. They came around the corner and he saw the souse-hole to the left below the boulder. He hugged the bank on the right, sweeping around the bend and over a small drop. The raft bucked as it dropped and water splashed up to spray their faces. Dana squealed.

Sam laughed, half from amusement and half from pure joy. A couple of strokes positioned them perfectly to make the next obstacle, an enormous boulder that bisected the river. He might have chosen the right if he were on his own, but this time he went left to minimize the impact into a series of small shudders instead of a heart-stopping drop.

Three more drops, and they were almost through the rapids. Dana was looking more confident now, her eyes shining as they swept the river. He saw her checking out the hole to their right. Good, she was starting to read the water.

The banks closed in tight, forming a chute. In this spot, he had no latitude for a choice of how wild to make the ride. He folded in the oars so they didn't accidentally snag something and let the rushing current carry them through like a bobsled. Frigid water sprayed over the sides of the raft.

Dana gasped, and then she laughed out loud and shook the water from her face. Her eyes sparkled from excitement. They twisted through a narrow bend and dodged another huge boulder before the river spit them out on the other end of the narrows, suddenly gentle once again.

Sam resumed oaring. Not far downriver, they passed a distinctive double-crowned cottonwood that Sam used as a landmark. With a couple of strokes of the oars, he pushed the raft onto the gravel shoreline, hopped out of the boat and tugged it higher on the beach.

He smiled at Dana. "We're home."

"Already? I was just getting into it."

"Don't worry. There's more tomorrow."

DANA WOKE THE next morning and lay still, listening to the birdsong. She recognized the chirrup of a robin among the twitters and squawks. Warm and comfortable inside Sam's spare sleeping bag, she tried unsuccessfully to convince her bladder it wasn't yet time to get up. Last night, when she inquired about bathroom customs in the woods, Sam handed her a folding shovel, a roll of biodegradable toilet paper and a can of bear spray. The DIY nature of personal hygiene in the wilds made staying in bed longer even more attractive.

What time was it, anyway? The sun was shining on the tent, but since it didn't set until midnight and came up at something like four in the morning, that didn't help much. She hadn't bothered to dig her cell phone out of the dry bag after rafting. She bit the bullet and sat up. Sam's sleeping bag and the spot where Kimmik had spent the night were empty.

Dana stretched, crawled out of the sleeping bag and pulled a pair of sweats over the thermals she'd slept in. She didn't immediately see Sam when she emerged from the tent, so she grabbed the bathroom kit and slipped behind some bushes. When she came back, Kimmik ran from down the river to greet her.

Sam followed, carrying a speckled fish. "Good morning. Ready for breakfast?"

"Sure. What have you got there?"

"We're in luck. Trout are catch and release in this river, but I finally hooked a Dolly. I thought that sounded better than powdered eggs."

Dana had to agree, although the freeze-dried chili mac they had for dinner the night before was better than she expected. "So why did we bring a cooler and dry ice if we're eating freeze-dried food?"

"To take home the king salmon we're going to catch farther downriver."

"Aha. In that case, I'm all about eating fish for breakfast. Did you say it's a trout?"

"A Dolly Varden, technically a char, but a close relative. They taste like trout."

Sam lit the camp stove that looked like a leftover from an Apollo space mission and set a pot of water on top. Considering they were what Sam called "primitive camping," he was equipped with a huge assortment of high-tech stuff. Dana wasn't sure if it was because he was an engineer, or if all campers carried ultraviolet water purifiers, magic paste that came in a tube like toothpaste and started campfires from damp wood, and an entire menu of freeze-dried foods.

Soon the water boiled, and Dana brewed coffee with a French press. Meanwhile, Sam heated oil in a folding skillet and fried the fish. It may have been due to the fresh air stimulating her appetite, but Dana had to rank Dolly Varden as one of her all-time best breakfasts.

Once they'd washed the dishes, Sam announced it was time to break down camp.

Dana rolled up their sleeping bags and pads and packed the cooking equipment while Sam took down the tent. Together they sealed everything in bags so it would stay dry and strapped the bags into the raft.

A limb lay on the ground where it had broken off a tree. The end had split down the middle and peeled away. Sam studied the branch a moment. He pulled what looked like a piece of jagged wire from a bag and used it as a saw to cut off a piece about two feet long. He tossed it into one of the mesh gear bags in the raft and turned to Dana.

"Are you ready to go?"

"Are we heading through rapids like we did yesterday?"

Sam nodded. "Today is the biggest white water we're going to see." Laugh lines appeared at the corners of his eyes. "Want to back out?"

Dana grinned. "Do I have a choice?"

He pretended to consider it. "Well, I suppose we could call for a rescue with the satellite phone, but they're not going to be happy if they find you're not in distress. Emergency workers have no sense of humor about things like that."

"We have a phone?"

Sam pointed toward a bag attached inside the rear of the raft with a carabiner. "In the red dry bag with the camera and cell phones. It's for emergencies." He reached inside a blue bag and pulled out their helmets. "Rescue ropes are in this bag, should it ever come up."

"Good to know, even if I have no idea what to do with a rescue rope." Dana accepted the helmet. "Actually, once I figured out I wasn't going overboard, I rather liked the fast parts yesterday."

"Oh, yeah?" Sam held out a hand and helped her climb into the raft. He whistled for the dog. "Better than a roller coaster, don't you think?" He shoved the raft free of the gravel shoreline and jumped in.

"Way better."

The day started out with an easy float. Sam rowed smoothly, keeping the front of the raft partly turned toward the shore and the tail toward the center of the river, as the current carried them along. All the while, his eyes swept back and forth, scanning the river.

He seemed a part of the wilderness, somehow. Maybe it was the confident way he moved, as if piloting the boat came as naturally to him as breathing. He'd been the same way in the kayak, treating the paddle almost as an extension of his body.

"Why do you keep the boat at an angle like this?"

Sam slowed his oaring. "By turning across the current, it gives the river more surface to push the raft along. I keep the head toward the bank and the tail away so that the current doesn't push us into the bank on sharp bends."

"Oh, I see. You're catching the vector of the current."

He raised his eyebrows. "You know about vectors?"

Dana shrugged. "It's just math."

"Yes, it is, but you're the first person I've ever had in my raft who mentioned it."

At his look of approval, she could feel her cheeks growing warm. She quickly changed the subject. "What is it you're looking for when you study the water?"

Sam explained about the ripples and currents, how to see where the main channels were and how not to get suckered into a side channel that led nowhere, and where he liked to position the raft on river bends. "The trick to getting through the white water is to understand where the water is flowing. That way you'll be in the right position to get around obstacles and reversals."

"What is a reversal? Where the river bends and goes the other direction?"

Sam shook his head. "In white water, a reversal is where the current reverses upriver and sort of swirls around itself."

"Like a whirlpool?"

"Yes. Or a hole, or sometimes a curler, a wave that folds back in on itself. A keeper is an exceptionally strong reversal that can trap a raft, very dangerous. You want to avoid keepers."

"No keepers. Got it." Dana spotted some animals moving in the shadows along the water's edge. "Oh, look. Are those beavers?"

"River otters." The fond look on Sam's face made it clear they were a favorite of his. He oared the boat into the slower water on the other side of the river and rowed backward to hold the raft in place. "Pull out the camera from that red bag if you want to take some pictures."

Dana managed to get the dry bag unclipped and unrolled and found the camera he'd mentioned. The otters had disappeared when they spotted the raft, but Sam held the raft in place, and after a few minutes Dana saw a head pop up, and then another. Soon, several of them climbed onto the riverbank. With the telephoto lens, Dana was able to get close-ups of the youngsters wrestling together and sliding down the muddy bank to splash into the water. Sam kept the raft in position until she'd taken all the photos she wanted.

"They are so cute. You'll share these pictures with me, won't you?"

"Of course, if you give me your email."

"I will." It was strange to think Sam didn't have her address. It seemed like a lifetime ago that she woke up to strange noises in a strange house and threatened to shoot him with the flare gun. Good thing he didn't panic as easily as she did. For a man held at gunpoint in his own house, he'd been incredibly calm that night. He hadn't even raised his voice, just talked to her soothingly. Cool under pressure—no wonder they'd put him in charge of giant oil rigs. He'd probably be a great dad, able to handle whatever troubles kids might throw at him. Her lips curved at the thought of a posse of miniature Sams climbing all over him.

"What are you smiling about?"

She shook her head. "I was thinking of the

expression on your face when you saw me holding the flare gun."

"Yeah, probably the image of sheer terror." He chuckled, and she clicked a picture of him with his head thrown back in laughter, the sun shining on his face.

"Not at all. You acted as though it was quite reasonable of me to question why you were in your own house. Such a gentleman."

"That's me. Okay, you probably ought to put that camera away and strap everything down. We'll be coming up to some rapids before long."

Dana packed the camera into the gear bag, rolled and fastened the top and clipped it to the carabiner on the raft ring. She finished donning her helmet just as the current picked up speed.

Dana grabbed the line and pushed her foot between the thwart and the bottom of the raft for extra security. A row of boulders blocked the left side of the river, leaving a narrow channel of frothy water on the right. The raft bucked over the small waves, flexing the thwart away from the bottom of the raft and releasing Dana's foot. So much for that theory. She held tighter to the line. Ahead, waves curled like the tops of soft ice-cream cones,

almost as high as her head. The raft dived low
into a dip and then rose over the wave, momentarily bouncing Dana off her seat. After a
few seconds to regroup, they dropped over a
ledge across the river. A huge splash washed
over them into the raft. Dana gasped and used
her sleeve to mop icy water from her face,
then looked back to find Sam grinning at her
as he rowed. She laughed and pushed her wet
hair from in front of her eyes.

He guided them past a school bus–sized
boulder on the right side and, with two quick
strokes, crossed the river so that they took
the next ledge on the left. It was another big
drop, with a corresponding splash of water,
but they avoided a frothy hole on the right
side.

The ride continued, bouncing and churning through the section of river at high
speed until all at once the river widened and
calmed. Dana looked back at Sam. Behind
him, Kimmik shook the water from his ears
and wagged his tail. Dana let go of the grab
line and turned to face them.

"That was so much fun."

Sam grinned. "You liked it?"

"I loved it. It's like a flume ride at an
amusement park, but without all the people

and lines and manufactured thrills. It's the real thing."

"A little too real for most people. That water's cold."

It was, but Dana didn't care. Thanks to the protective clothes and her helmet, only her hands and face were really wet, but the sun was out and the air was warm. She'd do it again in a flash. "Any more white water today?"

"Not today. We need to make a few more miles before camp. There will be some ripples, but just one more real rapid in this river, and we'll hit it late tomorrow."

"Good. I'm really starting to like this white-water stuff."

Sam laughed. "Who would have guessed you were a secret adrenaline junkie?"

"Not me." She smiled, thinking of the looks on the faces of her former coworkers if they could see her now, riding a rubber raft down a wild river. The Dana they knew would never have considered something so risky. But here in Alaska, the old Dana had given way to a bolder, more daring version of herself. Alaska Dana kayaked and flew in tiny planes and white-water rafted. Alaska Dana was a lot of fun. She'd miss her when she went home.

SAM BEACHED THE raft on a gravel island in the center of the river and folded the oars out of the way. He shrugged his shoulders in circles, loosening them up after a day of rowing.

Dana inspected the island. Two spindly spruce trees grew at the downriver edge of the island, one leaning precariously over the water. Otherwise, the island consisted of washed gravel and a few large boulders, littered with pieces of twisted driftwood.

She looked at him, her expression dubious. "We're camping here?"

Sam nodded. "The breeze along the river tends to knock down the mosquitoes a bit." Besides, if they were lucky, there might be some kings pooled up. He'd caught them there before.

"Okay," Dana said slowly, "but there's not a lot of privacy on the island."

Sam winked. "I promise to turn my back. You said I was a gentleman."

"I did say that, didn't I?" She laughed and started handing him gear from the raft.

They unloaded and set up camp. Sam was surprised at how quickly Dana had picked up the routines. Without prompting, she immediately started threading together the tent poles as he'd demonstrated the day before. She set up the rolling table and campstools while he staked the tent, and even set out the water purifier. For a girl who'd never been camping, she was remarkably efficient.

Nothing seemed to faze her for long. He'd expected her to complain about the mosquitoes or getting wet or having to dig her own latrine, but no. Instead, she kept those big brown eyes open wide all day long, as if trying to absorb everything around her.

"Sam." She held perfectly still and kept her voice to a whisper. "What's that?"

He followed her eyes to the far bank. Something moved, but the dappling of the shadows disguised the shape until the animal stopped and turned to look in their direction, and he could make out the disproportionately large tufted ears over a flat cat's face. "A lynx," he whispered back.

The furry cat watched them for several seconds before fading into the woods and disappearing. Dana gazed after it. "It was beautiful."

Sam nodded. "We're lucky. People don't see wild lynx often. They're mostly nocturnal." He looked at his watch. "Of course, it is almost nine. No wonder I'm so hungry.

What do you think—sweet-and-sour pork or spaghetti?"

Dana looked up at the silvery moon rising in the east even while the sun still shone in the northwest. "A full moon. Tonight, we should dine on Italian. Do you have tiramisu in your magic food chest?"

"Afraid not, but I do have freeze-dried Neapolitan ice cream."

She grinned. "No way."

"Way." The breeze died down, and Sam immediately felt a mosquito land on his neck. How did they find him so fast? "I'll get the water boiling, and you can light a citronella candle. We'll dine by candlelight."

The freeze-dried spaghetti tasted great. Although, after rowing all day and not getting around to setting up camp until so late, cement would have tasted like gourmet food. After the spaghetti, Sam dug through the food stash until he uncovered a pair of freeze-dried ice-cream sandwiches and offered one to Dana.

She eyed the package before she unwrapped it. "I didn't know dried ice cream existed."

"I think NASA popularized it."

"Hmm." She took a bite and chewed

thoughtfully. "It's not exactly ice cream, but it's not bad. I'm getting in a lot of firsts on this trip."

"First camping trip."

"Yes. And first lynx sighting. First time in an inflatable raft—any raft, actually. First time to eat trout."

"Really? You've never tasted trout before?"

"No."

The corners of his eyes crinkled. "Well, technically you still haven't. That was a Dolly Varden. Be sure and get it right if Game and Fish should ask so they don't throw me in jail. You've had salmon?"

"Yes, of course."

"King salmon?"

"Only the dip Ursula made."

"Right. Well, if we're lucky, tomorrow we'll catch a king and I'll make you my famous planked salmon. You're in for a treat."

"I can't wait." Dana carried her plate and fork to the river to prewash it before using the boiling water. She picked up the shovel and walked past the tent, toward the spruces. "Time for you to be a gentleman."

"Yes, ma'am." Sam turned upriver. He gathered a small pile of driftwood together and started a fire. Spreading his slicker on the ground in front of a boulder for a backrest, he settled in to watch the flames. He picked up the spruce limb he'd collected, pulled his knife from the holster on his belt and whittled away the excess wood and splinters, working it into a plank. By the time Dana returned, the fire was blazing nicely.

She held her hands in front of the flames. He set down the plank and spread his knees to make a space for her. "Come sit with me."

Without hesitation, she settled into the spot he'd created and leaned back into his chest, a loose strand of hair tickling his neck. He encircled her with his arms, not too tight, but enough to keep her there, pressed against him. She fit him just right, the top of her head tucked up beneath his chin.

Neither of them spoke. There was no need. Words would only have distracted from the perfection of the moment, from the gentle breeze, the first few stars becoming visible in the dusky sky, the sound of the river flowing. They watched the orange and yellow tongues of fire dance together, listened to the crackle of the fire. Occasionally, a tiny blue blaze would erupt with a soft hiss.

Kimmik wandered over from whatever he'd been sniffing and flopped down beside the fire. Dana shifted and Sam tightened his arms, encouraging her to cuddle closer. They sat together, staring into the flames, until the logs had reduced themselves to embers.

He pulled the stretchy band from her ponytail, releasing the silky strands, and nuzzled the top of her head. Her hair smelled like wood smoke and lavender shampoo. If only he could bottle that scent. He would remember this one perfect night always.

Dana turned slightly so that her head was against his shoulder and she could look up at his face. "Sam?"

"Mmm-hmm?"

"I'm really glad you asked me to come on this trip."

"So am I."

She gave a happy sigh. "Someday, when I'm an old lady sitting on a rocking chair in some nursing home, and people are telling stories about exciting things they've done, I'll tell them about the time I rafted down a wild river in Alaska with you."

"I'm sure you'll have lots of exciting stories to tell."

She shook her head. "No. The most exciting thing that ever happened to me before was probably winning the science fair in middle school. I'm not the kind of girl who takes chances."

"You took a chance coming out here with me."

"Maybe." She paused. "But it didn't feel like taking a chance. I trust you."

She trusted him. It was as simple, and as absolutely mind-blowingly complicated, as that. In spite of his mother's hatred of Raynotts, of his possible claim on her father's estate, of Chris's misgivings, Dana trusted him. It was a lot to live up to.

She turned those dark eyes up at him and stroked her fingers along the ragged stubble on his jaw. Maybe he should have brought a razor along. On the other hand, she didn't seem to mind it. "Sam?"

"Yes?"

"Are you going to kiss me?"

He wanted to, more than he wanted oxygen at that moment. But he had to think beyond tonight. One stolen kiss wasn't enough, would never be enough. They were on borrowed time. What he wanted from her he couldn't have, and pretending would just make it harder in the end. Instead, he smiled at her. "Better not."

"Why?"

"Because if I do, I might not be able to stop at one."

"Hmm." She didn't seem surprised, just thoughtful. After a few seconds, she shifted around so she was kneeling in front of him and rested her hands on his shoulders. Illumination from the twilight sky made the graceful lines of her face look like an ivory carving. Her breath escaped through parted lips, and it took all his willpower not to taste them. But he'd experienced one of her kisses, knew the power she had over him. Another kiss would be a keeper, dragging him into a hydraulic that he didn't have the strength to pull out of. Instead of giving in to the kiss, he backpedaled desperately, drinking her in with his eyes.

She spent a long time simply looking into his face, almost as though she could read his thoughts. Finally, she leaned forward and pressed her lips against his forehead. "Good night, Sam."

"Good night." He watched her disappear into the tent and then focused again on the fire as the embers reduced themselves to ashes, working the spruce plank until the surface was smooth, as much by feel as by sight.

He tried to congratulate himself for maintaining discipline, but who was he kidding?

All she had to do was gaze into his eyes and he was lost. He set the plank aside, picked up a pebble and tossed it into the river, listening to the splash as it broke the surface of the water, imagining it sinking steadily to the bottom, far below the surface. Kind of like him. As much as he'd like to deny it, when it came to Dana, he was in way over his head.

CHAPTER TWELVE

THE NEXT MORNING, the first thing Dana saw when she came out of the tent was Sam up to his knees in water at the edge of their island. He cast his line out into the water, pulled it in as the colorful feathers on the end drifted downstream, and then whipped it behind him in a graceful arc and cast it out again. Dana knew nothing about fishing, but she always thought it involved putting a worm on a hook and dangling it into the water. Maybe this was fly-fishing.

He looked like he'd been there awhile. Did the man never sleep? He didn't come into the tent for at least an hour after she crawled into her sleeping bag, and somehow he'd slipped out this morning without waking her.

Maybe he was avoiding her. Her cheeks flushed as she thought of last night, of almost begging for his kiss. Maybe she'd been too direct, scaring him away. But no, the way he'd looked at her wasn't the expression of a man trapped in an uncomfortable situation. He felt the attraction, too, but he hadn't acted on it. And as she thought about it, maybe not kissing her was the kindest thing he could have done.

Because they both knew in three more days, the floatplane would carry them back to Anchorage and it would be time for her to go home. Back to Kansas, back to her mother, back to reality. And most likely, she would never see Sam again.

She pushed that thought away. She had the rest of her life to live with regrets. Today the sun shone, and the birds sang, and the river flowed around her. She should make the most of this while it lasted.

Kimmik spotted her and came running up with a stick in his mouth. She threw it into the river on the other side of the island from Sam. Kimmik launched himself into the water and grabbed the stick, then paddled back to the island, gave a mighty shake and trotted up to her, holding the stick proudly in his mouth.

"Hey, sleepyhead. Ready for breakfast?" Sam called over the sound of the river.

"I'll make it. Powdered eggs?"

"I'm afraid so."

She followed the technique Sam had used

to light the stove, and soon had water boiling and made coffee. Sam left the river and came to sit beside her on the ice chest. She handed him a cup of coffee and poured the prescribed amount of water into the egg pouches. "No Dollies this morning?"

"Nope. There are some kings pooled up, though. I just have to convince one to take my fly."

Aha, he was fly-fishing. She smiled to herself and tried the eggs, which were flavored with cheese and bits of bacon. "These aren't half-bad."

"I suspect if you had them at home, you wouldn't think so. Everything tastes better outdoors."

"You're right. Being outside seems to do something to your senses. The colors are brighter. The sounds are crisper. Maybe fresh air wakes up your taste buds."

He shook his head. "I can't believe you've never been camping before."

"If I'd known it was this much fun, I would have. More coffee?"

"Yes, please." Sam held out his cup and she topped it up.

"So, are we spending the day here, fishing?"

"No. We need to break camp by about noon. We have one more tricky bit of white water late today, and I don't want to leave it too late. Evening shadows make it hard to read the river." He finished his coffee and set the cup on the ground. "So, if I'm going to make you my famous spruce-planked king salmon for dinner, I'd better get back to fishing."

Dana puttered around the camp, cleaning up breakfast and rolling up the sleeping bags while Sam fished. Funny, even chores seemed better outdoors. She wouldn't want to wash her dishes in the river every day, and the baby wipes she cleaned up with this morning were a poor substitute for a real shower, but for now, the novelty made everything fun.

"Dana." Sam spoke in a low voice. She turned to see him pointing across the river and a little downstream. A furry brown animal scampered down the bank. Her first thought was to wonder how Kimmik had gotten across the river, but she quickly realized it was a bear cub. Another cub, lighter in color, appeared from behind a bush and pounced on the first one. They tumbled into the water, where they drew apart and scurried back to the bank, the darker cub chasing after the lighter one.

Dana snatched the camera and zoomed in to focus on the siblings. She'd managed to snap half a dozen photos when she saw the mother bear step out of the woods. The shaggy bear raised her head, sniffed and looked in their direction. Dana continued snapping pictures. It wasn't long before the bear jerked her head and turned downstream, loping along the riverbank, the two cubs right behind her. She looked back once more before disappearing around the bend of the river.

Dana turned to see Sam watching her. "First grizzly?"

"First bear, period. They were so cute."

"Cute and dangerous. Remember, where there's a cub, there's usually a mama bear with a chip on her shoulder. I was probably in her favorite fishing spot. Lucky she decided to move on instead of challenging me."

"What would you have done?"

"Backed off. I don't argue with mama grizzlies."

Dana packed up the stove and breakfast gear. She glanced over at Sam. He stiffened suddenly, raised the tip of his rod and started reeling in the line. The rod bent in a deep arch. She hurried over to the shoreline to watch. Soon, the fish was close enough to be visible in the water. It was a monster, almost three feet long. It kept trying to move toward the faster water in the river, but Sam maneuvered the rod to keep it swimming in the shallow area.

"Could you grab that net?"

Dana found the net lying on the bank beside her. Sam stepped slowly backward, leading the fish toward her.

"Try to net it."

"Me?"

"Could you?"

Dana knelt down and leaned over the water to scoop the net over the fish. It thrashed violently, almost pulling the net from her hands, but she managed to hold on until Sam stepped closer and took the net from her. He lifted the fish from the water, still flapping wildly in the net.

"It's huge." The long silvery fish had dark speckles over its body and a blush of pink along its sides. The undershot jaw opened and closed as the fish grew quieter.

Sam inspected the fish. "Probably twenty-five pounds."

"In the water, it seemed as big as me."

"They're strong. You did a good job netting him."

Sam cleaned and filleted the salmon, packed the pieces into gallon-sized plastic bags and put them in the ice chest while Dana took down the tent. After a snack lunch of jerky and trail mix, they loaded up the raft and pulled away from the island, one king salmon richer.

THEY WERE A little late breaking camp, and it was early evening before they reached the braided section of river Sam was looking for. He folded the oars into the boat and rested for a few minutes. After wrestling that king to the shore this morning and oaring all afternoon, his muscles ached. They still had one more set of rapids to get through. He was tempted to set up camp here and take the rapids in the morning, but he remembered the river well enough to know there weren't any good camping spots on this side of the canyon. What looked like a grassy meadow was actually a marsh, and if they camped there, they would have to slog the gear all the way across it to the forest edge and sleep on knobby tree roots and rocks. He knew because he'd done it before.

There were some tricky narrows in the up-coming section. He considered pulling over and hiking up to the bluffs to scout the rap-ids ahead, but even with the midnight sun, he didn't want to leave the rapids too late in the day. The shadows of the canyon would make reading the water that much harder. Besides, he'd floated this river a dozen times, with high and low water. He knew the holes, knew the dangerous areas. He could do this.

Sunlight warmed the meadow, contrasting with the shadows of the forest beyond and a velvety green mountain rising behind it. The snow-capped peaks of Denali towered over the shoulder of the lower mountain. Dana pulled out the camera to capture the scene.

She continued to take pictures as Sam rowed with the current, hurrying them down-stream. He got caught up watching her fre-quent smiles and the way her eyes sparkled when she would look at him, which is how the rapids almost sneaked up on him. The sound of rushing water alerted him.

He oared backward, slowing their pace. "Better put that away. We're about to come into the canyon." He grabbed his helmet and jammed it on his head.

"Oh, good." Dana snapped one more of

him before she put the camera into the dry bag and rolled the top closed. They came around a corner and dropped over a ledge, jarring her. She tucked the bag away and pulled on her helmet as the raft rolled off a boulder. She grabbed the rope, her eyes wide, but looked at Sam with a big grin on her face.

Sam winked at her and transferred his attention to the rapids. His heart shifted into high gear, pumping the blood through his body, and he forgot his weariness as the raft picked up speed. He dipped an oar, making a minor adjustment to the angle of the boat before the next bend. He loved the adrenaline rush, caught up in the power of the river, maneuvering the boat through the rapids. This is when he felt most alive.

The next part was tricky, with a line to the left to avoid a boulder, then a sharp ferry to the right or they'd land in a hole. He skimmed the boulder and pulled hard on the oars, rotating off an outcrop on the right bank and moving downriver.

Dana stayed low in the boat, holding on to the grab line, but she studied the river and Sam's adjustments, instinctively leaning uphill as the raft navigated the rushing waters.

Her glance back at him was so believing, it made him proud.

Sam scanned the river, searching for the large hole that would be the last of the white water on this river as he worked his way to the right bank, better to bypass the reversal. They came around a bend and he saw a strainer, an ancient cottonwood, lying halfway across the river, blocking his line to the right. If they got caught up in that, they were goners. Sam dug in his oars, pulling frantically to move to the left of the hole. "Hang on, Dana."

They almost made it, barely catching the edge of the hole. The raft dropped in with a splash and tilted upward on the left, threatening to overturn. "High side!" Sam leaned uphill. Dana threw her weight onto the uphill side also, and the raft stabilized for a moment before the front of the boat soared skyward over the wave, bucking like a bronco and bouncing everything in the raft.

Dana slid off the thwart, but quickly recovered her balance. Sam lifted the oars from the water so they didn't catch and throw him, letting the raft ride out the wave. Out of the corner of his eye, he saw a flash of red go over the edge of the raft and Dana's look of panic. Before he could react, she grabbed at it just as they reached the crest of the wave and dropped down the other side. The jar sent her headfirst into the churning river.

Sam dropped the oars and stood, scanning the water, blood pounding in his ears. The loose oar hit something and landed a blow to his left side, sending a sharp pain shooting through his left arm and knocking him into the oarsman seat. He scrambled up again and spotted Dana, bobbing beside the raft. Thank God for the PFD. He grabbed the loop behind her head and dragged her into the boat.

The raft bobbed along in the choppy water below the rapids. Sam grabbed an oar with his right hand and used it as a rudder to guide the raft to the bank of the river, underneath a curving bluff. The boat beached on the gravel and they came to rest.

He sucked in a lungful of oxygen and ran his eyes over Dana, looking for signs of damage. Completely soaked, of course, her eyes huge, but she seemed okay.

She scrambled to her feet. "Sam, your arm."

He looked down. His left arm dangled uselessly just below the elbow. Blood ran from a jagged tear. A dispassionate voice inside his head warned that when the adrenaline wore off, this was going to hurt. A lot.

Dana scrambled to the back of the raft and burrowed like a terrier through the equipment until she unearthed a white case with a red cross. She pulled out a thick dressing and looked at his arm, then at his face, obviously not knowing what to do.

Sam took the wad of gauze and pressed it against the bleeding gash. "Thank you. Are you okay?" He could see a few scrapes on her arms but nothing serious.

"I'm fine. I'm so sorry, Sam." Dana checked through the contents of the kit. "What else do you need?"

"First I need to stop the bleeding." The wound wasn't spurting, so he hadn't ruptured an artery. That was a plus. What happened to cause her to go overboard? They were through the worst of it by then. He looked around. "Where's Kimmik?"

Dana stood and called him. The dog came running up the shoreline to the edge of the raft. He must have gone into the water when Dana did. He gave a mighty shake, spraying them both with river water. Not that it mattered. They could hardly be any wetter. Sam was glad to see he was safe, but he didn't need an exuberant Labrador in his lap right now.

"Kimmik, stay." The dog stopped and sat. "Good boy." Sam turned to Dana. "You know first aid?"

"No."

"Okay." Sam needed to assess the situation, but his brain seemed to be operating in slow motion. "Um, could you help me get this helmet off?"

Dana removed his helmet and hers, tossing them into the back of the raft. Her cheeks were pink, her breathing fast but not labored. No sign she'd inhaled river water. She might have some bruising, but seemed to be moving fine.

He, on the other hand, wasn't so fine. Judging from the ache each time he took a breath, he had a couple of cracked ribs as well as the compound fracture in his forearm. He pulled the thick dressing away from the wound, pleased to see it was starting to clot. He was going to have to rely on Dana.

She stood beside him, waiting for his next instruction. Better give her one. His safety training emphasized giving everyone in an emergency situation a job to avoid panic. Besides, he needed her help. He swallowed. "I'm going to need a splint."

Dana picked over the contents of the raft and pulled the plank he'd been polishing from the mesh bag. "Would this work?"

"Perfect. Can you break it in two lengthwise?"

Dana propped one side of the plank on some rocks and jumped on the middle, splitting it along the grain. She climbed back into the raft where Sam still sat on the oarsman seat.

At his prompting, she cleaned the edges of the wound with an antiseptic wipe, gingerly so as not to start it bleeding again. "Now, you'll need to line up the bones as best you can and sandwich them between the boards. Then use that stretchy bandage to wrap it."

Dana bit her lip. "I'm afraid I'll hurt you."

"I can almost guarantee it. But it will save me pain in the long run. Pull down and away so you can line up the bones."

She nodded and took a deep breath. When she straightened his elbow and pulled on his wrist, flashes of fire shot up his arm and through his spine. Sam closed his eyes and ground his teeth, waiting for the pain to stop.

Once she had the splint in place and made

the first couple of wraps, the shooting pain subsided into a throbbing ache. Sam opened his eyes. Dana's hands were steady as she wrapped the bandage around the splint. Tears streamed from her eyes and ran down her face, but she ignored them and continued to wrap his arm until she reached the end of the bandage and secured it. He had to give her credit. The woman had guts.

She looked up at him and managed a tight smile. "How's that?"

"Better. Thank you." He nodded toward the first-aid kit. "Use one of those antiseptic wipes to clean those scrapes on your arms. You don't want an infection."

She nodded and tore a foil package open. "Then what?"

"Well, since I'm basically useless, I suppose you'd better make camp." He looked at the splint on his arm. "I guess we won't be cooking that planked king salmon tonight, after all."

CHAPTER THIRTEEN

DANA HOVERED NEXT to Sam in case he needed help climbing out of the raft, but he managed on his own. He stumbled over to sit on a fallen log, hugging his broken arm. His expression seemed almost normal—only the tightness around his eyes and mouth signaled his pain. Kimmik came to sit at his feet and gave a low whimper. Sam used his good hand to give the dog a reassuring pat on the head.

After tying the raft to a tree, Dana started to unload the gear. By the time she'd finished, the quick-dry clothing she wore had almost dried. She found a bottle of water and brought it to Sam. Even in the late-day shadows, his face seemed pale. He took the water and drank, but his body was shaking and he spilled some of the water.

"You're cold."

He nodded. "Shock."

Dana tried to remember what she knew about treatment for shock, but since her education on this subject came entirely from old British novels, all she could think of was sweet hot tea or brandy. She was pretty sure they had neither. But if Sam was shivering, he must be cold. She brought a sleeping bag and wrapped it around his shoulders.

"What else do you need?"

"This is helping."

She lit the stove and set a pan of water to boil. While she waited on it, she flipped through the booklet from the first-aid kit and read about shock. Not good. She found some packets of instant cider in the food bin and carried a mugful to Sam.

"Here. Something warm to drink."

His hand still shook, so she helped raise the mug to his mouth and let him sip. He swallowed. "Thanks."

"You're welcome. Do you want to lie down?"

"I'm fine."

"If you're in shock, you should lie down, elevate your feet and stay warm."

Sam's eyes crinkled at the corners. "Since when are you a Girl Scout?"

She shrugged. "I can read. I'll build a fire, and then I'll spread out a sleeping mat so you can lie beside it and keep warm. Humor me, okay?"

"Yes, ma'am."

Dana gathered up a load of firewood and used Sam's knife to shave some of it into kindling. With some coaching from him and a dab of his magic fire-starter paste, Dana got the fire going and fed the dog. As the sun disappeared beyond the mountains, Sam dozed next to the fire, covered with a sleeping bag, his feet propped up on a section of log, and Kimmik stretched out beside him. Sam seemed to have stopped shivering.

Dana cut off a few chunks of king salmon and stewed them in boiling water, adding a packet of chicken and noodles. When she checked on Sam, he opened his eyes. She brought him a mug. "Here. This is the closest I can come to chicken soup."

With her help, he sat up, propped against a log. Dana handed him the soup. He took a sip. "Not bad."

She smiled and drank from her own mug. "I should start a new career writing a camping cookbook. I'll call it the *Freeze-dried Gourmet*. Maybe I'll become famous. What do you think?"

Sam snorted and then winced. "Ouch, don't make me laugh. It hurts."

"I'll try not to be funny." She brushed a strand of hair back from his forehead and her expression grew more somber. "What do we do from here?"

Sam took a breath as if speaking was an effort. "Since I can't oar, we have two options. We can call for rescue, or we can wait a couple of days until the group behind us catches up and get one of them to oar us to the pickup point. With hard rowing, we're only a few hours away."

Considering his condition, the choice seemed clear. "I think we should get you to a hospital sooner rather than later. How do we call for rescue?"

"With the sat phone."

Dana's blood ran cold. "In the red bag. The one with the camera and our cell phones."

"That's right."

"Sam, I'm so sorry. It went overboard."

"What?"

"I forgot to clip the carabiner when we got into the white water and when we went over that last bump, it flew out. I tried to grab it."

"That's when you fell in?"

"Yes." She slapped her hand against her

forehead. "I can't believe I was so stupid. This is all my fault."

Sam shook his head. "No, it's my fault. I wasn't paying attention and didn't give you enough warning before the rapids."

"I still should have—"

"Don't. We both made mistakes, and we can't change them. We have to move forward."

She would have argued more, but she could see the effort was tiring Sam. She nodded. "Won't the pilot report us missing when we're not at the pickup the day after tomorrow?"

"Maybe, but he won't necessarily think it's an emergency. He'll probably do a flyover up the river, but with the bluff here, I doubt he'll see us. We'll just have to wait for the next group to come by."

They could do that. They had plenty of food and fuel for the stove. If it weren't for Sam's pain, she would have enjoyed an extra couple of days on the river. "Is there anything I can do for you now?"

"Throw another log on the fire, and then come sit here beside me. Keep me warm."

DANA DOZED ON and off through the night, occasionally getting up to feed the fire. She considered moving them into the tent, but Sam seemed relatively comfortable where he was, and with the fire, two sleeping bags, and she and Kimmik pressed against opposite sides of his body, he seemed warm enough. At least it wasn't raining, and the mosquitoes weren't bad.

Sam seemed to drift between sleep and restlessness. Her only clue about how much pain he felt came during his interludes of slumber, when he would moan in his sleep. The sun had just peeked over the northeastern horizon when she finally fell into a deep sleep for a couple of hours. When she woke, sweat beaded on her forehead.

The fire had burned down, but Sam seemed to be radiating heat. Dana placed a gentle hand on his forehead and drew back almost as if she'd been burned. Fever. Not good. His breath seemed more labored. He didn't stir under her touch.

She slipped out from under the sleeping bag and checked the first-aid booklet. Fever, a symptom of infection, along with redness around the wound, and eventually muscle weakness, confusion and nausea. There weren't any antibiotics in the first-aid kit, but Dana did find a bottle of ibuprofen.

She returned to Sam, trying to decide whether to wake him or let him rest. The decision was taken out of her hands when Kimmik crawled out from under Sam's arm and gave a big shake, flapping his ears. Sam opened his eyes.

Dana knelt beside him. "Hi. How are you feeling?"

His eyes seemed glassy, unfocused, but he gave a little smile. "Not great. How about you?"

"I'm fine. But you're feverish, so I want you to take these."

"What are they?"

"Ibuprofen. To get your temperature down. And you need to drink water."

"Okay." With some effort, Sam sat up and swallowed the pills and some water. He struggled to his feet, wobbling a bit. He seemed noticeably weaker than yesterday.

Dana rushed forward to support him. "Where are you going?"

He raised an eyebrow. "It's a private matter. Can you pass me that stick?"

Leaning on the walking stick, Sam made his way into the edge of the woods, past a cow-sized boulder. At his pointed look, she waited on the other side of the rock until he gave the okay before returning to escort him back to the fire.

The medicine seemed to help, and Sam swallowed a few bites of scrambled eggs before he fell asleep. Dana did the camp chores. Still plenty of freeze-dried food along with all that fish. They weren't going to starve. But Sam's fever worried her.

A couple of days until they could expect the other rafters to come along. Surely, Sam could hold out until then. But a flash of panic shot through Dana as a thought occurred to her. What if the other group passed without seeing them?

She checked the first-aid book to see if there was some sort of distress signal, but that didn't seem to be covered. Maybe a white flag? Or was that surrender? Not that it mattered since she was fresh out of white flags. She tore a strip from the bottom of her light blue thermal top and used a charred stick from the fire to spell out HELP on the shore.

She tied the makeshift flag to a long stick and planted it along the bank where anyone passing on the river would be sure to see it. Then she went to check on Sam. His temperature was back up. She applied a warm compress to his arm and dosed him with ibu-profen again.

She kept busy the whole day gathering fire-wood, organizing the equipment and taking care of Sam. She was worried. As each dose of medicine wore off, his temperature seemed to spike higher. In between, he shivered with chills. He slept more and she could hardly coax him into eating at all. He said food made his stomach churn.

Once again, she spent the night beside him, giving him space when the fever would spike, wrapping the sleeping bag around them and pressing herself against him when he would shiver with chills. Finally, he fell into a fitful sleep and she closed her eyes and held him tight, as if she could somehow protect him from the infection. The sky had turned the pale silver of just before dawn when she heard him moan. She spoke softly. "You okay?"

"I don't think so." His voice was a hoarse whisper. "I shouldn't have dragged you here. I'm so sorry, Dana."

"I'm fine."

"If I don't make it—"

"Shh. You're just sick. You'll be okay once you get to a doctor."

"Be quiet a minute." The effort to talk was

obviously costing Sam, so she quit protesting and listened. "I want you to be safe. Just flag down the rafters when they come. They'll get you to the floatplane."

"I know. And you're coming with me. Hey, you promised me you'd show me how to make planked king salmon. You're not going back on your promise, are you?"

He smiled before his eyes fluttered closed. Dana scrambled to her knees. "Sam? Sam, don't you dare leave me."

"S'okay, Dana. I'm right here."

She gave Sam another dose of medicine, tucked the sleeping bag around him and kissed him on the forehead. Almost immediately, he fell asleep, his breathing rapid and shallow.

Once he was settled, Dana went to work, packing the raft. She was not going to sit around and wait to be rescued while Sam grew weaker. The floatplane was due at the lower lake today at noon, and one way or another, she planned to be there to meet it.

She made sure every single thing was strapped down this time. Then she woke Sam. "Hey, sleepyhead. Wake up. It's time for breakfast."

Sam made a face. "Not hungry."

"That's okay. It's only cider. You need a little sugar in you before we get on the river."

He struggled into a sitting position and took a sip of the hot liquid. "They're here?"

"No, but we're not waiting. The plane is coming at noon, so we need to get going."

He shook his head. "Too dangerous. You might get hurt."

"We're past the white water, right?"

"Still ripples, backwater. You're safer here."

"But you're not. Come on, Sam. You said it. I can drift or I can paddle my own boat. I've decided to paddle and you're coming with me."

He took another sip and met her eyes. "You've never oared a raft."

"There's always a first time. Today is mine. Let's go."

His legs shook when he stood, further proof she was making the right decision. With her on one side and the walking stick on the other, Sam made his way to the raft and eased over the side onto the floor, leaning against the thwart. Kimmik jumped into the raft and wagged his tail at her expectantly.

Dana carefully put away the sleeping bags. She managed to get the PFD over Sam's splint, and buckled it and his helmet before donning hers. She untied the raft and gave it a shove. Nothing happened. Okay, lesson one. Push into the water before loading the raft. But Sam had done it this way.

Kimmik jumped out and gave a bark. She got down lower and put her shoulder into it. This time, the raft slid six inches farther into the water. Good. Three more good shoves and it was floating. Kimmik jumped in and she followed, tripping over the equipment on the way, but eventually she made it to the oarsman seat.

She took the oars in her hands, measuring their weight, getting the feel of them. Sam gave a little smile of encouragement. She smiled back and gave her first stroke, just as she'd seen Sam do it. She felt it in every muscle in her core, but the boat leaped forward into the current, carrying them downstream.

After a minute of solid oaring, she had to stop to catch her breath. How did Sam do this hour after hour? The man was a machine. Fortunately, the current continued to carry them forward, and a slight downriver breeze helped push them along.

"You're doing great." She could tell Sam was fighting to keep his eyes open, but he watched her. "Don't wear yourself out. It's a long stretch."

Dana nodded and started oaring again, setting a more reasonable rhythm. Up, rotate, pull, up, rotate, pull. One stroke at a time, she was moving them down the river.

Up ahead, she could hear rushing water. Sam heard it, too. "Easy does it, just hug the outside bank, but put your tail toward the center."

Dana pushed the raft toward the outer edge of the bend, keeping the raft at a forty-five degree angle the way Sam had done it. Frothy water jostled the raft and she stiffened, but it carried them through the bend. The river took another sharp turn, and they bumped into an almost-submerged rock, rolled to the left and spun in a complete circle before another stroke gained her control once again. Dana let out the breath she hadn't realized she was holding.

"Good job." Sam gave her a thumbs-up with his good hand. She smiled at him. Her shoulders ached and her abdominal muscles protested each movement, but they still functioned. She could do this.

They continued the float downriver. Sam had drifted off, his head cushioned against the inflated tube. They reached a point where the river branched into three small rivers. Which one? Did it matter? She decided the one on the right seemed the least intimidating, with hardly a ripple in the surface. She soon realized her mistake, as the water became shallower and finally petered out into a marshy area too shallow for the boat.

She oared in reverse, pushing the boat against the current, but when she lifted the oars to make another stroke, she lost all the ground she'd made up. The muscles in her arms burned. *I give up.* Dana almost said it aloud, but after a glance at Sam's face as he slept, she knew giving up wasn't an option.

She reversed the boat so her back was up-river and rowed hard and fast, still losing one stroke for every two she gained, but eventually they were out of the backwater and into the main channel. This time she chose the branch where the current seemed the strongest. Roots from a fallen tree blocked part of the path, but she pushed off with the oars and they glided past. Soon the current picked up again and the branches of river joined together, gathering speed.

Dana rested the oars on the tubes and caught her breath. The sun was high in the sky now but not quite overhead, so it probably wasn't noon yet. Unfortunately, she had no idea how much farther they had to go. She resumed oaring.

Time passed. Dana spotted another set of ripples ahead. She didn't see any route to avoid them, so she went through the middle. The raft jostled as if they were driving down a rough road, but Sam didn't stir. She rowed harder.

They passed a bend and, before her, the river split into two sections. She didn't have time for another mistake. "Sam." He didn't respond. Dana called louder, "Sam, wake up!"

His eyes opened momentarily, then closed again. Dana rowed toward a tree leaning over the river and hooked the bowline around it. She climbed to the back of the raft where Sam rested and laid her hand on his forehead.

His fever had spiked again. She stroked his face. "Sam, wake up. You need to take some pills."

He stirred and seemed surprised to see her. "Dana?"

"Yeah. Here. Swallow these." She pressed the tablets into his hand and offered the water bottle. He swallowed obediently. "Sam, listen. We're at a break in the river. Can you tell me which branch to take?"

He blinked and then tried to struggle upward. Dana helped him into a sitting position on the thwart. He narrowed his eyes to slits and looked downriver. "Are we on Brazzle Creek?"

Yikes. He didn't even remember where they were. "Yes. Brazzle Creek." She had to get him to that plane, ASAP.

"That one." He pointed to the left branch.

"Are you sure?"

"Main channel."

"How far are we from the pickup area?"

Sam concentrated. "An hour?"

"Okay. Why don't you lie down again? We'll be there before you know it."

Sam slumped onto the floor of the boat, and Dana untied the bowline. In the haze of fever, Sam wasn't even sure what river they were on, but she had to trust his instincts. They were all she had.

He was correct. After weaving back and forth a few times, the left branch widened. Clouds had gathered to block the sun, so she couldn't tell exactly where it was positioned in the sky. Maybe it wasn't noon yet. Maybe if it was, the pilot would wait a little while.

Or if not, maybe the pilot would fly overhead and see them on the river. That was a lot of maybes. She rowed faster.

Cottonwoods hung over the banks here, blocking her view of the sky. The river widened more and slowed. Without the brisk current to carry them along, Dana had to supply even more of the power to push the raft forward. Every muscle in her body screamed, but she kept rowing.

They came around a bend, and the wide expanse of the lake stretched in front of them. Dana breathed a sigh of relief until she noticed the hum. There on the far side of the lake, a plane grew smaller as it pulled away.

Nooooo.

She slumped in the seat. Then her eyes fell on the bag Sam mentioned contained rescue ropes, and she remembered what else she'd found in the bag her first night in Anchorage. She tore it open and pulled out the red flare gun and a package of flares. It took a few precious seconds to figure out how to load the flare.

She pointed the gun far to the right of the plane, closed her eyes and pulled the trigger. She opened her eyes to see the flare shooting across the sky. It was much lower than the plane, but maybe it would grab the pilot's attention. Distress was three blasts, right? She repeated the process twice more as quickly as she could and watched for a moment before she saw the most beautiful sight in the world.

The plane turned in a wide arc and dropped onto the lake.

CHAPTER FOURTEEN

DANA GRABBED A cup of coffee and sipped it as she waited in the hallway for Sam's nurse to complete her examination. The ambulance had been waiting for Sam at the dock. Sam's pilot friend had volunteered to drop her off at the hospital and take Kimmik to his house, and Dana gratefully accepted.

When she arrived at the hospital, the grim expression on the face of the emergency room doctor was enough to send Dana's heart racing, but Sam rallied and they'd transferred him to a hospital room.

While they were getting Sam cleaned up and admitted, Dana borrowed a phone from one of the staff to leave a message for Chris, thankful she remembered the number. She should call Ursula, but with their cell phones somewhere on the bottom of Brazzle Creek, she had no way to contact her.

That was hours ago. Since then, she'd been sitting by Sam's side or lurking outside his door while the medical people came and went and did whatever it was they did. Sam slept a lot, whether because of his exhaustion or the drugs, Dana wasn't sure. Probably both. His breathing seemed easier, which made her breathing easier, too.

Now that he was safe, she could take time to examine the situation, and the truth made her cringe. Her carelessness, forgetting to clip the carabiner onto the raft, was the beginning of the chain of disasters that almost cost Sam his life. As much as she'd loved the wild river, the birds and otters and bears, it had been a mistake for her to go along. She was a hazard. She belonged in town, where traffic lights signaled when it was safe to cross the street, not out in the wilderness with Sam, where a tiny lapse in judgment could have such huge consequences. Thank goodness he was going to live.

Someone pushed a trolley through the hall, collecting empty plates from the various rooms, which must mean it was evening. Dana tossed her empty coffee cup into a trash receptacle. She should probably think about finding something to eat, but all she really wanted to do was be with Sam. The nurse came out and smiled at her. "His fever is down and Dr. Tucker says it's a go. We'll be taking Sam into surgery soon."

"That's good news." They'd already explained the need for surgery to clean out the wound and fight the infection, as well as put in a couple of pins to help the bones heal. They'd just been waiting for Sam's condition to stabilize.

Dana pushed her way into the room and reached for Sam's good hand, careful not to jar his IV. "Hi."

"Hi." Sam seemed more alert. When he met her eyes, that feverish, glassy look was gone. The antibiotics and whatever other drugs they had in there seemed to be working their magic.

"The nurse says you're scheduled for surgery."

"Yeah. The doctor says it should heal fine as long as they can get the infection under control." He squeezed her hand. "He also said if I'd waited another day I probably wouldn't be here. I owe you my life."

Oh, Sam. It was all her fault, but if she said that, he would just argue with her. "If you hadn't pulled me out of the river, I might not be here, either. You don't owe me anything."

Tears threatened, but she needed to keep this light. "Well, except maybe a salmon dinner."

He laughed and winced. "Hey, have pity on my ribs."

"Sorry."

"Speaking of salmon, did you get the king into the refrigerator?"

He was lying in a hospital bed, worrying about the condition of his fish. Were all fishermen like this? "Your friend at the flying service said he'd go back for your equipment and take care of everything, including Kimmik."

"Good. He'll probably vacuum-pack it and freeze it then." He squeezed her hand. "Seriously, Dana. What you did on the river—"

Before he could finish the sentence, the nurse bustled back into the room and injected something into the IV bag. "It's time. Are you ready?"

Sam met Dana's eyes. "A kiss for luck?"

"You bet." She pressed her lips to his as the nurse released the brake.

The nurse threw an amused smile over her shoulder as she pushed the bed down the hall. "You can wait in the room at the end of the hallway."

Twenty minutes later, Dana was sitting in

an orange vinyl chair, pretending to read a magazine, when Ursula burst into the room. "Where is he?"

"In surgery."

"I came as soon as Chris called. He'll be here in a few hours." Ursula dropped into the chair beside Dana, her face agitated. "Sam is always so careful. Even when he was a teenager, Tommy taught him to plan things out and take precautions. What happened?"

Confession time. Dana squared her shoulders. "We were on Brazzle Creek and hit a bad patch of water. The bag with the phones and the camera went overboard. I tried to grab it, but I got thrown out, too, and while he was pulling me into the raft, the oar came loose and broke Sam's arm."

Dana thought she saw a flash of fury in Ursula's eyes before she closed them and took a deep breath. When she opened her eyes, she studied Dana, a frown on her face. "You're a mess. Have you been here the whole time?"

Dana nodded.

"Go home. Take a shower. I'll stay with Sam."

Dana shook her head. "I want to be here for him."

Ursula crossed her arms in front of her chest. "Haven't you done enough? Go."

Slowly, Dana rose to her feet. Ursula was right. Sam's injuries were all on her. She never should have gone on the float trip. She never should have spent so much time with Sam in the first place. Because she didn't belong with someone like him. She should have foreseen that it could only lead to tragedy—maybe not broken bones, but it was predictable that somebody was going to suffer the consequences. She shouldn't have taken the risk.

Ursula's face softened and she pulled out her phone. "I'll call a cab for you."

By the time Dana made it to the front door of the hospital, a taxi was waiting. She slid into the back seat, gave Sam's address and collapsed against the cracked vinyl. She hadn't realized until this minute just how much she hurt. Sore muscles she didn't even know she had cried out in protest. But that was nothing compared to the pain in her heart.

THE SOUND OF humming and beeps forced its way into Sam's consciousness. He vaguely remembered waking up after surgery and seeing Ursula's face. His eyelids felt too heavy to lift.

The door latch clicked open. "How is he?" Chris's voice.

"Shh, he's asleep. They said he'll be fine as long as they can get the infection cleared up," Ursula whispered. "They've set the bones, and he's responding to antibiotics."

"How did this happen?"

"Sounds like that sister of yours fell out of a raft and in the process of saving her, he broke his arm."

"What was he doing taking Dana on a fly-in raft trip, anyway? She knows squat about wilderness camping. She was supposed to be on her way home."

"Heaven knows. And speaking of your sister, how come you never happened to mention you had one?" Ursula's voice was getting louder, more stern.

"It never came up."

"Oh, really? And I suppose the fact that your name used to be Raynott never came up, either."

"That's right."

"Are you trying to make me believe it was a coincidence that you never mentioned it?"

"I never said that. I figured that information would do more harm than good. I'm not a Raynott anymore, and I have no ties to them."

"Not until your sister showed up, anyway."

"Hey. Don't blame Dana. Whatever my father may have done, it's not her fault. She's just trying to do the right thing."

"I'm sure she is. I like her, in fact. She's a nice person. But Sam would have been a whole lot better off if she'd never come to Alaska."

"Where is she, anyway? Her message said she'd be here."

"I sent her home. The last thing Sam needs is some doe-eyed cheechako who has to be rescued every five minutes hanging around him. I'm sure she didn't mean to almost kill Sam, but we all know about good intentions and where that road leads."

"You might get your facts straight before you chase her off." Sam's voice was just a rasp across his throat.

Ursula turned, startled. "You're awake." She poured a cup of water and passed it to him. "How are you feeling?"

Sam sipped the water, then set it down and locked eyes with Ursula. "A whole lot better than I was this morning when that 'doe-eyed cheechako,' as you call her, dragged me half-conscious into a raft and oared us all the way from just below the lower rapids to the pickup point."

"But that's, like, fifteen miles," Chris said.

"I know. I told her to wait for rescue, but she wouldn't risk letting the infection get worse. The doctor told me if I'd been out another twenty-four hours, I'd have surely lost my arm, and quite possibly my life."

Ursula blinked. "Dana did that?"

"She did." He turned on Chris. "*And you.* You run away and leave your kid sister holding the bag on all the family responsibilities. Then when she manages to track you down, you leave her alone in the house and go fishing without a word of explanation. What's wrong with you?" The strain of talking scratched Sam's throat and he coughed. He gulped down some water and looked up to see them both staring at him. Rants weren't his usual style, but some things needed to be said.

He continued in a quieter voice. "I accept full responsibility for everything that went wrong on this trip. I should have scouted the lower rapids before we ran them. It was avoiding an unexpected sweeper that caused the accident. I made mistakes and because of those mistakes, Dana was in danger. I probably shouldn't have taken her out without support. But you know what? Up until then, she was loving it. She loves everything about Alaska, and she has more heart and more courage than anyone I've ever known."

Neither of them spoke for a few moments. Then Chris patted his good shoulder. "Man, you've got it bad."

Sam started to shake his head, but Chris went on. "And that's not good for either of you. Dana's always done exactly what the old man tells her to do, and he's set it up so she can't leave Kansas. Without him around, her mother is going to be entirely dependent on her."

Sam took a deep breath and almost welcomed the tug of pain in his ribs as a distraction. Chris wasn't telling him anything he didn't already know. "I'm aware she's going home. I just don't want her slinking off in the night, feeling like everyone blames her. She's a hero."

Ursula looked down before meeting his eyes. "You're right. I'll apologize." To Chris, she asked, "So, what's the deal with this father of yours? Why did you run away from home?"

Chris gave her the same story he'd given Sam and Dana. "So nobody knows for sure what went on in that bar the night it burned down, but considering my father's reaction to my finding my birth certificate, I have to assume the worst." He shot a glance at Sam. "That's why I'm having trouble accepting any inheritance from him. I don't believe it's his money to leave. It should be Sam's, but he won't take it."

Ursula tapped her finger on her chin. "What if you could find a witness? Would it matter?"

"Yes, it would matter." Chris stood up straighter. "What witness?"

"Give me a day or two. I'll let you know if she actually saw anything."

"Who?" Sam demanded.

Ursula looked away. "If she's willing to talk, I'll set up a meeting once you're out of the hospital. In the meantime, I have a humble pie to bake. Excuse me."

AFTER A HOT SHOWER, Dana felt slightly better. According to the nurse she talked to on the phone, Sam was out of surgery and recovering. Dana longed to see him for herself, but maybe Ursula was right. Maybe it was better if she wasn't there, bothering Sam.

Maybe when it came to Sam's family, the Raynotts were some sort of curse. She still didn't believe her father could be a murderer or a thief, but she couldn't dispute the fact that Sam had spent his childhood in poverty while her father's business flourished.

The sound of a key rattled the front door. Finally, Chris had arrived. The door opened, and Ursula walked in.

Dana's eyes opened wider. "Is Sam okay?"

"He'll be fine. The surgery went well, and the antibiotics are working. The doctor says he'll probably keep him through tomorrow and let him come home the next day. Chris is with him now."

"Good."

Ursula gave a sheepish smile. "In fact, Sam was feeling well enough to make it clear he didn't appreciate me jumping to conclusions. He told us you got him to the plane and probably saved his life. You left out that little detail."

Dana shrugged. "It was still my fault he got hurt."

"He says it isn't." When Dana started to

protest, Ursula cut her off. "I tend to believe what Sam says. He's not in the habit of lying."

"No." Dana hadn't known Sam long, but she would bet her last dollar on his always being honest.

"So, I came to apologize, and to thank you. Sam means the world to me, and you kept him safe."

Dana grimaced. He wouldn't have needed saving if she hadn't goofed up in the first place. "Anyone would have done the same thing."

"I doubt that. Sam thinks you're extraordinary, and I tend to agree. When did you learn to oar a boat?"

"This morning."

The lines around Ursula's eyes crinkled. "You must be incredibly sore."

Dana rolled her shoulders. "Like you would not believe."

"Did you take anything yet?"

"No. I just got out of the shower."

Ursula walked to the kitchen and pulled a bottle of aspirin from the cabinet. "Showers are fine, but you need a good soak. Here, take two of these, then go to Sam's bathroom and get into the whirlpool for a while. It will help you sleep. I'll be in the spare room down-

stairs. I promised Sam I'd get you to the hospital in the morning."

"Sam wants me there?"

"Oh, yes. Sam wants you there."

CHAPTER FIFTEEN

THE NEXT MORNING, Dana woke to the scent of cinnamon rolls. Ursula must have risen at the crack of dawn. Well, maybe not quite that early since sunrise happened at about four, but close.

The soak had done wonders for her muscles, although she was going to be stiff for a few days. She'd stayed in the whirlpool until her fingers pruned up, reluctant to leave the luxurious swirling water and the comforting scent of Sam's bodywash. She couldn't wait to see him, to make sure he was really okay. She wondered what time visiting hours started at the hospital. Or did they have visiting hours anymore?

She drifted to the kitchen, where Ursula was frosting the rolls with a white icing. Cream cheese, she guessed.

"Those smell incredible."

"I make them at the inn when I think someone might be tempted to sleep in too long. It usually gets everyone out of bed."

Dana laughed and settled on a barstool. "Well, it worked with me. Can we sneak one into the hospital for Sam?"

"I believe so. I made enough to bribe the nurses."

Footsteps sounded on the stairs, and a few minutes later Chris appeared, his curly hair in a wild tangle. "Cinnamon rolls? No fair. I was trying to sleep."

He walked over and wrapped his arms around Dana's shoulders. "Hey, short stuff. I hear you did some pretty fancy boating out there."

She shrugged. "I doubt it was pretty, but it got us there."

"I thought you were on your way home to Kansas."

"Sam offered to let me tag along on his float trip, and I couldn't resist. I may never be in Alaska again, after all."

"Right." He moved around the bar and kissed Ursula's cheek. "Good morning, Auntie." He stuck a finger into the icing she was spreading and she slapped his hand.

"Let me finish. You're not going to starve

to death in the next five minutes. Go pour your sister a cup of coffee and sit."

Dana envied the easy way they teased each other. She didn't have that kind of relationship with anyone, not since Chris left home. A tear formed in her eye and she blinked it away impatiently. Chris was right here, handing her a cup, and instead of enjoying his company, she was feeling resentful of all the time they'd missed. Ridiculous.

She smiled her thanks. "What time did you get home last night?"

"The nurse ran me out about midnight or one. She said my snoring was disturbing the patient."

"When can I see Sam this morning?"

"As soon as you can convince Ursula to take you. I'm going to grab a little more sleep."

"You're not going back to work?"

"Not yet. I want to wait until Sam comes home." He turned to Ursula. "Have you done any more checking with that person you mentioned?"

"I've hardly had a chance yet." Ursula set a plate with a gooey roll in front of each of them. "I'll let you know when I find out."

"What are we talking about?" Dana asked.

Chris and Ursula exchanged glances before Ursula explained to Dana, "Chris told me about the bar in Fairbanks that burned."

Dana broke off a piece of cinnamon roll, but set it on her plate without eating it. "I admit it looks bad, but you didn't know my father. He wasn't an affectionate person, that's true, however this... I can't believe he would do something like this."

Chris shook his head. "You don't want to believe it."

Ursula frowned. "Maybe it's better if we never know."

"No." Chris's voice was firm. "It's always better to know the truth."

Ursula raised her eyebrows. "This from the man who hid his identity for so many years?"

"And see how it bit me in the butt? Sam's still irked. If you can find out something, I want to hear it."

"What can she find out?" Dana asked.

"She says she might know of a witness who was at the bar the night it burned."

Dana stared at Ursula. Maybe this witness could vindicate her father. But... "Why didn't you mention this earlier?"

"It's complicated. I'm not sure she saw anything. If I can reach her, I'll find out today."

WHEN THEY ARRIVED at the hospital, Sam was sitting up in bed. A green cast covered his left arm, and an IV line ran to his right elbow. He was using the tines of his fork to pick at something unnaturally yellow on his plate.

"More powdered eggs?" Dana smirked.

The smile that lit his face when he saw her convinced her he was well on the road to recovery. "They're not as good as yours."

"Then it's a good thing Ursula sent this." Dana opened her bag and pulled out a plastic-wrapped cinnamon roll.

"Oh, man. I love these things." Sam broke off a piece and popped it into his mouth. "Mmm. Where is Ursula?"

"At the nurses' station, giving them rolls and checking up on you. You look a whole lot better than you did yesterday."

"I feel a whole lot better, too. The doctor says I can go home tomorrow."

"Great." Which probably meant it was about time for her to go home, too. But she didn't want to think about that yet. Not until Sam was completely out of danger.

"Good morning." Ursula bustled into the room, patted Sam's cheek and slid a hand to his forehead. "No fever."

He grinned. "Yeah, the numbers on the monitor there could have told you that."

"I prefer the hands-on method." She glanced down. "Eat your roll."

"Yes, ma'am." Sam stuffed a bite into his mouth.

Ursula turned to Dana. "I need to run an errand. Will you be okay here for a while?"

"Absolutely. Anything I can help you with?"

Ursula shook her head. "No. I just need to look up an old friend. Call me if you need me." A little line formed between Sam's eyebrows as he watched her go.

This must have something to do with the conversation this morning about a possible witness, and Dana guessed from his expression Sam knew it, too. "Chris says Ursula might know someone who has information about the bar fire."

"That's what she said."

"I wonder why she didn't mention it when the subject first came up."

"I suspect she's protecting someone."

"Who?"

Sam shrugged, more as in he didn't want to answer than he didn't know.

"Ursula never lived in Fairbanks, right? How would she happen to know someone with that sort of information? The odds of her randomly meeting someone who witnessed what happened with your father have to be—"

"Astronomical." Sam nodded. "Exactly."

THE NEXT MORNING, it took Sam a ridiculously long time to put on the fresh clothes Dana had brought. It had taken him twenty minutes just to get the T-shirt over both his cast and his head. Maybe a button-up shirt would have been better, assuming he could manage buttons with one hand. But eventually he was dressed, he had prescriptions and instructions from the doctor and Ursula had gone downstairs to pull the car around while Dana waited to accompany him out.

The only thing delaying them was Sam's reluctance to follow hospital procedure. After all, it was his arm that had been broken, not his legs. He could walk. But the nurse was having none of it.

"Get in the wheelchair or get back into bed. Those are your choices." She obviously wasn't backing down. Dana grinned as Sam yielded to the inevitable and settled into the chair. He felt like an idiot being wheeled around, but if that's what it took to get out of this place, he could handle it.

Dana walked beside him on the way to the

elevator and down to the lobby. Ursula's car was waiting outside the front doors. Before the nurse could embarrass him further, Sam got up from the chair and climbed into the passenger seat. Dana settled into the seat behind him.

Ursula pulled the car onto the street and stopped at the corner, waiting for the light to change. She gave him an odd look before she spoke. "Looking forward to going home?"

"Sure am." He was especially looking forward to a night in his own bed, with nothing beeping at him and nobody dropping by to poke him every few hours.

"Do you want to go straight home or are you up to a little visit with someone who might have some answers for you?"

Sam paused before replying, studying Ursula's face. She didn't meet his eyes. "Who are we visiting?"

"You'll see."

It had to be her. Did he really want to do this now? Definitely not. But she was the only one with the information they needed. "How long have you known where she is?"

In the back seat, Dana shifted and leaned forward. Sam was sure she wondered what they were talking about, but he wasn't ready to go into long explanations.

Ursula looked straight ahead, not answering his question. The light changed to green. "Are we going or not?"

"I guess we're going." Sam closed his eyes and rested his head on the seat. To his relief, Dana held her tongue.

"Good. Chris is meeting us there." So Sam really hadn't had a choice. As usual, Ursula thought she knew what was best for him. And she was probably right. She drove toward the tall buildings of downtown. "She called me about a year ago. She'd seen one of the flyers for the inn and recognized my picture. She wanted to know how you were."

"Why didn't you tell me?"

"She asked me not to." Ursula parked at the curb in front of a medium-sized hotel. It had obviously seen better days, but looked to be in good repair.

Sam frowned out the window. "This is that place for homeless alcoholics who won't give up drinking."

"Yes." Ursula sighed. "But some of them have reduced their drinking now that they have a place to live."

"Some of them?"

Ursula put her hand on his. "I don't know, Sam. But I talked to her on the phone a short while ago, and she sounded sober."

A knock at the window startled him. Seeing Chris peering into the car, Sam rolled down the window.

"Is this the place?"

Sam shrugged. "Apparently."

"So, you ready?"

Sam looked at Ursula and she nodded. Then he twisted in his seat to catch Dana's eye. She'd been protecting the memory of her father all along, refusing to believe the worst about him. Chris, on the other hand, refused to believe in his innocence. If Chris was right, what would that do to Dana, to her image of her father? Sam didn't want her hurt. "What do you think? It all happened a long time ago. Does it really matter now?"

There was fear in those eyes of hers, but also determination. She nodded. "Let's see if we can get to the truth."

"Okay."

They all climbed out of the car and followed Ursula inside and up the stairs to a unit at the end of the hall on the second floor. Ursula knocked. A moment later, the door opened a crack and familiar blue eyes peered at them. Her face had grown haggard, aged beyond her years. She seemed shorter, but then Sam was a foot taller than the last time he saw her. Her posture drooped, and her shoulder-length hair was the texture and color of straw with gray-streaked roots showing at the part. Ursula gave an encouraging smile and she straightened a little.

She looked past Ursula's shoulder and her eyes found his. She drew in a breath. "You look just like your father."

"I wouldn't know." Of course, thanks to Chris's photo, he knew she was right, but she'd never even shown him a picture of his father. At his icy tone, her shoulders sagged. Well, what did she expect from him?

"Come in. Ursula says you need some answers, and heaven knows you deserve them. I haven't given you much of anything else."

They followed her into a small apartment, obviously converted from two hotel rooms. This room contained a tiny kitchen at one end. The rest of the room held a small table with four chairs, a sofa, a coffee table and a low bookshelf with a television on top. Through an open doorway, Sam glimpsed a double bed, carelessly made up.

She was staring at his cast. "Ursula said

you got hurt in a rafting accident. Are you okay?"

"I'll be fine."

"Good. Uh—" She looked helplessly at the group and at the sofa. Chris grabbed chairs from the dining table and set them around the coffee table. The woman turned toward Dana. "Hello. I'm Ruth."

"Dana R—"

Sam broke in. "These are my friends Dana and Chris." He raised his chin a fraction and met Dana's eyes. "Ruth is my mother."

He saw the momentary shock before she hid it behind a friendly smile. Dana offered her hand. "Hello." Ruth's hand shook as she reached out to shake Dana's.

Ruth shook hands with Chris, too. "Please, sit down. Can I offer you something to drink?" At Sam's frown, she elaborated. "A glass of water?"

"I'd like one." Ursula gave her a smile. "Thank you."

Ruth filled two glasses with tap water and handed one to Ursula. Her gaze traveled to the others. "Anyone else?"

"We're fine, thank you." Sam sat stiffly in his chair. He wasn't here for a reunion, just the facts as she knew them. Once they had the information, they could go. "We won't take up much of your time."

"All right." She sat beside Ursula on the sofa across from him and set her glass on the scarred coffee table. "What do you need to know?"

"Is it true you were a witness to what happened the night my father died?"

"I…" Her breath came faster and her eyes darted around the room. "I was…"

Dana sat perfectly still, almost blending into the background. Chris seemed to be trying to do the same. Ruth looked at them quickly, then darted a glance at Sam and winced as though his gaze burned her.

Ursula leaned toward her and offered a comforting smile. "Let's start at the beginning." Her voice was soothing. "How did you meet Roy?"

Ruth settled and stared past Ursula at the wall, where a dark square in the paint indicated a picture had once hung. "My father was a preacher in a little church at the end of a dead-end road in Fairbanks." She offered a wry smile. "He wasn't a very successful preacher. The congregation was tiny. Papa said it was because we were so far out nobody could find us. He did odd jobs to make ends meet, and I worked at the fountain in a drugstore in town. Anyway, one day we saw some activity at an old building about a half mile up the road. Papa asked around and found out a couple of men were fixing it up to make it into a bar. He was livid. I swear, the man turned purple, he was so mad."

She took a sip of water. "That was around Christmastime. We didn't hear much else for a while, just saw a few trucks and deliveries. In January, we had a big storm while I was at work. On the way home, my car got stuck in a drift right outside that bar. I was scared to go in there. I mean, Papa had been ranting about the evil they were bringing to the neighborhood, but it was that or risk freezing to death walking. So I knocked on the door." She continued to stare off into the distance as if she'd lost herself in the story.

"What happened then?" Ursula urged.

Ruth blinked and focused on Ursula. "Roy was there, working. He had the nicest face, and once he smiled at me, I wasn't scared at all. He limped when he walked, and I wondered what happened to him. He invited me in, said I should warm up first and later he'd dig me out of the drift. It sure felt good next to that woodstove after being out in the cold,

I tell you. I sat there by the stove while he sanded the bar, polishing the wood until it was smooth as glass, and all the while he talked to me." A smile crossed her face, and Sam could see a trace of the woman he remembered from some of the happier moments in his childhood.

Ursula smiled back. "How old were you?"

"I was seventeen, just graduated from high school a semester early. I hardly knew what to say to a man. My papa hadn't ever let me go on a date, but Roy was easy to talk to. He told me about their plans. He'd been working on the pipeline, but was in an accident and broke his leg. It healed up shorter than the other one and he couldn't work there anymore. So they gave him some money for the accident." Her face hardened. "That's when Raynott came into the picture. Wayne Raynott. He worked on the pipeline, too. He'd saved up some money, and he had this idea. The workers needed a place to drink. They could pool their money and buy a liquor license. Wayne would buy this old building, and Roy would use his money to fix it up into a bar. They'd be partners."

She looked at Sam. "Roy was from a village. He didn't understand about contracts or protecting himself. It never occurred to him that he should have insisted Wayne put his name on the property, too. They agreed to be equal partners and they shook on it, and that was that." She winced. "He found out later that Wayne got that old building in a tax sale for next to nothin', maybe a tenth of what Roy put into fixing it up, but they were bringing in lots of money by then, so he didn't much care."

Sam glanced over to see how Dana would react to that. She shifted in her chair, but she didn't say anything. Chris's expression remained neutral. Sam directed his attention back to his mother's face, but she seemed to be waiting for something.

"Did he ever dig you out?" Ursula asked with a laugh.

"Oh, he sure did. I didn't tell Papa about it. Sometimes after that, if I thought I could get away with it, I'd drop by when Roy was working and we'd talk. Once when I stopped by, Wayne was there. He hustled me out so fast it would have made your head spin. After that, I always looked in the window to make sure Roy was alone before I came in.

"Wayne and his wife had moved into the little house on the back of the property. They were expecting a baby, and he was spending time fixing up the place while Roy fixed up the bar, so I was able to sneak in to see Roy without him seeing me."

"Why didn't Wayne want you there?" Ursula asked.

Ruth twitched her shoulders. "I didn't know at first, but Fiona told me later my papa had been by, preaching at them about the evils of drink. Wayne had seen my car and knew I was his daughter, and he didn't want more trouble with Papa."

"What did your mother think of all this?" Ursula asked.

"I didn't have a mama. Papa said she got real depressed after I was born, couldn't take the dark and the cold, so he sent her to her family in the lower forty-eight for a visit, and she just never came back."

Sam nodded slowly. All very sad, but other than the fact that his grandfather had been a preacher who disapproved of drinking, he hadn't heard anything he didn't already know or suspect. She needed to get to the point. "Eventually they opened the bar, I assume."

"Yes. Every night the parking lot was overflowing. It drove my papa crazy that all them people wanted to go drink and he couldn't get anybody to come out to hear the Gospel. By that time, I'd turned eighteen, so sometimes I'd tell Papa I was visiting a friend and stop into the bar. I remember the first time I ever tasted a beer, I spit it back out. Roy just laughed and gave me a ginger ale."

Sam gave a mirthless snort. Somewhere along the way, she'd developed quite an affinity for the taste of beer, and wine, and whiskey. Hard to imagine she was ever that innocent. Ruth ignored his outburst and directed her story toward Ursula.

"I met Fiona there. When it got busy, which was almost every night, she'd put the baby down to sleep in the back room and help out at the bar. She looked after me, made sure none of the men there bothered me. She was a real lady, and the men, they mostly treated her with respect. It was a good thing, too, 'cause Wayne, he was the jealous type. He tossed out more than one man who he thought was getting too familiar with his wife."

"What was she like?" The words seemed to slip from Chris's mouth.

Ruth glanced his way as if surprised to see him there. "Fiona? Oh, she was a beauty. Had this head full of curly red hair, like an angel. She had the face of an angel, too, kinda peaceful and sweet. Her mother was from Ireland, and Fiona talked a little bit like they do, kinda like she was singing, ya know? She loved that baby. Always called him Christopher. Said it was such a pretty name it would be a shame to shorten it. She used to carry Christopher around all day, hugging and kissing him, and she'd sing him lullabies and tell him stories just like he understood. Maybe he did, because I never saw a happier baby."

Chris nodded, apparently satisfied with her description. Ruth didn't seem to make the connection between baby Christopher and the man who had been introduced as Chris, but then, Chris had presumably changed a bit since he was an infant.

Ruth's face clouded. "Although, I was playing with fire. Eventually, my papa called and found out I wasn't at my friend's house and went looking for me. He found me at the bar and dragged me out, shouting curses at all the sinners there. Roy tried to stop him, but Wayne and two other men held on to him. They said not to interfere between a father and a child." Ruth wrapped her arms tight around herself.

Ursula placed a hand on her shoulder and asked gently. "What happened then?"

Ruth shuddered. "In spite of what he said about drinkers, Papa always had a bottle of whiskey hidden away in our cabin, in a box in the back of his closet. I found it once when he had me polish his shoes and I put them away. I could tell from his breath that he'd been nipping into it that night. When he got me home he preached hard at me about the evils of drink, and told me if I ever set foot in that place again, I'd wish I'd never been born. I said if whiskey was so evil, why was he drinking it? He didn't think I knew about his secret bottle, you see. That made him so mad he said he was going to beat the devil out of me." Ruth stared at the table in front of her. "He almost did. Almost beat the life out of me while he was at it."

Sam's jaw clenched. The hypocrite. Getting drunk, beating his own daughter because she had dared to defy him. His good hand curled into a fist.

Ursula scooted closer and put an arm around her shoulders. "I'm so sorry, Ruth."

Ruth stole a glance at her. "Papa finished off the bottle that night and started on another one. Once he passed out, I slipped out and went to the bar. It was summer then, so I walked. Good thing Papa broke my nose and not my leg. It was after closing, but Roy was there, and so were Wayne and Fiona. Roy took one look at me, picked me up and put me into his truck. He took me to the emergency room and they patched me up. Roy wanted me to call the police, but I wouldn't turn Papa in. Roy told the nurse to take pictures of me, and he somehow made sure Papa got the word that if he ever came near me again, he'd be in jail.

"I don't know how she managed it, but Fiona convinced Wayne to let me live with them so I wouldn't have to go back to my papa's house ever again. I offered to help out in the bar, but Wayne said I should take care of the baby at night while Fiona worked. I think he liked having her close by where he could keep an eye on her."

Ruth picked up her water and took a deep drink. "Christopher was the sweetest baby, and every day, I got to see Roy when I cleaned the bar. Wayne didn't approve of Roy and me. I heard him tell Roy he oughta stay away from me, that he was just asking for trouble with my papa and it'd cause trouble for the bar, but Fiona always found little errands and excuses to let me and Roy spend time together. She said what Wayne didn't know wouldn't hurt him. I stayed with them for almost a year, and it was the happiest I'd ever been in my life."

Sam leaned forward. "What happened the night of the fire?"

Ruth sighed. "Roy and I fell in love, and one thing led to another, and of course, I got pregnant. I was kinda scared to tell Roy, but he was happy about it. He said he'd always wanted a son, and that we should get married right away. We decided it would be better to elope, so there was no chance of my papa getting wind of it and trying to stop us. Roy said not to tell anybody, but Fiona guessed about the baby, and so I confided in her. She was happy for us and promised she wouldn't say anything to Wayne.

"So, late one night, after the bar closed and Wayne and Fiona were in bed, she waited for him to go to sleep and slipped out of their house to meet Roy and me in the bar. She said she wanted to give me a wedding present before I left. She'd sewed me a silk nightgown, white with little pink rosebuds embroidered on the neckline. It was just the prettiest thing you ever saw. I took it outside to pack in my suitcase in Roy's truck." Ruth stopped talking and sat motionless for a few seconds, her eyes staring sightlessly at the table.

Ursula squeezed her shoulders. "Can you tell us what happened next?"

"Wayne came in. He was raging mad. Somehow, he'd gotten it into his head that Fiona and Roy were having an affair. I came in behind him and saw him yelling at them. They were trying to explain, but he was too angry to hear what they were saying. He took a swing at Roy and knocked over one of the tables with a kerosene lantern we'd lit when we'd come in. A tablecloth caught on fire. They could have all still got out then, but Wayne wouldn't stop trying to fight Roy and Miss Fiona wouldn't leave them. She kept telling Wayne to stop, that he didn't understand. I was so scared, I couldn't move. I just stood there and watched." She swallowed.

"Wayne hit Roy hard in the jaw and knocked him down. Fiona went running over to him, and Wayne went stumbling back. That's about the time the flames really started spreading, and it got between Wayne and them. I think that was the first time he realized the bar was on fire. He backed up toward the door, and that's when he noticed me. He grabbed me and pushed me out of the bar."

Ruth stood and paced around the room, shaking her head. "The fire spread so fast. I tried to get in to Roy and Fiona, but Wayne held on to me. I screamed at him, told him Roy and me were gonna get married and have a baby and I had to save him, but Wayne wouldn't let me go. That must have been when he realized he'd been all wrong about Fiona and Roy, 'cause he looked real upset. He said it was too late, that they were probably already dead. He pulled me into his house and told me to take care of Christopher, and he called the firemen.

"I stayed on with him while he settled everything out. He told me not to tell anybody what I'd seen. He said it was an accident, but the insurance might not pay out if they knew he was there in the bar when it happened. I needed money for the baby, so I kept my mouth shut.

"It dragged on for six months and I had the baby. A son, just like Roy wanted." She finally looked up at Sam. "Samuel, from the Bible. Finally, the insurance company finished looking into everything and paid out on the building. Wayne said he was taking

Christopher and moving back to the lower forty-eight. I asked for Roy's half of the money. Wayne just looked at me like I was crazy. The title for the bar was in his name. The insurance was, too. I didn't have any proof of all the money Roy put into fixing up the bar.

"I tried to convince Wayne to do the right thing, that Roy's share should go to his son." Her face distorted into a sneer. "He said I had no proof Sam was Roy's baby, that he could be anybody's brat. But he said, since I'd been good to his wife, he'd help me out, give me a little money for the baby. I told him what he could do with his crumbs. I wasn't going to let him salve his conscience with a few hand-outs after he killed Roy and stole his money. Later on, I found out where he'd moved to and wrote him letters, told him to send Roy's half of the money. A few times, he mailed back a small check. I guess he thought I'd be grateful." She snorted. "I never kept none of his checks. Not a single one."

Tears ran down her cheeks. "I tried, Sam. I really did. But without Roy, it was too hard. I just couldn't make it through the day without taking a few drinks. I know I was a bad mother. I decided you'd be better off with somebody who could really take care of you. I'm sorry."

Sam watched her for a moment. A shudder ran through his body. After everything she'd been through, all she'd suffered, it was no wonder she broke. He stood and reached for her with his good arm. His mother blinked at him for a moment before stepping into his hug, sobbing against his shoulder. He patted her back. "I had a good life with Ursula and Tommy."

"I know. I saw your name in the paper for honor roll, and all those scholarships. An engineer. I'm so proud of you."

Ursula stepped forward and Sam pulled her into the hug, too.

DANA WATCHED AS Sam embraced his two mothers, the one who gave him life, and the one who raised him into the fine man he'd become. She had no doubts that Ruth had been telling the truth. Dana had to face facts. The man she'd spent her life trying to please, the man she'd always held up as a role model, the man whose reputation she'd defended over and over was a cheat, a liar and, for all intents and purposes, a murderer. Yes, it may have been an accident, but Wayne Raynott was the man responsible for the death of Sam's father. It was no accident that he cheated Ruth out of Roy's share of the insurance money and left her to raise Roy's son in poverty, and the offer of an occasional handout didn't make it any less wrong.

And Dana had come to Alaska to convince Chris to forgive their father and accept the inheritance. Chris had been correct all along. It was tainted money, and neither of them had any legitimate claim to it.

Dana touched Chris's arm. "Can we get out of here?"

Chris glanced over at the two women weeping in Sam's arms and nodded. "Let's go."

Dana stared through the windshield of Chris's pickup. The mountains behind Anchorage were as green and peaceful as ever, but she wasn't seeing them. All she could see was a smoke-filled room and the two people trapped inside, changing the fate of two innocent baby boys.

Chris touched her hand. "You okay?"

Dana nodded. "You were right about him."

"I'm sorry. I wish I wasn't."

"I know." She gave Chris a little smile.

"Good thing you took after your mother. She sounds like a wonderful woman."

"She does, doesn't she? I wish I could remember her."

"Me, too. I'm glad you had a mother who loved you."

Chris gave her a sharp glance. "Your mother loves you, too, as best she can."

"Does she?"

"She tries." Chris patted her knee. "When you were a baby, she used to pack you into a stroller and she'd take you and me to garage sales in the neighborhood."

"Typical."

"Yeah, but she was looking for things we'd like, toys and baby clothes. Then she would take us to the park and let us play in the playground. You liked playing in the sandbox, even though she had to watch you constantly to make sure you didn't eat the sand. When you were about four, she bought you a storybook about a penguin. You loved that book. Every day at least once, you'd ask her to read it to you. She'd stop whatever she was doing, pull you into her lap and read you the story. I think it was when you went off to school that she got lonely and sort of lost control."

"I don't understand her. What is it about shopping that consumes all her interest?"

"She's obsessed with things because things are the only affection she ever got, from her parents and from Wayne."

Dana lifted her eyebrows. "You've got this all figured out, huh?"

"Maybe I do. She shops because it distracts her from having to face the emptiness of her life. She's not strong like you."

"Me? Strong? I let people walk all over me."

Chris shook his head. "You've always been the glue that held the family together. Even when you were just a kid. Don't sell yourself short."

Dana was so confused. Was she strong? Strong enough to do the right thing, even if it was hard? She honestly didn't know.

AN HOUR LATER, Sam sank into the passenger seat of Ursula's car, suddenly aware of his exhaustion. They had talked, caught up. Ruth—he still couldn't think of her as Mom—insisted on hearing every detail of his work, of what he had accomplished. She drank it in like water in the desert, as though she'd been longing for this information all her life.

He closed his eyes and rested during the drive home. Nothing like an emotional catharsis two days after surgery to test a man's limits. But at the same time, he felt lighter. The weight of the anger he had carried for so long was gone, replaced with pity. He finally saw Ruth for what she was, not a selfish monster who abandoned her child, but a woman with a heavier burden than she was equipped to carry alone.

Now that he could get past the sting of her abandonment, memories of better times came back. Of his mother tucking him into bed, cutting his hair, making him a peanut butter sandwich. If she was awake when he left for school, she would remind him to zip his coat and wear a hat, and always gave him a congratulatory hug when he brought home a good report card. The booze made it hard, but she tried.

His mother wasn't a strong woman. But she had recognized her weakness, and she'd given him up so he could have something better than what she could give him. She'd understood and trusted Ursula and Tommy's commitment to him, and she'd been right.

Maybe running away was the best way she could manage to show her love.

Faced with difficult circumstances, she simply couldn't cope. If she'd been in that situation on the river... She wasn't like Dana. It would never have occurred to Ruth she could take responsibility and do whatever it took to get him to that plane.

Sam sighed. Dana, who carried the load for her entire family with never a thank you. Those dainty shoulders of hers could hold the weight of the world, and yet she was vulnerable enough to be moved to tears at the sight of a family of swans.

He was worried about her, about the effect this revelation concerning her father might have on her. She'd insisted for so long her father was a good man, that he was simply misunderstood. Sam wasn't sure how Dana felt about Ruth's story, but he wanted to hold Dana close and make sure she understood that she bore no responsibility for her father's actions.

The past was the past. Mistakes were made, people were hurt, but here they were, he and Dana. They were themselves, not the sum of their parents' choices. They were survivors. Dana needed to know.

Ursula pulled up in the driveway. Sam climbed the stairs and opened the front door, with Ursula close behind him as though she expected him to collapse any moment. The living room and kitchen were empty, and he realized, belatedly, that Chris's truck wasn't in the driveway. Maybe they had stopped for groceries or something. He sank into a living room chair.

"How about a drink of water? The doctor said you need to stay hydrated." Without waiting for his answer, Ursula bustled into the kitchen to fill a glass with ice water. When she came into the living room, she handed him the glass and an envelope with his name on it in rounded script. "This was on the island."

Sam frowned and tore open the envelope. Typical of Dana, the message was straightforward.

I'm sorry, Sam. I'm sorry that the selfish behavior of my father had such a devastating effect on your childhood. I'm sorry I defended him to you and refused to believe the truth. Most of all, I'm sorry my carelessness almost cost you your life.

But I can't bring myself to be sorry I met you. You showed me beauty I never knew existed, and even more, you showed me how to live. You took the rotten hand life dealt you and you made it into something wonderful. You showed me it's possible to avoid the obstacles life throws at you and paddle your own boat to the places you want to go. Now I have to paddle mine.

The time I spent with you is the highlight of my life, and regardless of what brought me there, I'll always be grateful I came to Alaska. I hope life gives you everything you deserve.
Dana

Sam looked at the note again, trying to read something different in the words, but the message was clear. This was goodbye.

Ursula watched him, her face concerned. "From Dana?"

Sam met her eyes. "She's gone."

CHAPTER SIXTEEN

DANA SAT AT the desk in her cottage and added up the slips for all the merchandise she'd returned. The sum was probably close to three thousand dollars. She punched in the last amount and hit total. Two thousand nine hundred ninety-seven. Math, she could do. If only real-life problems could be solved so easily. Dana gave a wry smile and filled out a deposit slip for her mother's checking account.

She put the calculator away and sat back in the chair, letting her gaze roam around her kitchen. Only three ceramic canisters marred the smooth expanse of countertop. The yellow daisy print on the café curtains at the window added a touch of color. If she opened a drawer or a cabinet door, the tool she needed would be there, easy to spot. She'd always loved this house, from the second she'd moved in. So why did the peace she'd always prized now seem too quiet, too dull?

She could think about that later. The bank closed at noon on Saturdays. She scooted back the chair, grabbed the pile of cash and the deposit slip and hurried out the door.

Thirty minutes later and the deposit made, she parked in front of her parents' house. The towers and gables of the regal Victorian reached for the open Kansas sky. The bright green lawn, professionally maintained since Chris left home all those years ago, ran up to the boxwoods at the base of the porch. Two wicker rockers on the porch looked like an inviting place to drink a glass of lemonade and catch up with family, but as far as Dana knew, those chairs had never been used. No one had ever offered her a glass of lemonade, or invited her to sit and talk. Her family didn't do that.

Remembering the expression on Ursula's face when Sam climbed out of the truck at her inn, how she'd hugged him and made his favorite foods, left Dana feeling wistful. Then she remembered how Ursula came into Sam's life and the feeling faded. So her parents weren't the most affectionate people in the world. Dana always had a home, and food, and all the clothes and school supplies she'd needed. Actually far more than she'd needed. She was one of the fortunate people.

And maybe this emotional distance from her family was partially her own fault. She wasn't a child any longer. If she'd wanted things to be different, she could have made changes. She could have engaged her parents in conversation, tried to get to know them better. Heck, she could have made lemonade.

But there wasn't any use crying over the past. It was time to move forward. Dana used her key to let herself in via the kitchen door. "Mom? Are you here?"

"Dana." Her mother came from somewhere in the back of the house. "I was just looking through a catalog and I found the cutest pillows for your bedroom."

"That's sweet, Mom, but I don't have room for extra pillows so please don't order them. I returned the things we talked about yesterday and put the money in your checking account."

"I'm so glad you're home. That Ginny person couldn't keep my account straight. She actually said I was out of money."

Dana suppressed an eye roll. "You were out of money. I moved money from my savings into your account, and she still had to pay the electric bill late, along with an extra twenty-five-dollar service charge."

"Well, anyway, I'm fine now."

Dana opened the refrigerator and poured them each a glass of iced tea. "Sit down, Mom. We need to talk."

Her mother frowned suspiciously. "About what?"

"Just sit." Dana settled into the chair next to her and reached for her mother's hand. "I love you."

"What?"

"I love you. I know we never say things like that out loud, but it's something you need to hear. Sometimes I get aggravated with you, and I'm not always patient, but I do love you. You know that, right?"

"Well, of course. I love you, too."

Dana smiled. "I know. That's why you're always trying to buy me new pillows or things." She squeezed her mother's hand. "That's why you're always buying yourself things, too, isn't it? To make yourself feel loved?"

"Dana, what are you talking about?"

"This shopping habit of yours. Since Dad died, it's gotten even worse. Mom, it's got to stop."

Her mother raised her chin. "But I never buy anything that isn't on sale. I save a fortune by careful shopping."

"It's not a savings if it's for something you don't need." Dana paused until her mother looked at her. "You're an intelligent person. You know how much money the trust transfers into your checking account each month, and you know how much your bills amount to. I've seen you calculate sixty-five percent off an eighty-five-dollar sweater without blinking. You are perfectly capable of doing the math to stay in your spending budget. You didn't need Ginny to tell you you'd bought too much."

"I made a mistake. But you took those things back to the stores, and everything's okay now."

"It's not okay. But we can make it better." Dana pulled a card from her pocket and handed it to her mother.

"What's this?"

"It's an appointment card, for Monday at ten. Dr. Stevens can help you get control of your obsession with buying things."

Mom crossed her arms in front of her chest. "It's not an obsession, and I don't need a doctor. I'm fine."

"You're better than fine. You're smart, you're attractive and you're worth so much more than the things you own. I talked with the doctor yesterday, and she explained some things to me. She's worked with other people who feel the way you do, and they're happier now."

"I'm already happy."

"Are you? What was the last thing that made you happy besides buying something?"

"I, uh. Yesterday I… Well, that's just silly, putting me on the spot like that."

"Are you happy I found Chris?"

"Of course." She latched on to the lifeline. "How is Chris?"

"He's good. He has his own business and also does commercial fishing. He loves Alaska."

"Good." Mom turned the iced tea glass in circles.

"He knows about his birth mother. You don't have to keep that secret anymore."

Mom looked at her with wide eyes. "What did you find?"

"The truth. About Chris's mother, about her death and about the death of Dad's business partner. How much do you know about it?"

Mom shook her head. "Nothing. Only that

Chris was born when your father was in Alaska, but it was important to Wayne that nobody knew I wasn't Chris's mother. He never talked about his life before I met him."

"That's what I figured." Dana sighed. "Dad did some bad things. Not illegal, per se, but things he knew were wrong. His wife and his partner were killed in an accident, an accident he caused, and he cheated the man's family out of his share of the insurance money."

"No, that can't be right. Wayne went on and on about being honest. He got so angry if I told even a little lie about when I bought something."

Dana raised her eyebrows. "And yet he had you lie to Chris about his mother all his life."

"That was different."

"How was it different?"

"He did that for Chris's sake. So he wouldn't feel left out."

"Did Dad say that?"

"No, but why else would he do it?"

Dana kept asking herself the same question, and could only find one answer. "For his own sake. He didn't want any questions about Alaska or his first wife, and so he pretended it never happened. How did you explain to your friends and family how you came to have a three-year-old son as soon as you married?"

"I wasn't from here. I moved here from Idaho and went to apply for a job in Wayne's store. He hired me as a nanny instead. Two months later, we married. I never saw my parents after our marriage, just talked on the phone a few times."

"You never went to visit, or had them come here?"

"We were never close. Wayne said it didn't matter, that I had a new family now."

Dad certainly played that well. A caretaker for his son and a cover story all wrapped up in a neat, obliging wife. The only trouble was, Dad showed his wife no more affection than an employee. Did he feel guilty that he didn't love her? Maybe that's why he tolerated the out-of-control shopping and hoarding. Because it was easier than facing their problems.

"Mom, Dad didn't treat you the way you deserved to be treated. He used you."

"No. I was his wife."

"Yes. And you deserved more than he gave you. You deserved to be loved, not just indulged. You still deserve love."

Mom frowned at her. "You've always adored your father, but now you're talking about him like he was a villain. What's gotten into you, Dana?"

"He was closer to a villain than a saint, but I don't think he was evil. He did some bad things, but he did try to make up for them, at least in a small way. He was human, like the rest of us, and it's healthier if we recognize that. He made plans for us, plugged us into certain roles, but he's gone now. We're free to break out of those roles if we want. I think this doctor can help you be happier."

Mom fingered the card. "Dana, I don't know."

"Go to the appointment. Talk to the doctor. What can talking hurt?"

"It's a waste of money."

There was a hint of hysteria in Dana's laugh. "Are you really going to use that as an excuse?"

Mom hesitated before she spoke. "Chris is happy in Alaska?"

"Yes, he is."

A smile tugged at the corners of Mom's mouth. "I've missed him. He was such a sweet, funny boy, always laughing." She tapped the corner of the appointment card against the table. "Okay, I'll go on Monday. But I'm not promising anything after that."

"I understand." Time to lighten the mood. "It's too hot to cook. How about I make us a nice Caesar salad for dinner tonight?"

Mom's eyes brightened. "I'd like that. I just bought the nicest salad bowl."

DANA GLANCED AT the time in the corner of her computer screen. Mom should be with Dr. Stevens now, and having met the doctor, Dana was fairly sure she would be able to convince Mom to keep coming. She was warm, patient and compassionate, and able to give her the attention Mom was so hungry for.

The web page popped up and Dana returned her attention to the college application form. It was a little scary to contemplate returning to school after all this time, but exciting, too. Before she could start typing, her phone rang.

"Dana? It's Heather."

"Hi. Thanks for returning my call."

"Sorry it took so long. I had to wait until lunch. I didn't want to take a chance on Jerry overhearing."

"I understand. I just wanted to check in with you to see if things had gotten better at the office."

"For about five minutes. But now Jerry is on this frugality kick and has started cutting people's hours. The maintenance guys are blaming me. Revenues are way down."

Dana realized she was holding a pen like a dagger. She set it on the table. "How bad is it?"

"It's bad. And I don't know how much longer I'm going to be here. Jerry was digging through my desk the other day, asking questions. I think he's trying to get rid of me."

"Why would he do that?"

"Because that way, if anybody asks what's going wrong, he can blame everything on me." Heather paused. "Dana, I'm going to have to start looking for another job before he fires me. I can't afford to be unemployed."

Dana pressed her hand against her forehead. Now that Dana had quit, Heather was the only one at the office who understood the books, the scheduling and the systems. It really hadn't been fair of Dana to dump it in her lap and disappear, the way Chris had done with her. She probably should have stayed. A good part of Mom's income depended on the business. They couldn't afford to lose Heather. "I just wish the trustees had put you in charge, instead of Jerry."

Heather snorted. "Me, in charge of hiring and firing and all that HR? Right."

"You underestimate your abilities. You practically run the place, anyway. Honestly, you'd probably be better off going somewhere else where they'd pay you what you're worth, but I'm still going to ask a big favor. Can you stay a little longer, just to give me a chance to investigate a few things? I think I can make things better, for you and for the business."

"You really think so?"

"I do, but I'm going to need your help. What do you say?"

Heather paused, but when she spoke, her voice was firm. "Let's do this."

Dana spent the next few hours poring over the spreadsheets Heather sent. At three thirty, she shut her laptop and stretched. Today was her day at the shelter.

As soon as she walked through the door, Jane came running over to wrap her in a hug. "I'm so glad you're back. We've missed you."

"I've missed you, too. What are the numbers today?"

"We're at capacity. Tyra found a job and moved her kids into an apartment, but we got a new family—three kids and Mom is pregnant."

"And the dad?"

Jane shrugged. "Went for cigarettes and never came back. They just moved here when he took a new job, so they have no family or backup."

Dana nodded. It was a familiar story.

"Any kids who need help with math before dinner?"

"There always are."

"Good. I'll be in the quiet room."

Dana went to check with the kids doing their homework. She explained multiplication by a two-digit number to a fourth-grade boy and then managed to talk a middle schooler dealing with fractions down from a ledge. Her final project was a ninth grader trying to make sense of an algebra lesson. It took them both some digging, but eventually Dana managed to find the concept the girl had missed in a lesson from two weeks before, just about the time they got evicted and moved into the shelter. Once she grasped that, the rest fell into place without too much trouble.

This felt good, natural. Explaining math concepts to kids gave her a sense of satisfaction she'd never gotten from the equipment and tool rental business. But somebody had to look out for Mom's interests. Could she do both?

She drove home and walked past the For Sale sign in her yard to collect her mail before she went in. A lumpy padded envelope sat atop the usual bills and credit card offers. She tore the flap and carefully poured the contents onto the kitchen table.

Her cell phone tumbled out, not the replacement phone but the one she'd had with her on Brazzle Creek. A red flash drive rested beside it. She reached inside the envelope and found a short note from Chris. Apparently, a group of kayakers found the dry bag hung up on a tree and returned it to Sam.

Wow. She never expected to see that phone again. And what was on the drive? She plugged it into her computer.

Pictures. Copies of all the photos on Sam's camera. Come to think of it, she'd never given him her email address. The otters were there, sliding down the bank. The bear cubs. Pictures of the trees and sky and the river. Pictures of her she hadn't even known Sam took, playing with the dog or gazing off into the distance. She looked silly in her oversize waders, but she was always smiling.

Dana clicked through the photos until she

reached the last one. The one she'd taken of Sam oaring the raft just before they reached the rapids. Strong arms pushing the oars through the water, a smile on his face, blue sky behind him. Strong, competent, wise.

What was it he said? *You can either paddle your own boat, or you can throw up your hands and let the current carry you wherever it will.*

She gazed at the picture until her computer slipped into sleep mode. *I'm trying, Sam, paddling as hard as I can. I just hope it's enough.*

CHAPTER SEVENTEEN

SAM PAID THE taxi driver and unlocked his front door. Silence greeted him. According to Chris's text, he'd taken Kimmik and gone camping with a German backpacker he'd just met. Odds were good she was a blonde. Chris specialized in blondes, especially the ones with a built-in exit strategy like overseas citizenship. Sam went to the refrigerator for a beer and took the first swallow without any sign of a deranged woman bursting into the room pointing a flare gun at him.

He smiled to himself and took another sip. Typical Dana. Grabbing the first weapon she could find to confront what she thought was an armed intruder instead of hiding and calling the police. A hundred and ten pounds of raw courage, and she didn't even know it. Damn, he missed that girl.

He rubbed his elbow, still sometimes stiff but healing nicely. He'd had to skip a rotation to Siberia due to the injury, but they'd managed to juggle personnel until his cast came off. Sam had just finished a four-week hitch, successfully completing two wells that had come in far above forecasts. Ethan would be pleased.

In fact, his boss had hinted he had some important news once Sam was back in town, which probably meant Sam's time in Siberia was coming to an end. Everything was coming together exactly how he'd planned it. Odd that he didn't feel more excited about the whole thing. But then, he had been traveling for three days. Maybe after a good night's sleep, the world would look better. Yeah, he'd go with that.

IN THE MEETING the next morning, Ethan greeted Sam like a long-lost brother, almost gloating to the other supervisors about the success of the Siberian project. Sam made sure the other members of his team got credit, too, but to hear Ethan talk, you'd think Sam had performed some sort of miracle in Russia instead of simply doing his job. Finally, the spotlight turned to other business.

"Walt Chrism has announced his retirement in three months."

Sam looked up. Walt was a fixture up on

the slope, part of the glue that held the whole operation together. Right out of college he'd worked under Tommy, and Tommy had nothing but good things to say about him. Since that time, Walt had stayed in Alaska, working his way up until he was one of three heading the whole operation at Prudhoe Bay. The organization would be hard-pressed to find anyone with the experience and commitment to Alaska to fill his shoes.

Once the meeting was over, Ethan slapped Sam on the shoulder. "Got a few minutes?"

"Sure." Ursula was in town running errands and Sam had agreed to meet her for lunch, but that wasn't for another hour.

"Then let's step into my office. I have some things to show you." Ethan tossed a folder onto Sam's lap. The papers inside spelled it all out. A promotion, overseas posting with frequent travel and an impressive bump in pay. Plus, various overseas bonuses and perks.

It meant leaving Alaska and living in an apartment in a big city. Not the sort of place he was likely to hear the call of a loon or see eagles and moose on the trails right outside his backyard. But it was a significant step forward in the company, not to mention a lucrative one. And he would be meeting with people all over the world, growing his reputation within the company and in the industry.

It was all happening like Tommy said it would, back when he encouraged Sam to take advanced classes in high school. *You have the brains. Make the grades. Earn yourself some scholarships and with an engineering degree under your belt, you can go far. If you're willing to put in the work, the rewards will come. I guarantee it.*

Tommy would probably be amazed at the salary figure quoted. Not that money was the driving factor. If it were money he was after, Sam could have taken the funds from Wayne Raynott's estate, but he didn't want it that way. He wanted to earn it himself, to show Tommy he was right to have faith in him.

When Dana disappeared, she'd taken the legal papers with her. Chris urged him to make a claim against the estate, but Sam couldn't. He'd had a lawyer draft up a document renouncing any interest in the Raynott estate and had Chris send it to Dana. She needed the estate settled quickly to get the money for college.

No response. Sam wasn't sure if she'd claimed the inheritance or not. From what

Chris said, when she left she had no intention of accepting money from her father, even to spend on tuition. He just hoped she'd changed her mind.

After all, she had nothing to feel guilty about. How could she be responsible for what her father had done years before she was ever born? Her father may have been, at best, a greedy opportunist, but Dana was just the opposite. She always did the right thing for the people who depended on her, like her mother, and the kids she tutored at the shelter, and even Sam when he was injured.

If only the right thing hadn't been to return to Kansas. Yes, her mother needed her. So did the shelter. But darn it, Sam needed her, too.

Wait—where did that thought come from? Yes, he liked having her around, but he didn't need her. He didn't need anyone. Sam was self-sufficient. Maybe he'd felt something for Dana he'd never felt for any other woman, but Dana was gone and it was time to concentrate on his career. He would be fine. More than fine. He'd be great.

"Sam, hello? Don't you like the offer?"

Sam snapped back to the present. Wool-gathering when his boss was trying to make him a job offer. Real professional. He focused on Ethan's face. "It's a great opportunity. When do I need to let you know?"

Ethan frowned. "I didn't realize you'd need time to think about it."

Sam shrugged. "Always take time to study a situation before a major decision. Didn't you tell me that?"

Ethan laughed. "I guess I did. Okay, take a little time. But not too much. It'll require some work behind the scenes to move everyone around and cover all the positions."

"I'll do that." Sam stood and shook his boss's hand. "Thanks, Ethan."

When Sam arrived at the diner, Ursula was already waiting in a booth, sipping a cup of tea and studying the menu. She must have finished her errands more quickly than she expected. She stood to greet him. "So, how was the meeting this morning?"

"Just fine. I got the promotion they've been hinting at. It's based out of London and involves traveling around the world, troubleshooting."

"That's wonderful." Ursula wrapped him in a hug. "Tommy would be so proud."

"I wish he could be here."

"You and me both." Ursula stepped back

and they settled into the booth. She studied his face. "So why aren't you happy?"

"I am happy."

"I've seen happier faces waiting in line at the DMV. What's wrong?"

Sam shook his head. "I don't know. I guess now that it's here, I'm realizing I'll have to leave Alaska. I'll miss Anchorage." He shrugged. "I'll miss you and Chris."

"I'll miss you, too, but I thought this was what you wanted."

"It was." Sam sat up straighter and spoke more decisively. "It is. Tommy always said I could do it if I tried, and he was right."

She paused for a moment before speaking. "Tell me about the job."

"Basically it's advising. I'd be traveling around the world helping out with the most difficult projects in places like Norway, Azerbaijan, Trinidad and Dubai."

"It sounds important. They must have big plans for you."

"I think so."

"As long as you're sure."

"I'm sure." Sam opened his menu, cutting off any more discussion. He'd worked hard to prove himself, and this assignment traveling the world was exactly the life he wanted.

Maybe if he kept telling himself that, eventually it would be true.

JERRY STOOD WITH his back to the door, bending over a golf ball when Dana arrived. She knocked on the door frame. "Jerry? Got a minute?"

He putted and missed. Scowling, he turned to lambast whoever had upset his concentration, but faked a smile when he saw it was her. "Hello, Dana. I always have time for Wayne's daughter."

"Good, because there's someone here to see you." Dana motioned to a man wearing a red power tie with his dark suit that had been standing behind her.

He strode into the office and offered his hand. "Mr. Brinkman? I'm Morris Hollister, one of the trustees for Mr. Raynott's estate."

"Hello." Jerry shook the man's hand as if it were a ticking bomb. "Have a seat. Dana, perhaps we can talk later."

"Actually, I'd prefer that Dana stay."

Jerry shot her a questioning look but nodded and settled into his desk chair. "What brings you here today?"

Mr. Hollister gestured for Dana to sit in one of the chairs in front of Jerry's desk and claimed the other one. "I understand you've been checking on the performance of some of the employees."

"I don't know how you know that—" Jerry shot a look across the office toward Heather's desk "—but yes, I have. Got to stay on top of things, you know. Can't settle for the status quo. Have to make sure the employees are earning their keep."

"I'm glad to hear we're on the same page." Mr. Hollister opened a folder and pointed to something on the top page. "Because according to these figures, revenues for the store have decreased thirty-six percent since you took over as manager."

"Well, there is a learning curve. Wayne knew the business inside and out. Now that I've learned the system—"

"Since Mr. Raynott's death, that trend has only accelerated." He turned a page. "I have several documented customer complaints that common tools they need are unavailable or not working properly."

"Let me see that. Who's complaining?" Jerry reached for the papers. "Did Heather tell you that?"

Mr. Hollister held them out of his reach. "These reports were given on condition of anonymity, and Mrs. Johnson's performance isn't the problem. You are hereby relieved of your position, effective immediately." Mr. Hollister slapped a stapled stack of papers on the desk. "This outlines the conditions of your severance package. Please read it over and sign."

"Severance?" Jerry stared at the man. "You want me to leave?"

"Yes. So if you'll just read over this agreement—"

"Today?"

"I said immediately. The trust has a fiduciary responsibility to make sure the business is competently run, and it is our opinion that it's in the best interest of the company if you depart as soon as you sign the papers."

Jerry glowered at Dana and then at Mr. Hollister. He puffed out his cheeks like a blowfish. "You'll wish you had me back when you try to make sense of the chaos around here. Who are you going to find who can just step in and run the place?"

Mr. Hollister smiled at Dana. Dana watched as realization finally dawned on Jerry's face. She looked him square in the eye. "That would be me."

CHAPTER EIGHTEEN

SAM PADDLED HIS kayak across the lake. A few yellow birch leaves floated on the still water. The loon family was all grown up now, practicing their flying skills in preparation for their upcoming migration.

The last of the pink fireweed bloomed along the bank, signaling the end of summer. It wouldn't be long before winter arrived in the Anchorage bowl, painting the town in shades of silver and white and changing it so dramatically a summer visitor would be hard-pressed to recognize it as the same city. The profound hush of falling snow, with the city lights casting a glow that seemed to come from inside the forest itself, often gave him the sensation of being inside a snow globe.

Usually the first glimpse of snow on the peaks of the Chugach range was all the motivation he needed to pack away his summer gear and put a coat of wax on his cross-country skis. He would look forward to gliding along the groomed trails that meandered through the city or snowshoeing across the virgin snow of the hillside, breathing the crisp air into his lungs. But today, he couldn't seem to generate any enthusiasm for the end of summer.

Maybe it was the new job. He'd tentatively accepted, starting when his twenty-eight-day rotation was over. In the meantime, Ethan was working with the management in London. If all went as planned, by the time Sam reported back to work, the position would officially be open, and assuming Sam passed the interview process in London, which Ethan seemed to think was a slam dunk, he would receive a formal job offer.

Sam hated to leave Alaska, but other places had charms of their own. He might have a chance to ski in Norway, or sea kayak in Trinidad, or fish in Scotland. Then again, he probably wouldn't. When they called on him to troubleshoot, it would be because they were desperate for answers. There wouldn't be time to play.

That was probably just as well. He didn't seem to be very good at playing lately. Here he was, in the kayak he loved, in his favorite lake, but he wasn't happy. It didn't feel right.

It was like looking at a beautifully prepared meal, but when he tried to eat it, it turned to sand in his mouth. Nothing felt right anymore. A piece of his heart was missing, and without that piece, nothing functioned the way it should. And it had been like that ever since Dana left.

How could a couple of weeks in the company of one woman change everything? He'd been fine before, content even. If he'd never met her, he would never have realized anything was missing from his life, but now that he had tasted her company, he craved it constantly. Whoever said it was better to have loved and lost was an idiot.

At least he knew from experience how to handle desertion. Move on and keep paddling. He threw himself into work, boning up on the newest technologies while his arm healed, and then putting in fourteen- or fifteen-hour shifts in Siberia, trying to make up for the time he'd missed. He hadn't had time to think much about Dana then, but now that he was back in Alaska, the strategy wasn't working so well. Everything he saw reminded him of her. He couldn't even watch a flock of geese graze on his lawn without wanting to call her to the window to watch. It was pathetic.

At least it made the decision easier. Since he couldn't enjoy Alaska, anyway, he might as well take the overseas job. He could keep his house here, let Chris continue to rent. He was sure Ursula would adopt Kimmik. Maybe someday Sam's heart would heal and he could come back and once again feel he was home.

He paddled toward the dock. It was settled. In a month or two, he would be moving across the ocean and starting a new job. A new chapter of his life. Moving up, getting ahead, just as he'd always planned. He stowed the kayak on top of his truck and drove home.

The speed bump on his street caused a jolt that knocked over the almost-empty coffee cup Chris had left in the truck, spilling the contents on the floor. Sam muttered a few choice words under his breath. He ought to make Chris clean it up. But Chris's truck was absent from the driveway, so he ended up doing it himself before he went into the house.

Kimmik came to greet him, tail wagging, when he stepped in from the garage. At least someone was having a good day. "Hey, buddy. Where's Chris?"

"He's gone to Seward." Dana stepped out of the hallway and walked across the living room, stopping several feet away from him. "Something about his friend needing help to sail his boat to Valdez." She nibbled at her lower lip, watching him with those big brown eyes.

Sam just stared, groping for words. All he could come up with was to state the obvious. "You're here."

She nodded. "Chris met me at the airport."

"He didn't tell me you were coming." Which explained why Chris found an excuse to take himself out of the line of fire before Sam got home.

"I know. I asked him not to. I wanted to surprise you."

"I'm surprised all right." He took a few steps closer and crossed his arms over his chest. "But not as surprised as I was when you just disappeared without a word."

She looked at her feet and then met his eyes. "I'm sorry. Did you get my note?"

"The note? Oh, yeah, I got the note." His

mouth tightened. "It explained everything, except why you felt like you had to sneak out without even telling me goodbye. Do you want to tell me why that was?"

She paused. "You want the truth?"

"That would be nice."

Dana sighed. "I was afraid if I tried to give you a goodbye kiss, it would be too hard to stop at one."

Sam shook his head, a smile tugging at the corners of his mouth. Throwing his own words back in his face. "Touché."

Her eyes swept over him, stopping on his elbow. "How's the arm?"

"According to my doctor, it healed fine."

"That's good news." She licked her lip in that nervous gesture he recognized.

She was here, standing in front of him. How could he stay mad? Sam grinned and opened his arms. "Come here, and we'll try it out."

Dana laughed and ran to him, throwing her arms around his neck to hug him tight. He pulled her close against his chest, and the frozen ball of disappointment he'd been carrying around seemed to melt away, at least for now.

"Oh, Sam." There was a hitch in her voice.

He put a finger under her chin and tilted back her face. Tears trickled down her cheeks.

"What? What's wrong?"

She shook her head. "Nothing's wrong. I'm just—" she sniffed "—so glad to be here with you."

"Hey, I'm glad you're here, too. No need for tears." He grabbed a dish towel from the counter and wiped her cheeks.

Her smile was like a sunbeam breaking through the clouds. She reached up to stroke her fingers along his face. "I'm sorry. I didn't mean to get all weepy."

"Don't be sorry."

He should ask her to sit down, offer her something to drink, but he was loath to let her out of his arms. He compromised by easing her over to the couch and settling her beside him. He put an arm around her and she leaned against his shoulder.

"So, what are you doing here? Not that I'm complaining, but Chris said you took over running your father's business."

"I did. Just long enough to establish better systems and give one of our senior employees some time off to take a couple of workshops in management and human resources. Heather's taken over as manager, and she's doing a great job. How is Ursula? And your mother? Have you seen her again?"

"Ursula is fine. Busy. The inn had a record number of guests this summer, and the local newspaper ran a feature on her. I've seen my mom a few times. We're okay, I think. She's put herself on a waiting list for a rehab program. As to whether she'll actually go when she gets to the top of the list is anyone's guess, but she seems to be trying. And how is your mother?"

Dana's face brightened. "She's much better. She's seeing a therapist, who's helping her come to terms with her shopping addiction. Just recently, she started volunteering at the shelter. Spending time with people who have almost nothing has been a real reality check for her. The only problem is the temptation to go buy them all the things they need. But she's donated a lot of her surplus furniture and clothes, and any size-six women who pass through the shelter will have plenty of nice interview outfits to choose from."

"That's great. So, Chris wouldn't tell me. Did you get the inheritance and enroll in the college classes you need?"

"I signed up for classes." Dana paused. "But I didn't use the inheritance."

"What?" He frowned. "Why not? If anyone deserves that money, it's you."

"Not if it's not legitimately my money. My father stole Roy's investment and used it to make his fortune. Most of that fortune is locked into a trust, but as for that hundred thousand, Chris and I agree we can't accept it."

"So what happens to it? Your mother spends it on junk?"

"We took it and put it aside. It's in an account, waiting to be returned to Roy Petrov's family, where it belongs."

"No." Sam was firm. "I don't need it and I don't want it."

Dana nodded. "Chris said you'd say that. But what about your mother?"

Sam shook his head. "My mother is an alcoholic. A sudden influx of cash would do her more harm than good."

"That may be true now, but if she ever gets it together, it might help give her a fresh start. It's Roy's money. I would think he'd want it to benefit his wife."

"She was never his wife."

"She should have been."

BETH CARPENTER

359

"Yes, she should have been." They were on their way to be married the night he died. Maybe Dana was right. Mom did seem to be getting better. She'd lost that defeated look, especially after he told her about how Chris had come looking for him. She had signed up for a rehab program on her own without any urging. Maybe she was ready to start over.

"Before you decide, Chris says to tell you if you don't accept the money, he's donating his share to the Martin Reynolds reelection campaign. Something about bigger speed bumps."

Sam laughed. "You win. I'll set aside the money for my mother."

"I'm so glad."

"So, if you didn't use the inheritance, how'd you find the money for college?"

"I sold my house and used the equity."

"You did what?"

"I sold my cottage in Kansas."

"Instead of using your inheritance, you gave up your job as manager and sold your house to pay for college." Sam spoke slowly as the magnitude of her deed soaked in.

"Yes. I'm homeless and jobless." She grinned. "But I have a plan."

"Tell me this plan."

"I've been accepted to the University of Alaska Anchorage. It will take two semesters to bring my teaching credentials up-to-date. They tell me the Anchorage School District is always looking for math teachers."

"Here?" He felt like a kid who just got a pony for his birthday. "You're going to college here in Anchorage?"

"Yes. I already have a part-time job on campus."

"That's fantastic, Dana. You'll be a great teacher."

"Thanks. Classes start next week. I also signed up for a wilderness safety class so, you know, I won't be such a hazard." She smiled at him and then looked away, as though suddenly shy. "I was hoping between hitches to Siberia, we could spend some time together. If you want to."

"I want all the time you can give me." A brilliant idea occurred to him. "In fact, you should live here. We have an extra bedroom." And he'd be able to see her every morning, her bright eyes shining, whenever he was home, and when he came back from his rotation— No. He'd forgotten all about the new job. "Actually, I'm not working Siberia anymore. I got a promotion."

"That's great. In the Anchorage office?"

"No." He closed his eyes and took a deep breath. "Based in London."

"Oh." Her face fell, but then she managed a brave smile. "Congratulations."

"Thanks." He paused. "I'll be taking vacations in Alaska, of course. And maybe sometimes I'd work on projects here. We could see each other then."

"Yeah. That would be great." Her enthusiasm seemed forced.

He didn't want her dropping out of his life again. "We can call and video chat. And you, you could visit me. Have you ever been to the UK?"

"No, I've never been out of the country."

"We'll plan a trip for you next summer when you're off school."

She looked a little happier. "I'd like that."

"I have two weeks left before I have to go back to work. There's still time for some summer fun together." He stood and reached for her hand. "In fact, I have something to show you."

"What's that?"

"Remember the loons we saw?"

"Of course. I'll never forget that cry of theirs."

"Well, the eggs in the nest hatched and now they're all grown up. Want to see if they're still at the lake?"

That sparkle he loved so much shone from her eyes. "I do."

"Come on." He pulled her up from the couch. "Let's go."

SAM WAS AFRAID the loons might not be there when they arrived, but before he and Dana had even reached the dock, all five birds swooped over the trees and landed in the lake right in front of them. The grayish coloring distinguished the youngsters from the crisp black and white of their parents, although they were almost the same size.

Dana ran forward, dragging him along. "Look how big they are. They're flying now."

"They'll be migrating soon."

"But they'll be back. And I'll be here to greet them next spring." She swept her gaze across the lake. "The leaves are already turning. It's gorgeous."

Sam put an arm around her shoulders and she leaned into him. They watched until the sun was gone and they could no longer see the loons on the water. He led Dana toward the parking lot, guiding her around a low spot. "Careful. There's a puddle. Don't step in the mud."

"Mud?" Dana snorted. "I'm an Alaskan girl now. Mud doesn't scare me."

He stopped walking and turned toward her. "It doesn't, huh?"

"Nope. I like mud. It means there's an adventure coming."

"And you like adventure?"

"I love adventure. I just never knew that until I met you."

Sam faced her. The last traces of sunset painted her cheeks pink and reflected in her bright eyes. He pulled her close, and with deliberation and care, he kissed her. A gentle brush of his lips against hers, once, twice, and then a tender kiss that deepened as her arms tightened around his neck.

The sound of a child laughing in the distance reminded him they were in a public place. He stepped back, catching both her hands in his and smiling at her. "Come on. Let's go home."

DANA SCRIBBLED NOTES as the instructor described the assignment. She was slightly nervous to be in a classroom again after so many years, but it was all coming back: syllabi, lesson plans, group projects. She could do this.

After class, she collected her notebook and walked toward the parking lot. Her transportation budget was limited to the money she'd raised from selling her car and furniture in Kansas, but Sam insisted she needed four-wheel drive, so while she was busy with classes and her new job in the dean's office, he made it his mission to locate a reliable SUV she could afford. She clicked her key fob and unlocked the door of the sporty blue jeep he'd found for her.

"Hey." A girl she recognized from class waved at her and walked closer. "A bunch of us are going for coffee at Kaladi's. Want to come?"

Dana was torn. She'd love to get to know her fellow students better, especially since they would be doing several group projects, but she wanted to spend as much time as possible with Sam while she still could. She smiled at the girl. "I'd love to, but I have plans tonight. Sorry."

"No worries. Next time."

Dana waved and climbed into the jeep. She was enjoying being back in an academic setting. Things were going well in general. During their daily phone call that morning, Mom had given her encouraging news about a new preschool program at the shelter. She was volunteering daily now and seemed happier than she'd ever been before.

So was Dana. She liked her campus job and her instructors, but it was her time with Sam that made life perfect. Her heart beat faster as she drove home, knowing Sam would be there, waiting for her. They'd spent every available moment together the past two weeks.

Coming to Alaska had been a huge leap of faith. Those negative voices inside her head tried to tell her Sam was an illusion, that once she spent more time with him, she'd find he wasn't the man she thought he was. Those voices were wrong.

Sam was everything she admired—strong, kind, loyal and thoughtful—and the more she was with him, the more her feelings grew. These last two weeks together just confirmed what she already knew. She loved him.

And she was going to lose him. Tomorrow he reported back to work, and the process would start to send him halfway around the world. A cold knot formed inside her chest. By unspoken agreement, they'd avoided talking about the new job since the first day, but they were almost out of time.

At least with modern technology, they could stay in contact with daily phone calls and video chats. It wouldn't be enough, but she would never tell him so. Sam worked his tail off to get ahead in the company. He deserved this promotion, and if it meant a long-distance relationship, she could handle that. More than anything, she wanted him happy.

She parked in the driveway and pasted a smile on her face before she opened the front door. Kimmik ran to greet her. Thankfully, Chris and the dog would be staying, keeping her company. Chris was fishing again, but in another couple of weeks he would be back in Anchorage for the winter, and they'd finally get a chance to make up for the time they'd missed.

Sam met her at the top of the stairs with open arms and a warm kiss. "Hi. How were your classes?"

"Good. My Alaska history teacher was telling us all about the sixty-four earthquake. He was there when it happened. It sounds devastating."

Sam nodded. "I've seen pictures. There was a place downtown where one side of the road dropped several feet below the other side. And speaking of downtown, I made dinner reservations at Orso's. Hope that's okay with you."

They'd been to the restaurant once before. Dana loved the cozy, old-world atmosphere. "Nice. What's the occasion?"

Sam shrugged. "Do we need an occasion?" He smiled at her, but there was a sadness in his eyes. She suspected he was feeling the future bearing down on them, too.

She kissed him once again. "In that case, I'll change and we can go."

Dana wore a blue dress that was Sam's favorite. Even though he was waiting, she took a few minutes to add mascara and lip gloss and brush her hair. The appreciative look in his eyes when she walked into the room made her glad she'd made the effort.

The heavenly scent of roasted garlic greeted them at the door of the restaurant. The hostess led them past a wood-paneled divider to a quiet table near the back.

They kept conversation easy during dinner, talking about her classes and local news. Someone in Dana's class had mentioned cross-country ski trails around campus, and

Sam gave her advice on where to find ski equipment and lessons once the snow fell.

It wasn't until they'd finished eating and were sipping the last of their wine that Dana brought up the subject she'd been dreading. "I guess tomorrow's the big day."

Sam nodded. "Ethan emailed me. I'll officially apply for the job tomorrow and they'll set up interviews for me in London."

"So the job isn't a done deal?" A spark of hope flared. Maybe she hadn't understood the procedure.

"Not officially, but Ethan says they've seen my résumé and they want me, assuming I don't bomb the interviews."

A selfish streak inside her hoped he might, but she knew better. Talking to Sam face-to-face could only make them want him more. "You'll do great. When do you think you'll go over?"

"Probably next week for the interview, and maybe report in a month or two after that, depending on personnel and work visas and such." He spoke matter-of-factly.

Dana raised her glass. "To success in your new job. May it bring you all the happiness you deserve."

He nodded, but he didn't smile. She took

a drink of wine while Sam watched her, an expression she couldn't quite decipher on his face. He seemed to be turning something over in his mind. After a long silence, his eyes softened. "Do you know how beautiful you are?" He leaned across the table and ran his finger over her cheek. "Marry me."

"What?"

"Marry me, Dana. Be my wife. Come to London with me."

"We can't get married."

"Why not? I need you. You just wished me happiness, but there's no happiness without you."

"But you don't love me."

"Of course I love you." He laughed aloud. "I love everything about you. I love your smile, and your laugh, and the way your eyes light up when you see something wonderful. Most of all, I love your big, beautiful heart. I loved you almost from the moment I met you." He winked. "Once you set the gun down."

"Oh, Sam." Her heart fluttered. "I love you, too."

"Then let me do this right." Sam slid off his chair and knelt before her, taking her hands in his. "Dana Raynott, I do love you.

You make me smile and fill my life with good things. Please do me the honor of becoming my wife."

The normal sounds of conversation and dining suddenly stopped all around them as everyone paused to watch. Dana blinked back a tear. "Is this for real?"

"Absolutely. It's a genuine, bona fide offer of marriage." Sam waited.

"Yes. I would love to be your wife." She leaned forward to kiss him, and the restaurant broke into hardy applause. Dana felt her cheeks grow warm, but she couldn't hide the smile on her face as he returned to his seat without ever letting go of her hands.

He grinned. "Sorry I don't have a ring, but I promise we'll find you a good one."

"You already gave me a ring." Dana slipped the silver feather ring off her right hand and handed it to him.

He laughed. "That will do for now." He slid it onto the ring finger of her left hand. "I wonder if there's a waiting period."

"For what?"

"For getting married. The sooner you're officially my wife, the sooner we can start making arrangements. Is that all right with you? Or do you want a big wedding?"

She blinked. It was all happening so fast. If quitting her job to start teaching in Alaska seemed like a leap of faith, marrying Sam and moving to London was like jumping out of an airplane. But if it meant she could be with Sam… "The sooner, the better."

Sam squeezed her hands. "Let's go home."

ONCE THEY WERE inside the house, Sam led his lovely fiancée to the couch and pulled her onto his lap. He was going to have a wife, the most wonderful wife in the world. He pulled her against his chest and nuzzled her silky hair. "I love you."

"I love you." She cuddled even closer. "So," she murmured, "how will this work, exactly? With the company, I mean?"

"I'm not sure, but I suspect once I officially accept the position, they'll want me as soon as they can arrange for a work visa. That will give us time to get you on my health plan and everything, and arrange for an apartment."

"Oh." Her hand went to her mouth. "I just remembered—I don't have a passport."

"Then we'll get you one. We can get it expedited."

She traced a finger along his arm. "Tell me

about your new job. What will you be doing in London? Do they have oil wells there?"

"It's advising. I'll be consulting with the various assets around the world. When they're implementing new technology or having complications, I'll be there to support them. Sometimes, I'll be working from the office in London, but a good part of the time, I'll be flying to different places around the world, helping with problems."

"I see." She nodded slowly. "But you'll be coming back to London in between? Kind of like with your Siberian rotations?"

"I'm supposed to be in London about half the time. And I should have most weekends off to spend with my wife." Of course, he'd assured Ethan he had no wife, no ties, that he was free to travel. But Ethan would just have to adjust his expectations.

"Okay." Dana paused and looked thoughtful. "I guess while you're gone, I can explore. They have all kinds of museums and things there, right? It will be like a really long vacation."

"Yeah, it will be great." He tried to sound confident, but the more he thought about it, the worse this idea seemed. How much fun could it be for her, living alone in a busy city where she didn't know a soul, waiting around for him to get home from work or from a trip, where he'd stay just long enough to repack his suitcase and head out again?

Dana went on, gamely making plans. "So, I guess I'd better contact UAA tomorrow and drop my classes. I'm still within the refund period. And I'll give notice on the job so they can give it to someone else."

This wasn't right. It was beyond selfish to expect her to drop everything to go with him. Dana deserved better. "No. Don't give notice. Don't drop out."

"No?" Her eyes opened in alarm. "You've changed your mind?"

"Yes, I have. This isn't fair. You've wanted to teach your whole life, but you gave up your own ambitions to meet your father's expectations. I won't ask you to do that for me."

"But, Sam, I want to be with you. You're more important than any job, including teaching. I'm sure I could be happy in London. Lots of people would give anything for a chance to live in London."

"Maybe someday we'll decide to do that,

but not now. Right now, you need to go to college and get your career started."

"But—"

"I'll turn down the assignment. There's a job opening on the North Slope I think I might be good at. Walt Chrism, a supervisor in Prudhoe Bay, is retiring. It's a two-week-on, two-off position, so I'd still be away half the time, but during the two weeks I am home, I'd be free to spend it all with you. Not like London, where I'd be in the office every weekday when I wasn't traveling."

"What if you don't get it?"

"Then I'll find something else."

"Are you sure about this? Sam, I know how important it is to you to advance in the company. If you turn down a promotion, you might never have another chance."

He thought about that. "You know the idea doesn't upset me nearly as much as it would have a few months ago." He put his finger on her chin and tipped her face so she was looking into his eyes. "Do you love me?"

Her eyes softened. "Yes, I love you."

"Then marry me. Make your home here. Let me share Alaska with you."

"When you put it like that, how can I refuse?"

"Then it's settled. Tomorrow I'll decline the offer in London and apply for the job on the slope." He kissed the top of her head. "And then we'll find out how to get a marriage license."

"Perfect."

Sam, picturing their future, could see nothing but happiness. "We'll raise our kids here and teach them all the things Tommy and Ursula taught me. You do want kids, don't you?" Because he did. Suddenly, he wanted the whole package, a wife and a kid or two, or three or four. Whatever Dana wanted.

She gave him a slow grin. "I do."

"You're going to be a fantastic mother." He nuzzled against her hair. "And teacher." He brushed his lips against the corner of her eyebrow. "And wife."

She turned her face up to receive his kiss. He leaned in, but instead of a kiss, he rubbed his nose against hers.

She giggled. "Eskimo kisses."

"By definition, all my kisses are part Eskimo."

She slipped her hands behind his head. "Is that what makes your kisses so good?"

"No. You're what makes my kisses so good."

She raised her eyebrows. "So am I going to get one or not?"

Sam chuckled. "It's going to be hard to stop at one."

Dana tightened her arms around his neck. "I'm counting on it."

* * * * *

If you enjoyed THE ALASKAN CATCH, don't miss Beth Carpenter's next heart-tugging NORTHERN LIGHTS *romance coming in December 2017!*

Available at www.Harlequin.com.

Get 2 Free Books,
Plus 2 Free Gifts—
just for trying the
Reader Service!

Get 2 Free Books,

Plus 2 Free Gifts—

just for trying the Reader Service!

HOMETOWN HEARTS ♥

Get 2 Free Books,
Plus 2 Free Gifts—
just for trying the Reader Service!

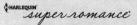

Get 2 Free Books,
Plus 2 Free Gifts—
just for trying the Reader Service!

Love Inspired HISTORICAL